www.**randomhouse**.co.uk

Also available by
Anthony McGowan:

Hellbent

Henry Tumour

ANTHONY McGOWAN

Definitions

HENRY TUMOUR
A DEFINITIONS BOOK 978 0 099 48823 1

First published in Great Britain by Doubleday,
an imprint of Random House Children's Books

Doubleday edition published 2006
Definitions edition published 2007

1 3 5 7 9 10 8 6 4 2

Set in 11/15pt Sabon by
Falcon Oast Graphic Art Ltd

Definitions are published by Random House Children's Books,
61–63 Uxbridge Road, London W5 5SA

www.randomhouse.co.uk

Addresses for companies within The Random House Group Limited can
be found at: www.randomhouse.co.uk/offices.htm

THE RANDOM HOUSE GROUP Limited Reg. No. 954009

A CIP catalogue record for this book is available from the British Library.

Printed and bound in Great Britain by Cox & Wyman Ltd,
Reading, Berkshire

For Gabriel Dante McGowan

CHAPTER 1
ARSECHEESE

Arsecheese.

Well, that's what I heard. I don't know if that's what he really said because that was his first word and I don't know if he was just learning to speak then or if maybe I was learning to hear but that's what it sounded like.

Arsecheese.

I stopped what I was doing. What I was doing was reading, although I wasn't really reading, more just turning over the pages with the letters floating around like astronauts in zero gravity.

'What?'

I must have said it aloud because some of the other people in the waiting room looked round at me. A woman with big hair and a face like a collapsed lung shuffled her chair a few centimetres further away from me, like *that* was going to make a difference if I was going to turn psycho and stab her. In fact, it raised my wanting-to-stab-her score by about seventy-two per cent.

Whoever had said *arsecheese* the first time didn't say it again, and I assumed I'd imagined it. I'd been imagining a lot of things lately and that was one of the reasons I was there. Not the main reason. The main reason was that I'd had headaches so bad I thought the little dude from *Alien* was going to burst out of my eye socket. The first one came on while I was watching a music video, and my mum thought I was freaking out to the music, but really I was writhing around on the floor in agony. Shows how my mum's got her finger on the pulse of popular culture. That's sarcasm, by the way, but she'd take it straight, because she thinks she has.

I'd been in the clinic since nine o'clock. It was boring, but I didn't mind too much as it meant that I wasn't at school. Except that at school there'd be my friends to keep me company, and not this load of derelicts and mutants. Apart from the lung-faced lady with the big hair, there was a man who looked like a scrunched-up brown paper bag, and another with a beard that started at his eyebrows and went down to his stained crotch, and a boy with a feature-less head like a balloon, and a youngish woman who looked like all her bones had been taken out and then put back in the wrong place, and a librarian type who had something similar going on with her teeth (I mean, big ones like molars at the front and small sharp pointy ones at the back, and I knew all about her teeth because she kept smiling at me, as if I was the freak here, the one in need of sympathy).

'Hector Brunty.'

'Er, yeah.'

That was me. I mean, that was a nurse in a brown nylon uniform like something you'd find adorning one of the mildly retarded – I mean 'special' – shelf-stackers in Tesco. You know, the ones who, when you ask them where the

2

beans are, first take you to the Thomas the Tank Engine toddler ride and then start shouting at you about cheese.

I stood up. The nurse smiled at me, and for the first time I began to understand that my life was going to become less pleasant. At the time my best estimate was about twenty-six per cent less pleasant, but I've since recalculated and it currently stands at between ninety-eight and ninety-nine per cent less pleasant (you have to allow a margin for error). Although since that first day in the clinic there have been blips taking the graph both ways, but we'll come to those later.

'Is your mother here?'

'No.'

'Oh.'

I felt that I ought to try to explain, but I didn't have the faintest idea how to do that in less than an hour, so I looked at my feet. And looking at my feet was seldom a good idea as it hammered home the fact that what was happening down there was all wrong, meaning I had on shoes made out of an elephant's foreskin, and not cool or even luke-warm trainers like everyone else. I shouldn't have said elephant's foreskin, because Mum is no more likely to buy elephant-skin products than she is to go harpooning whales. I just meant shapeless blue-grey buboes, as if something big – OK, let's stick with elephant – waddled over and shat on my feet.

I told my mum a joke once. I said, 'I went to the Wailing Wall. In Jerusalem.' Pause. 'It was rubbish.' Pause. 'I didn't harpoon a single whale.' You see it relies on the fact that 'wail' and 'whale' are homonyms, that is two words which sound the same but mean different things. Anyway, she looked at me with this expression of disgust on her face, as though I'd just shown her a boil with a maggot in it, because the joke bit of what I said was completely lost by the horror of the killing-whales bit, when we all should know that they are our brothers, and peace-loving Gentle Giants of the Ocean, even though nobody ever asked the krill what they thought about it.

'This way then,' the nurse said, and I followed her into an examination room that managed to be stuffy and cold at the same time. There was a window with a view over the complicated rooftop of the hospital, all pipes and vents and skewed angles. It made me feel dizzy, and for a second I thought I was going to have to puke in the sink. The sink had one of those taps with a long handle so you could turn it off and on with your elbow. Or your chin. Or you could stand backwards on a chair and do it with your arse.

But why would you want to do that?

Well, what if you had no arms?

Then you'd probably develop cleverly expressive feet, for which taps would be a piece of cake.

What if you lost your feet?

Well then you could use your knee, still much better than an arse.

So what if your legs were amputated just below where they join onto your body? In an accident with some intricate piece of farm machinery, a turnip spangler, say, or a hay thrummer, or a many-bladed pig-splayer.

Well, then you couldn't get up on the chair to use your bum, could you?

Aha! That's where the *special* chair comes into play. The special chair with a hydraulic arm that lifts up your limbless trunk, swivels it round and presents your arse to the tap.

'Hector?'

A man looking a lot like a doctor was staring at me. I had a nasty feeling that I might have been acting out being hoisted bum-first towards the tap. I'd always done a lot of that – I don't mean acting out, I mean the internal-dialogue thing. I sometimes wonder if that's got something to do with Henry, I mean how he came into being, how he was how he was.

I nodded.

'I'm Doctor Jones.'

I nodded again. He hadn't said anything yet that I felt like disagreeing with.

'As you know, this is a teaching hospital. Would you mind if some, ah, *observers* sat in?'

Before I had the chance to mind, a group of gormless-looking students began filing into the room. Not all gormless-looking. There was one exceptionally pretty girl, with the kind of straight black hair I like.

It meant I was going to get an anal probe for sure.

I felt the electric tingle of a blush as the whole scene played out before me: the pink rubberized truncheon they were going to use, the sparking electrodes at the end, the giggle from the students at the trumping noise produced as the probe was extracted, my stuttering efforts to say it wasn't me but the probe that made the noise.

'So, you've been having some problems?' said Doc Jones.

Problems! Where did I start? My mum was a hippy, my dad was nowhere, my school was a shit heap; I was bullied by Neanderthals and ignored by the girls, and my friends were the Wretched of the Earth.

But that wasn't what Doc Jones meant.

'Headaches,' he said, looking at his clipboard. 'Blurred vision.'

'Yeah,' I said.

'Anything else?'

Should I tell him about the voices, the strange echoing effect I sometimes heard or felt, as though I were being called from another dimension?

'Been a bit tired. Get dizzy sometimes.'

'That's good, that's good,' said the doctor mysteriously. 'Why don't we have a little look at you?'

There followed ten minutes of probing, none of it anally-oriented. The doctor shone a light in my eyes and moved it around, asking me to follow it. He stood behind me and asked if I could hear his watch tick, first on one side, and then on the other. Then he tested my reflexes, which I thought only happened in films. All the students had a go, banging randomly around my knee area with a rubber hammer. Then I had to touch my nose with my finger, alternating left and right with my eyes closed. Then I had to walk in a straight line, again with my eyes closed.

All sounds easy, doesn't it? Except with all those people staring at me, and especially the pretty one, I didn't do that well in the nose-touching and straight-line-walking parts. There were more questions, more tests. Did I know who the prime minister was? Could I say the days of the week backwards? Did I know my arse from my elbow?

Throughout it all I could feel myself getting more and more sullen-teenagery, and that's not my normal way. I couldn't think of any clever things to say.

And then it was over.

'That's just grand, Hector,' said Doc Jones. 'We'll make an appointment for a CAT scan, and sort this all out. We'll send the appointment card. Try to fit you in early next week. Or perhaps later this week. We sometimes get cancellations. And in urgent— Well, we might be lucky. OK?'

'OK.'

And although I knew what a CAT scan was, I still had this quick mental image of a sort of Star Trek TriQuarter, only shaped like a cat, and Spock with his hand up its bum, passing it over my body and detecting alien life forms in there.

CHAPTER 2
BUGNOB

So I was out of there, none the wiser. I got the bus to school, and the driver gave me the eye, thinking I was on the skive, and I started to explain that there was something up with my head, but then I couldn't be bothered.

The trouble with all this was that I got to school just in time for morning break, which you'd think was a good thing, unless you knew what my school was like. Because it's called the Body of Christ, which is what the priest says when he puts the bread in your mouth, people who don't know it think my school must be all singing nuns and good grades, but it's not like that at all. It's full of headcases, and the worst of them hang out around the school gates, smoking and sniffing butane during break, and God help anyone who has to get past them while they're on duty. The teachers don't bother them because at least they're out of the way when they're at the gates, and they might even act as a deterrent to any casual truants thinking of making a run for it.

It's a bit like migrating wildebeest on the telly, where they go trotting across the Serengeti until they come to a river. And the river is full of big hungry crocodiles. So all the wildebeest bunch up, scared shitless by the shadows in

the water – you know, *I'm not going in there, no way* –
until one of them goes for it, and the first one usually
makes it, so a few more have a go, and they get majorly
chomped, and then the rest of the herd dives in, and most
of them get through because of the safety-in-numbers thing,
but then any stragglers at the end get all eaten to fuck as
well, until all you can see is blood in the water, and a half-
eaten head, and a slice of leftover hoof and a baby
somewhere bleating for its mother.

So, yeah, it's a bit like that, but with less eating and
more taunting, crocs being superb killing machines, but not
naturals on the old repartee front. You can imagine them:
'Hey, *you, er, aw, what's that word for a boy wildebeest
that likes other boy wildebeests more than he likes girl
wildebeests? Oi! Come back, I've not finished taunting you
yet. Ah, shit, Ralf, I've lost another one. Any chance of
sharing? C'mon, man, a hoof's all I'm askin'. Yeah, up
yours too.*'

Small brains, you see, crocodiles. A guy came to our
school once, talking about them. He had a skin and a skull.
I mean, belonging to a crocodile. Of course the man had a
skin and a skull too, or he'd have looked pretty stupid, not
to mention dead. We all filed up to feel them. The
crocodile's bits and bobs, that is. There was a tiny little hole
at the back of the skull. The man said it was the brain
cavity. A snug fit for your thumb. Or something else. In fact
I had a little fantasy while he was talking to the class, in
which I was left in charge of the thing, and I got horny and
as no one was around (in the fantasy, maybe a fire alarm or
something), I gave it a quickie, but then the man and the

class all came in again, and I turned round with my knob in this crocodile skull, wearing it like a Gothic codpiece.

OK, so I'm back from the Serengeti, and I've shaken off the crocodile underpants, and I'm praying that I'm too insignificant to attract the attention of the sentries, or maybe that they've got themselves a really good vintage paint stripper to inhale. (*'Well, Cecil, I detect citrus tones, undercurrents of leaf mould, juniper and MELT-YOUR-HEAD HYDROCHLORIC ACID.'*)

So I walked around the social club next to the school, my insides beyond the jelly stage, and I see straight away that something a bit weird's going on. There's normally about ten of the morons slouching about, tangled up like they've just been puked out by a tumble-drier, but now they're all staring in the same direction, their mouths hanging open. At first I thought they were looking at me, and that made me begin to initiate the countdown to shitting my pants, but then I realized that it wasn't me but the wall of the social club they were staring at.

Now this wall was the main outlet for the creative urges not just for our budding artists, but for all the local vandals, and it was regularly daubed with witless graffiti and crude drawings, generally of genitalia. Sometimes inadvertent poetry would result. There was a brutal PE teacher called Truelove, and the two-metre-high letters spelling '*tRuELovE is a wANkEr*' achieved a pleasing kind of bittersweet resonance.

Every couple of months the school or the council or someone would paint over the graffiti, but that just left a clean and tempting canvas, and a day later the same stuff would be back again, with maybe the obscenity ratcheted up a notch. So they'd finally covered it up with some kind of special coating that, in theory at least, you couldn't paint on, and the wall had been blank for a couple of months.

I turned and looked at it. At first I couldn't see anything. Then I began to make out the faint outline of a sinuous form emerging from the pale grey coating. It really did seem as though the *thing*, whatever it was, was somehow working its way through to the surface. And it certainly wasn't any of the usual stuff: you could see that right away. Even though I couldn't tell what it was, I could see the elegance of the form, the beauty of the line. It looked like a real work of art, like something in a gallery or a book.

Bugnob.

'Huh?'

There it was again. The voice. This time I stopped myself from looking round. This time I knew it didn't come from outside.

I didn't like it.

But at least it snapped me out of the strange trance thing I was falling into, looking at the whatever-it-was emerging from the wall. I quickly slipped past the guard of honour, who were all still staring like zombies.

CHAPTER 3
THE JUSTICE LEAGUE

I walked along the red-gra pitch. There were a couple of soccer matches going on, but none of my mates were playing. No surprise there. As I suggested earlier, they weren't exactly natural athletes on the whole.

Scattered here and there were clumps of girls in microskirts, pink legs whipped by the cold wind. They reminded me of flamingos, and anyone who thinks flamingos are pretty, frankly just hasn't looked at them, with their upside-downy heads and mad eyes. It must be a pink thing, I mean why people think they're pretty. But there's nothing so great about pink. Lots of pink things are ugly – you only have to find a porn mag on the back of the bus to realize *that*.

There was one girl standing on her own, not part of a group, but even more flamingoish than the others. She was tall and gangly and she had long, straight, strawberry-blonde hair. She also had a port-wine birthmark in the shape of Africa on her face, and it was hard not to stare at it, especially if she put on make-up to try to hide it, which she sometimes did and sometimes didn't – the worst of all worlds, if you ask me. Her name was Amanda something. For a second our eyes met, and I thought that she might have smiled, and I looked behind me, thinking there was someone there, and when I looked back, Amanda Something was looking down, and for no good reason I felt like a heel.

I found my gang hunkered down by the fence. All three of them.

'Where you bin?' asked Phil Tester. We called him Gonad, because gonad means testicle, and 'Tester' is like the first part of that, and Phil rhymes with the last part and, all in all, that's enough, we reckoned. Gonad was a gentle giant type with short fair hair and ears that looked like they belonged on some other, much smaller creature, a vole or something.

'Hospital.'

'What's up with you?'

'Nothing.'

'Oh.'

'What did I miss?'

'Double maths, single RE. We did quadratic equations.'

Numbers were my thing, or one of my things. My mum didn't approve. She'd have preferred it if I'd been good at almost anything else. She thought numbers were evil and stifled your creativity and she tried to make me learn the piano and the bassoon and write poetry.

There was one time when she thought she'd cracked it. In our house nothing works, and one of the things that doesn't work is the bathroom door. If you don't slam it shut, it kind of bangs all night in a random, rhythmless way that drives me mad. I told Mum every night to make sure it was shut, but she never did, because she's in a dream world.

So I stuck a note on the door, with writing in black felt tip. It said:

If you go in the night for a wee or a poo,
Close the door properly, please, when you're through,
Because if you don't it'll rattle and shake,
And keep hypersensitive Hector awake.

It did the trick, door-wise, which tells you something about the Power of Poetry, but I didn't write any more of it, because my other problems were the kind that no amount of poetry could fix and there was always a chance that someone at school might find out and punch me in the head for it.

All of the gang had a thing. Gonad's thing was history. He knew everything that had ever happened. Not just from watching the History Channel – he'd read everything in the library. Shout out any date and he'd tell you what happened then.

'Seven ninety-three.'

'Easy: raid by Vikings on Lindisfarne.'

'Seventeen fifty-nine.'

'English defeat French at Quebec in the Seven Years War.'

'Nineteen sixty-three.'

'The end of the *Chatterley* ban and The Beatles' first LP.'

That kind of thing.

Although he knew everything that ever happened, Gonad wasn't, in other ways, very bright, so you often found yourself explaining things to him, like what some joke meant, or what you have to carry in a long division, or which shoe went on what foot.

Stanislaw's thing was chess. We called him Stan. His granddad was Polish. He was like the exact opposite of Gonad: little and dark, quick in his movements, his eyes always darting about, looking for danger. And there usually *was* danger, and I don't mean from a Queen-and-Bishop pincer movement.

Simon Murphy, usually called Smurf for obvious reasons, was best at English. He was always having to read his work out in class, which tended to get him hated above and beyond what you'd expect for a swot and a nerd. Smurf was normal in everything except for his lips, which were fleshy and protuberant, and which therefore earned him another widely used name of Rubber Lips. This hurt him a lot, for he was a sensitive soul. If you were to rank us all in order of niceness, then Smurf would be top.

As well as our special things, we had other stuff we were all more or less equally good at. Or not good at. We knew about computers. We knew about getting our heads kicked-in by the Neanderthals. We didn't know anything about girls, and we were rubbish at sport. I suppose you could say we were a bit like the Justice League, that glittering super-hero collective spawned by the wondrous DC comic empire in the 1950s and more recently given new life in a surprisingly authentic cartoon.

What, this bunch of hapless nerds like the Justice League? How, exactly?

You know, the way that each has a special skill, but then they can all do other stuff as well. The Flash can run really quickly; Green Lantern has his power ring; J'Onn J'Onzz, aka Martian Manhunter, can dematerialize; Batman has his Batgadgets; Superman can fly; Wonder Woman has her indestructible steel bracelets and her lovely legs; and Hawkgirl her electro-hammer-bashing-thing. But then they can all fight and think and generally open a whole can of kickass as well. Except maybe The Flash, where the running-really-quickly thing just about exhausts his special powers, but that's why everyone likes him best, because he's a bit of a screw up.

God, now I've begun on the Justice League I see I'm not going to be able to stop. I don't normally like kids' stuff, but for some reason the Justice League really gets me. You see it's all these superheroes fighting together to save us, but there are all sorts of tensions working away beneath the surface. Batman and Superman don't like each other; Green Lantern wants everyone to obey him, and practise and improve efficiency, but nobody else wants to, and he's also in love with Hawkgirl, and she might love him back, and I'm not sure how I feel about it because I secretly hope that there's a future for me and Hawkgirl (her beautiful feathery wings close around me, I take off the hawk mask and kiss her soft, superheroine lips . . .); and The Flash really fancies Wonder Woman, but she thinks he's a lightweight, and he is, but she's too stuck up, which is her problem, and she actually has a soft spot for Batman. And the whole thing hovers always on the edge of tragedy and defeat, but still you know they're there for you.

And I also know there's something fascist in the idea of looking to these demi-gods for salvation, when really you should be looking inside yourself, but sometimes when you look inside yourself there's nothing there, or what there is is no good, and that's why you need the Justice League.

Yeah, well *now* you know why they call us the nerds.

'Whistle!'

The cry came a second before the searing pain. Of course I knew who and what it was.

'Whistle!'

I blew frantically. But when someone grabs hold of your nipple and squeezes it like a vice, the one thing you can't do is whistle. You blow and blow, but all that comes out is air. I tried to wrestle him off, but the little bastard was like a monkey and I couldn't get a grip.

Explanation.

This was Flaherty. Flaherty wasn't really part of our gang, wasn't really a nerd at all. What he was was a nutter, but not one of the evil ones, just a nutter plain and simple. He was a spiky-haired perpetual-motion machine, always fidgeting, spinning, jerking, chattering. Free-floating, independent, of no party but his own; the biggest pain in the arse known to mankind. His dad was a notorious local criminal, but his dad didn't live with his mum, and everyone said Flaherty was more like his uncle, who'd been a musician, but had died some squalid death in London. He hadn't, as far as you could tell, inherited any of Uncle Flaherty's musical talent, although he was pretty nifty on the old acoustic catarrh. But anyway, the reputation of the dad meant that nobody touched him, however irritating he might be, and that was handy, because he was as likely to get up the noses of the school hard cases as annoy us. What

I'm saying is, he was mad but funny, sort of. And now he was on my back, squeezing my tit.

'You know how to do it,' he whispered, like a guy from ground control trying to talk down a rookie pilot with the instruments all shot to pieces and zero visibility. 'Keep calm, two deep breaths, take it easy and WHISTLE.'

And it was true. That was the only way. I tried to forget the pain, forget the panic, block out the laughter of the others (they laughed partly because they'd all been whistled too, in their time, and because Flaherty wasn't really dangerous, just a pain). I blew again, and a low, barely audible whistle came out.

It was enough. Flaherty jumped off my back.

'You little tosser,' I said, rubbing my bruised tit, but laughing. You just couldn't be mad at Flaherty. Might as well be mad at the grass for giving me hay fever.

Flaherty's tie was halfway round the side of his neck, and his shirt was out and his trousers were all over the place, but there was still something cool about him, despite looking like he'd just fallen out of a tree.

'Got a joke,' he said. 'Biology joke; did it for homework.'

That was typical Flaherty – biology homework was supposed to be memorizing the carbon cycle, and instead he had made a joke.

'How do you make a hormone?'

'Don't know,' we all chorused back except Gonad, who tutted.

'Don't pay her.'

'Heard it before,' said Gonad.

Flaherty looked crestfallen for all of two seconds, and then he was away, flitting through the playground like a sprite or a spirit, or a really annoying kid who you couldn't hate even if you wanted to.

'Nutter,' said Stan, and we all concurred, smiling. And pretty soon the bell went and then it was school as usual, except for me worrying a bit about the *arsecheese* and the *bugnob*, and a lot about whatever else was happening in my head that made Doc Jones want to look in there with his CAT scan.

CHAPTER 4
THE KICK INSIDE

When I got home that afternoon I was feeling more tired than I'd ever felt before. It was as if I could sense the weight of the air on me, which is quite something given that every square centimetre of your body has a kilogram of air pressing down on it, and the only reason you don't get squashed like chewing gum on the street is that you have the same pressure pushing out from the inside, and that's why you explode if you go out in space without a spacesuit, because the pressure inside has no balancing pressure outside, so *boom!*

Mum was in the kitchen doing something with mung beans or aduki beans or some other bean you've never heard of. She was wearing one of her floaty dresses made from string and dandelion clocks. Her hair was down. It looked like a salt-and-pepper waterfall. I'd told her already that old people with long hair look like bunny-boilers, but it didn't sink in. I suppose she had some kind of mental image of how she looked which had probably stayed the same since she was twenty, and nothing was going to shift it.

She lifted her face from the pot of beans and smiled her dazed smile. Strands of hair fell down across her eyes and she tried to blow them away. A last few beams of late-afternoon sunshine came through the grimy kitchen window, and for a second I could imagine how she must once have looked, and I could see that her hair-blowing thing must once have been considered pretty cute by those in the market for cuteness.

'Hey, Heck!' she said.

'Hey, Mum.'

She'd obviously forgotten that I'd been to the hospital. I should have grown used to it by now, but it still got to me, sometimes, when I wasn't feeling great.

'How was school?' she asked, but I could tell even before the words were fully out that she'd drifted off again, back into the world of dreams and imagination, away from the reality of mung beans and schools and hospitals.

I went to my room. Had some homework. Atomic weights. Periodic table. Osmium. It took me ten minutes. I love the periodic table. It tells you everything about the material world, everything about what it's made from, about what combines with what, about how everything comes together. I sometimes think that if our universe was destroyed an alien power from another dimension could reconstruct it all just from the periodic table, right down to me being here now thinking these thoughts. And the way that Mendeleyev thought it all up without knowing any-thing at all about the structure of the atom, just by writing down everything he knew about individual elements on cards and then arranging them in groups according to similarities. All just mind-blowing. But not the sort of thing you could own up to thinking, at least to anyone outside my gang.

Arsium.

I jumped.

Shit.

The voice again.

'OK, who, I mean what the fuck is this?' I'd spoken before I realized I'd even opened my mouth.

Somehow the voice here in my room with Hawkgirl on the wall and my own duvet and pillows and stuff was much worse. It was an invasion.

There was a gap, when all I could hear was the blood pumping in my ears, and I felt like a twat for talking to myself. And then, just as I was beginning to relax:

It's me.

Well, that was even worse. The voice was definitely talking to me, answering back. It was deep, a bit theatrical, with a rasping edge to it.

I closed my eyes, trying to shut out the voice with blackness.

Knock knock, open up. Bored in here. Turn on the lights.

I shook my head from side to side. Then I opened my eyes and stood up. I went and looked at myself in the mirror. I was pale and my hair was sticking straight up, but that wasn't so surprising as it was always sticking straight up unless I gelled it down, and then it would eventually ping back with a noise you could hear from across the classroom.

Good Christ, what a mess. You look like a whorehouse bog brush.

I'd been watching closely, and my lips definitely weren't

moving. It was inside my head and it was talking to me.

'Who is "me"?'

That was me talking, the 'me' being him. It. Whatever. My voice was frail and quavery.

Ah, a . . . philosophical question. Who is me? Is that a question anyone can answer?

'T-try.'

Bugger it. I was adding stammering to the list of rubbish things I did.

Why, Hector – if you'll pardon my slide into familiarity – I am you.

I turned back to my bed and got under the duvet. It had footballs on it. And football boots. And some goals. And some animals. The animals were playing football. All in all it was a very busy duvet. I made a mental note to burn it.

You can't hide from what's inside.

The voice was taunting, but did not sound malicious. It was the way a friend would take the piss, feeling out your weaknesses without exploiting them.

I concentrated hard and worked at controlling my breathing.

'Was it you that said "arsecheese"?'

Jesus, I was talking back to the voice. I was losing it. I was a crazy man.

Oh, I was young then. I'd only just discovered the part which deals with speech.

'The part? The part of what?'

Keep up, boy. Have a guess.

I tried to think, tried to logic my way round this, or into it.

'My brain. You're in my brain.'

The voice did a sort of trumpeting fanfare by way of reply.

'You're in my brain,' I carried on, wonderingly. 'You're the thing that's making me dizzy. Am I mad?'

I don't know. Are you?

'Well, I've got a fucking voice in my head. Are you going to tell me that Satan is my master and I've got to go on a killing spree?'

Why should I do that?

The voice sounded wounded. I mean, playing at being wounded.

'It's what voices in your head usually say.'

I'm not that kind of voice. By the way, is Satan your master? It would put a slightly different slant on things.

'Not unless he's disguised as Mr Truelove.'

Humour! Good. I'd hate to end up in a bore. Take me back to the mirror, will you? I want to have a proper look at us.

'No.'

I could make you.

'Bullshit.'

Don't tempt me. It's early days yet, and I might make a mess of things. But I'd get you there.

'Horsepiss.'

If you insist.

And then I felt a weird thing. I mean, well, everything had been weird today, but we were now on a new level of weirdness, warp-factor-twelve weirdness. My arm started to slide out from under the duvet. I wasn't doing it. It was just moving. All by itself. No, not by itself. Just not helped by me. It wasn't my arm any more, it belonged to someone else. I grabbed it with my other hand and pulled it back. There was a moment of resistance, and then I was in charge again.

OK, OK, said the voice, sounding a little out of breath, *so I need a bit more practice before I try the old Mutiny-on-the-Bounty routine. But I can make life tricky for you, if I want. I'm talking here about making you step in dogshit or fall down in front of girls. Or boys, if that would work better. Let's have a little look down there. Mmmm . . . No, no, it seems girls will do the trick.*

'What? Down where? Where are you looking?'

Oh, just the old brain stem. Seat of the animal instincts. Desire, rage, hunger. Come on, to the mirror.

'I'll go if you stop playing games and tell me what you are.'

The voice sighed. *I wasn't playing games when I said that I'm you.*

'But you can't be me: I'm me, and you're . . . something else.'

Let me clarify. I'm made from you.

'Made from me?'

From your cells.

'My cells?'

Your brain cells.

'My brain cells?'

Yeah, OK with the repeating.

'Sorry. But this is a bit hard to take in.'

Keep going, you'll get there.

'So you're a thing in my brain made from my brain cells. How did you get there?'

Well, I grew, naturally.

And then I got it. So, I was slow on the uptake, but it had been a tough day and besides,

I Had a Fucking Brain Tumour.

No, let's be a bit more precise:

I Had a Fucking Talking Fucking Brain Tumour.

Hey, easy boy. Got a major adrenaline rush there, said the Tumour, as I now had to think of it. *Don't get me wrong, I love it, adrenaline, and we're going to make sure we get plenty more of it while I'm around, but now isn't the time. We're reflecting here. We want repose and tranquillity. What about a bit of a chant, like Mum? After me now, mmraangnuaangnoooooooooor.*

I'd been numb, but now something of the horror of it all was getting through. Thoughts rushed into my head like the cold frothing sea pouring into the hole in the *Titanic*.

Cancerdeathpainscalpelbloodwastingskullcancerdeath-painbloodcancerdeath.

'Shut the fuck up. Shut the fuck up.'

Then the door opened. Mum stood there, draped in towels, dripping from the bath. My head was ringing and reeling, and I guess I looked pretty white.

MUM :   Hector, what is it?
ME: Nothing.
MUM: But I heard you shouting.
ME: It was chemistry homework.
MUM: You've got to relax more.
TUMOUR: *That's just what I said.*
ME: Shut up.
MUM: What did you say?
ME: Nothing.
MUM: You told me to shut up. [Tears in her eyes.] You know it's the one thing we must never do. We must never shut up. We must always be able to speak. [Proper tears now. I'm feeling like a hound.]
ME: I'm sorry, Mum, it wasn't you. It was the . . . chemistry. Getting me down. Periodic table. Osmium.
TUMOUR: *Arsium.*
ME: Shut . . . shut . . . Shuttleworth's theory of molarity. You know, Mum, science.'

Of course, Mum would understand how science could upset you. She dried her eyes on the towel, and I got an unwelcome eyeful of Mum-tit. It hadn't been long since Mum stopped wandering about in the nude, so I suppose I should be grateful for small whatevers, but it didn't mean I had to enjoy it.

TUMOUR: Hubba hubba.

I didn't know if it was an ironic hubba or a real one, but either way I didn't like the implications. I bit my tongue, and Mum went sniffing out, carefully closing the door behind her.

ME: Don't hubba my mum, even in jest.

TUMOUR: *Hey, she's well hubbable.*

ME: No way!

TUMOUR: *Way!*

ME: Don't say 'way' like that. It doesn't suit you. You sound too old. It's Dad-at-the-disco time. And you're missing the point. If you *hub* her, and you're me, then I'm hubbing her, and I don't want to go there, or anywhere near there, or even in the same galaxy as there.

TUMOUR: *As they say, Oedipus schmoedipus.*

ME: Don't tell me you've read Freud. Why do I have to get an overeducated brain tumour?

TUMOUR: *I've read everything you've read. And what do you expect – I'm a brain tumour, not some dipshit of a colon cancer, or one of those frankly illiterate growths on your pancreas.*

ME: [Alarmed] My pancreas?

TUMOUR: [Soothing] *Pancreases in general. But you get the point. You see, I'm up here in the command module. I've got all the panels, all the displays, all the data. Everything you've ever learned is here, everything you've ever heard or seen or* smelled, *even stuff you've forgotten. It's never lost. There's always a neurone pathway somewhere with the memory intact, a memory of a memory, if you dig deep enough. And digging's what I do. If I need some data, then I can send off a tendril, reach out and take it.*

ME: You sound creepy. Like some kind of monster.

TUMOUR: *Monster? No, not me. I have a . . . cousin, you could say. Teratoma. It comes from the Greek word for monster. You don't want one of those. You really don't want one of those. Like having a lion loose in your underpants, but not in a good way. No, I'm not a monster. I'm your friend. I'm you. We're us. And we're tired. Let's have a kip. Might be out for a while. Need my beauty sleep. Nightie night.*

ME: Nightie ni— *Shut up!* You're my imagination. I'm already dreaming.

Then there was a time without any talking from either of us, but just before I fell asleep, I found myself asking: 'What shall I call you?'

Call me? Mmmmm, Henry. Henry Tumour. That has a ring to it. A royal ring.

CHAPTER 5
THE GREAT EARTH
SPIRIT WHO IS FATHER
OF US ALL

I woke up. I'd been dreaming. The images dissolved before I could get hold of them, but I knew they weren't nice. For five minutes I didn't move and just stared straight up at the ceiling. It was still pock-marked with Blu-Tack. The Blu-Tack had once held lengths of white thread in its gummy grip. The white thread had been attached to the fuselage of – if I remember correctly – a Gloucester Gladiator biplane (very tricky to make with all those struts and that whole extra wing business), locked in mortal combat with a Grumman F14 Tomcat jet fighter. My plucky biplane had been giving that Tomcat one hell of a seeing to – I suppose that looking on the Americans as the bad guys is one of the things that Mum passed on to me. But the Gladiator and the Tomcat had come down a year before when I realized that it probably wasn't what a foxy chick would want to look at as she lay on her back and I brought her to heights of ecstasy she'd never dreamed existed.

Yeah, well.

I was listening, my whole body tense, like a matchstick you flex between your thumb and forefinger, feeling for the breaking point. I could hear the morning noises: the birds bitching outside; a baby crying somewhere; car doors slamming like it was a contest; Mr Walsh in the next house having his absurdly long morning piss, the sound clear and loud as a clarinet through the paper walls. But as for voices in my head, well, there weren't any. I'd imagined it or dreamed it or imagined I'd dreamed it or dreamed I'd imagined it.

I mean, a talking brain tumour? Pah!

It'd be a singing verruca next, or a bum-boil doing stand-up comedy.

I dragged myself out of bed and went and made Mum a cup of rhubarb-and-nettle tea. Or maybe it was alfalfa-and-horseradish. Or dandelion-and-hemp. I should have looked on the box. Anyway, it smelled like something you'd scoop out of a tramp's belly button.

'Thanks, love,' she said. 'What time is it?'

'It's in the morning.'

Without putting the radio on it was hard to be more precise. None of the clocks told the right time, and some differed by several years, so if you went by the one in the kitchen the Spice Girls were still showing their knickers on *Top of the Pops*.

I sat on the duvet next to her and drank my coffee while she sipped her liquorice-and-piss infusion.

'You remember I went to the hospital yesterday, Mum?'

'Of course I remember, sweetie. What kind of mother do you think I am? I called the doctor afterwards. He told me all about it, and said you had an appointment next week for a scan.'

That made me feel better. I really did think she'd just forgotten the whole thing: the headaches, the first trip to the GP, the works.

'I'm a bit frightened, Mum.'

She always liked it when I said things like that. And I was, a bit. Frightened, I mean.

She put her arm round me.

'It'll be fine.'

She kissed the top of my head, which ordinarily would have been out of bounds, me being at least twenty centimetres taller than her. But now it felt like the right thing to do.

She sniffed.

'When did you last wash your hair?'

Now, I suppose that's the kind of question lots of parents ask their teenage kids, with the implied suggestion that now would be a good time to do it, BECAUSE YOU STINK. It was a bit more complex than that with Mum.

'Yesterday.'

She looked disappointed.

'You know it flushes out the natural oils.'

'I don't like the natural oils, Mum. It's just another name for grease. People take the p— People make fun.'

'You should be a bit less concerned by what other people think.'

I hated it when she said that kind of thing. It wasn't her that was having the piss ripped. And that was probably why I said the stupid thing, because I wanted to get my own back, even though it meant ruining things.

'I wish Dad was here.'

Instantly I felt her flesh change, turning from something soft and warm to something cold and hard, as if she were being fossilized at a billion times the usual rate.

OK, time for a bit of family history.

My mum was a political activist, back in the olden days when they still had them. 'Activist' maybe isn't the best word for someone who spent five years staying in one place. She joined some kind of demo outside a nuclear-missile base back in the middle of the 1980s, and ended up staying there until the Americans decided that the Russians weren't about to attack on account of the fact that they had nothing to attack with and probably didn't want to attack anyway, and the base closed down.

And somehow, despite the fact that it was supposed to be an all-girl peace camp, my mum managed to come out of it holding on to a mewling, puking me, wrapped up in a home-crotcheted poncho bedecked with CND badges and stinking of woodsmoke.

She's never told me who my dad was, but she did love to drone on about everything else that happened – the riots when the local council tried to evict them, the break-in to the base when they spray-painted flowers on nuclear bombers, the solidarity, the singing, the blaming men in general for all the bad stuff in the world. It was obviously the time when my mum felt she was most alive, and when she talks about it her face takes on this glow, and she looks like the stained-glass window in the school chapel, the one with Mary being told by the angel that she's up the stick, and as far as me knowing who my dad is, the two conceptions were equally miraculous.

So, she's quite happy to wax lyrical about the time ten thousand peace marchers held hands around the base, but if I mention how I came to be here, it's always the fossilization thing.

'You haven't got a father,' she said. 'Except for the Great Earth Spirit Who is Father of Us All.'

'OK, Mum,' I said, and got up and went to school.

CHAPTER 6
HECTOR BRUNTY:
LOVER AND FIGHTER

I got to school thinking about nothing much. My walk had become a lot more boring since I stopped kicking stones. For maybe three years I'd played this game with myself where I'd find a stone and try to dribble it all the way to wherever I was going. Usually school. And then back again. I'm not saying that it beat strip poker with Uma Upshaw, but it was a hell of a lot better than just mooching along, *not* kicking a stone. And the game had its complexities. I used to award myself points for style, say for bouncing the stone off a wall in such a way that it would roll back to me and I could take it on again without breaking stride. And for kicking it over or round obstacles. And for getting it across the road in one long curving punt. And there were bonus points for using a tricky stone, larger than the average, say, or smaller, or one with an especially irregular shape. You get the idea.

But then a couple of months ago I was forced to realize that it was another of the things (like having model aeroplanes hanging from your ceiling) that was unlikely to appeal to girls. This lesson was administered when I kicked my stone (a piece of angular flint, difficult to control, so I began with fifty bonus points) into the aforementioned Uma Upshaw's heel.

Now, Uma Upshaw is nothing like the other girls in our year. For a start, she looks about nineteen years old, and I mean *all* over. She's got black hair and red lips, and boy does she fill her school blouse. And even her initials, UU, look like two perfect bra-busters. I'm not quite as convinced as some of the other kids about her features – nose, eyes, ears and stuff – which to me look undistinguished, but the overall package is undoubtedly phenomenal.

So Uma Upshaw turns round slowly, after my stone has scuffed into the back of her shoe (black, pointy, with a forbidden high heel). I'm not sure she's ever noticed me before, but now she's doing some noticing, sadly not the good noticing. This is bad noticing. Uma is looking at me the way a lioness looks at a warthog – like I was something ugly, but she just might eat me anyway.

'Did you do that?' Her voice was flat, emotionless, haughty. Like some kind of death goddess, although that makes her sound a bit too Goth, and she isn't one of those. (We have three Goths in our school and, like all their ilk, they have very thin legs and very long fingers and their acne bubbles away under their face paint, and they are gentle creatures, but they play no part in this story and I won't mention them again.)

'What?'

So why is it right *now* that my voice, which is perfectly well broken, decides to come out like a castrated choirboy? Compared to Uma I sound, and feel, about fifteen centimetres tall, although we're really the same height, at least when she isn't wearing the heels.

'You heard.'

Now Uma isn't one of the tough girls. She's not frightening the way Susan Sutcliffe is frightening. Susan Sutcliffe fights with razorblades. Susan Sutcliffe will happily suck your eyeball out and piss in the socket.

Uma's scary in another way. A way that is all to do with the knowledge that she has something everyone wants, and the supplementary knowledge that you definitely don't have anything that she wants.

'Sorry.'

Shit: I've gone even higher. I could probably use that squeak for echo-location, like a fucking bat.

She looked for a second like she was going to continue the discussion, but then her dignity stepped in and told her that even talking to the kind of kid who kicked stones along the street for a living and squeaked like a bat was damaging her cool. And so she turned away again without so much as a consoling *fuck you* or *up yours*, and never mind a *put your head between these babies and flub away*.

So that's why I stopped with the stone-kicking, and let no man say that I am deaf to the stern tutor that we call Experience.

I said I got to school not thinking about much, but that was an effort. I knew that if I relaxed I was going to be thinking about the thing in my head. The voice. And the thing that owned the voice.

''Sup, Heck?'

It was Stanislaw. I'd got through the gates without

incident. The sentinels there were doing more of the staring-at-the-painting-on-the-social-club-wall thing, but this time I didn't stare with them.

'Oh, hi, Stan. Nothing much. Still stuck in the same place. Gets frustrating.'

We began to walk across the red-gra, heading towards the school buildings. A drizzle was falling, although it was so fine it seemed to hang about in the air, floating up as much as it fell down. But some at least had reached ground level and turned the red-gra pitch into meat paste. I could feel it gently sucking at the soles of my shoes.

As I may previously have intimated, I hated my shoes. Mum got them from a special catalogue and they were made from knotted tree vines and carob nuts. Not really, but you get the idea. They were rubbish at keeping the wet out, but truly excellent at making me look stupid.

'I've told you, you can't get further without a power-up. You think you're wasting time stopping, that you should just plough on, but you've got to collect those energy packs or you'll never get out of that place. Power-ups are the key. You've got to be thinking ahead. Speculate to accumulate.'

Stan was a fast talker, once he got going.

'Yeah, yeah, but when you stop, they get you.'

And then they got him. I didn't even see them coming. The first I knew was that someone had Stan in a headlock.

It was Sean Johnson.

Johnson wasn't one of the evil kids. He was too thick to be evil. In fact, on his own, he was an affable, harmless character, if a bit smelly. He was led astray by the Evil Ones, who told him what to do. There was an Evil

One with him now, Chris Tierney, telling him what to do.

'Hold him, Sean,' said Tierney, a bit superfluously, as that's exactly what Sean was doing. Tierney was small – not that much taller than Stan – and neat and quick. He dipped his fingers into Stan's pockets, looking for his money. This happened sometimes in our school.

Stan looked at me, his eyes wide and frightened. I felt sick, helpless. My legs wouldn't work. Tierney turned round, following Stan's line of sight.

'What you fucking looking at?' he said matter-of-factly, as if he was asking the time.

My mouth opened, but nothing came out. Tierney waited patiently.

'Kissy, kissy, kissy, ooooooo, baby.'

Flaherty had appeared out of nowhere. He was writhing around, fondling himself, making out that Tierney and Stan were engaged in a passionate embrace.

It was very funny.

If you weren't Tierney.

Kids started to snigger. It was brilliant, but it didn't last. Flaherty, bored already, whirled away to find mischief else-where. But the spell had been broken and I found that I could speak.

'Why don't you leave him alone,' I managed, finally. It was about as brave as I got. It had all the impact of a butterfly landing on a machine-gun.

Tierney paused, his hands still in Stan's pockets. I stared back at him, or rather at the air a metre or so above his head, and even that proved a bit too much for me and I felt my eyelid begin to twitch. I became aware of the watching

kids, of the shapes around us. Tierney took his hands out
of Stan's pockets and swaggered over, a narrow grin on his
weaselly face.

'*Leave him alone*,' he said, mimicking me, but making
me sound more of a poof. He was trying to make up for the
Flaherty embarrassment. Then he stopped smiling. 'You
gonna make me?'

'Just leave it out, will you, Tierney?'

I was trying not to sound too aggressive, trying to keep
things sane. Appealing to the profound wells of love and
gentleness in Tierney's soul. Trying not to run away crying
like a baby.

'Or what? You'll tell your dad? Oh, wait, *you haven't
fucking got one, have you*?'

Oscar Wilde eat your heart out.

Then Tierney pushed me firmly in the chest. I fell over.
Another of the Tierney gang had knelt on all fours behind
me. It turned the whole confrontation back into a comedy,
with me this time as the butt. People were laughing. Some
pink-flamingo girls turned sneeringly away. Amanda
Something, the strawberry girl, was there again, standing as
ever apart from the group. She didn't turn away, but looked
at me, sprawling like a fool on the slimy ground. My
humiliation swamped any anger I might have felt about
what Tierney had said.

About not having a dad.

The good side to all this was that Tierney and his mob
seemed content with what they'd done and started to amble
away, like hyenas leaving a stain on the grass that used to
be a zebra.

'*Thou whoreson obscene greasy tallow-catch!*'

Whoooa! What the hell was that?

It wasn't in my head. I mean it *was* in my head, but it was also in my mouth. I mean screamed at full volume, all decibels blazing. And not just screamed, but filled with a kind of laughing contempt.

Tierney and his stooges turned round.

'What did you say?'

I genuinely had no idea. And I don't suppose Tierney knew what it meant any more than I did. Maybe that's what saved me. That or the fact that the playground supervisor, Mrs Trimble, was stumping towards us on her varicosely lumpy legs, her grey hair sticking out like she'd been hooked up to the Van der Graaf generator in the physics lab.

'Come on now, boys,' she said. 'In you get. It's after nine.'

In general nobody took much notice of Mrs Trimble, but that didn't mean that kickings could be administered freely in her presence.

'C'mon, Heck,' said Stan. 'Let's not miss registration.' And then, as we got going, he added, 'What was that thing you said to Tierney?'

'I don't really know, Stan. I don't know what happened. It just came out. It sounded olden days, like Shakespeare or something. I must have picked it up in English.'

Mrs Hegarty, our English teacher, was a Shakespeare nut, and she was always getting us to do read-throughs, even of plays that weren't on the syllabus. She only really trusted us with the bit parts, and took all the main roles for herself, so she'd often end up having to kill herself or chat herself up.

There was a bit of a pause. The sound of Stan thinking.

'Thanks, though.'

'I didn't do anything. It was Flaherty really, making him look stupid.'

'Yeah, but you tried. I hate him.'

'Tierney?'

'Yeah, Tierney. Johnson's just a tool. A monkey, I mean. And Tierney's the organ-grinder.'

'Small organ,' I said, which didn't really bear analysing, but we laughed anyway.

'Minuscule,' said Stan.

CHAPTER 7
DOWN AND OUT

And then we were in the classroom, and we were late, and still smiling about Tierney's little organ, which never looks good (the smiling, I mean, not the little organ) when you enter a classroom late, and so Mrs Conlon began to shout.

When Mrs Conlon was still Miss Walsh – and it was only a few months ago – she never used to shout. The shouting was all to do with Mr Conlon. Before Mr Conlon she had been one of the nice ones – nice *and* pretty. She was still pretty, in a small, blonde way, but she wasn't nice any more. And being shouted at by someone who you fancied added extra levels of unpleasantness, unless you happen to be a perve, which I'm not, at least not yet, because you never quite know how you're going to turn out.

My class was 9M. We stayed together for registration, PE, RE, citizenship, domestic science and other stuff that didn't need brains. Everything else was streamed. 9M was, therefore, about thirty-two per cent psychos, fifty-six per cent normals, ten per cent retards, and two per cent brainy.

'Get out,' screamed Mrs Conlon.

Stan and I looked at her meekly, trying to show that we were not worth her wrath.

'Nobody runs into my classroom. Not grinning like an idiot. What do you think this is, the Wild West?'

It seemed a curious comparison to make, but occasion-ally, in her rage, Mrs Conlon's imagination would run away with her. She once yelled at us: 'Who do you think I am, Catherine the Great?' which baffled us completely, and not even history boffin Gonad could guess at what she meant, although the next day he came back after some research and told Stan, Smurf and me that one rumour had it that Catherine the Great perished while trying to have it off with a horse, but that that was probably just a lie put about by her enemies. I wished he hadn't told me that, because for a while afterwards I kept imagining Mrs Conlon ... Well, you can imagine what I imagined.

'No, Mrs Conlon. But we were—' And then there was more shouting.

And then – I don't quite know how – I was on the floor. I suppose it was some kind of faint, but fainting makes me sound like a girl.

Swoon?

No, much worse. Sound like a wuss.

Collapse, that's it.

I collapsed.

I think I might have seen some colours, and there was a smell of something in between flowers and burning plastic. And then I was looking up at the polystyrene tiles on the ceiling, thinking how the pockmarking of little craters in each tile must be different, so every tile was unique, and there must be billions of them in the world, like people.

And then there were faces around me: the gawping faces of kids – psychotic, retarded, normal, brainy – and then, looming over them, the concerned face of Mrs Conlon, who had thankfully stopped shouting and might have turned briefly back into nice Miss Walsh.

'Pick him up,' someone said.

'No, leave him, he might have a neck injury.'

'He fell on 'is arse, not his neck.' *Slap*. 'Ow! Sorry, miss. Bum. Ow! I mean backside.'

'Is he dead?'

'Miss, if he's dead can I have his desk?'

'He's not dead, he's in a coma.'

'His eyes are open.'

'That happens sometimes.'

'Maybe he's a zombie.'

'I think he's a poof.' *Slap*. 'Ow!'

I stood up, disappointing those who favoured death or coma, although the zombie supporters remained hopeful.

'Are you OK, Hector?' Mrs Conlon still wasn't shouting.

'Yeah. Must have slipped or something.'

I was embarrassed and felt a blush coming on, unstoppable as stampeding bison. Blushing is one of my things. I really wish it wasn't because it makes you look stupid and weak.

'Do you want to go to the sick bay?'

The sick bay was a small room next to the office. It's where the sticking plasters were kept. And a tube of Savlon. And a bucket. For the vomit. It often smelled of vomit (the room, not just the bucket), which is why it was called the sick bay. Actually, there were two buckets, both vomit-oriented. As well as the bucket for actually spewing into, there was also the sand bucket, used post-spew to strew the spew with sand, although why puke must be covered with sand prior to cleaning is one of those arcane mysteries like why the dinosaurs died out, or what happened at Area 42, or just what is going on down the front of Uma Upshaw's blouse.

There was also (in the sick bay, not down Uma's blouse) a slightly grisly head-and-torso dummy used for practising mouth-to-mouth resuscitation in citizenship classes. It was a lady one, perhaps pretty once, but a decade of heavy use had seen her fall into a decline, and her hair was all matted and greasy, and the paint was flaking off her and one of her eyes had come out and was on the floor next to her, waiting for a visit from the grisly-head-and-torso-resuscitation-dummy doctor.

(That, by the way, is a good use of the hyphen. If I'd said the 'grisly head-and-torso-resuscitation-dummy doctor', i.e. leaving out the hyphen after 'grisly', then it would mean that the doctor was grisly, and not the head-and-torso resuscitation dummy. I suppose that the doctor might also be grisly, in which case I should have said the 'grisly grisly-head-and-torso-resuscitation-dummy doctor'. And I've just thought that if that doctor himself got sick, then he'd go and see the 'grisly grisly-head-and-torso-resuscitation-dummy doctor doctor'. And if that doctor was, in turn, grisly, then—)

Enough already.

What?

Just get on with the story.

OK, Henry. Where was I?

'No, miss.'

I really didn't want to go to the sick bay. You'd have to be mad to go to the sick bay. You'd have to be sick to—

On the way to double chemistry, Stan asked me if I was feeling all right. He looked concerned. OK, so he always looked concerned about something, but that something wasn't usually me. I thought about telling him about my head troubles, Doc Jones, the works, but for some reason I couldn't. It wasn't even the sort of embarrassment that might stop you talking about your undescended testicles or pubic lice. It was a deeper reluctance, and it was dark and shrouded. And it had gotten itself mixed up with annoyance. So I went on the attack.

'Shut up, will you, Stan? You're the one who's allergic to the world. I mean, is there anything, and I mean literally *anything*, in the universe that doesn't make you sneeze, or make your eyes water, or bring you out in welts?'

It wasn't supposed to be unkind, but I think it probably came out that way. In any case Stan wasn't the sort to engage in repartee. He was more the sort who'd go off and hate himself in a corner, so I shouldn't have taken that path with him.

'You're just as bad.'

'It's only nuts, with me. You're everything. I mean, kiwi fruit? Who ever heard of being allergic to kiwi fruit?'

'So?'

'And latex.'

'Uh.'

'And pollen. All pollen.'

Stan shrugged. 'You've got that too, remember.'

'And wheat, and milk and . . .' But by then I was talking to his back and feeling like a sod. At least I hadn't mentioned his twitches and tics.

He had two main sorts. The first sort involved closing one eye, while the same side of the face made a kind of fluttering movement. It was a bit like a wink performed by a ham actor in a Restoration comedy with wigs and frock-coats and ornamental snuff boxes – our class went to see a performance of *The Fondling Fop* by Sir Humbert Halfninney (1643–1701) at the theatre in town, so I know all about this. The second sort of tic involved at least one additional eye in a sequence of rapid blinking, his face otherwise immobile.

I'm honestly not trying to be mean about Stan, who I love like a brother. I just want to give you the whole picture, and if you miss out on the blinking and winking (oh, and the compulsive knee shaking) then you're not seeing him like he is, in the round.

Anyway, he went and sat on one side of Gonad, and I sat on the other and, given Phil's bulk, that was a long way apart.

We were doing colloids. I had a soft spot for colloids. A colloid is a mixture of two different things: a mixture, but *not* – and this is the important bit – a compound. There's no chemical reaction between the two, nor any physical bonding. Just two or more things rubbing along together. So, a gel is a liquid suspended in a solid, an emulsion is a liquid in a liquid, smoke is a solid suspended in a gas, a fog is a liquid suspended in a gas, and a foam is a gas suspended in a liquid.

I could go on.

I told you I liked colloids.

Mr Brightman taught chemistry, and he was one of the teachers who mysteriously seemed not to hate us. He told us jokes and tried to make chemistry interesting with stories about what stuff explodes and what gases are the most poisonous, and how much of them it would take to kill, say, a million people, or an elephant. He was very tall, but yet drove a tiny Ford Fiasco, which was also quite funny, and which tended to earn him not insults but rather points for a good visual gag. Seeing him climb in and out of the little car was like watching a giraffe trying to have sex with a tortoise.

As I was getting my books and pens out, Gonad said, 'Heard you fainted.'

'Didn't faint.'

'He did,' said Stan from somewhere beyond Phil.

A girl called Sarah Wrigglesworth said, 'Yes, he did. He fainted, and he dribbled.'

She wasn't talking to anyone in particular, just adding her bit to the general humiliation. I didn't remember dribbling. Dribbling's one of the things I'd most like not to do in life, and it's not even one of those things you could imagine getting into in certain extreme circumstances, like cannibalism or sheep-shagging. It's just a complete no thanks, and I don't care how many parallel universes there happen to be.

But then Mr Brightman came to my rescue, and it was colloids for the next hour and twenty minutes.

CHAPTER 8
SMURF IN LOVE

We'd all given up on school dinners. It wasn't just the stuff they gave you – the eyeball-and-scrotum burgers, the pilchards, the mashed swede (Olaf, we called him) – it was more what might happen to it before it got into you; the things done to it while your back was turned, or even in your plain sight. As a bare minimum your water would be spat in and you'd find chewing gum or fag butts in your sago pudding. (OK, so that provided a mild improvement in flavour, but still, not a good thing to have happen.)

I once had to watch while Johnson, acting under orders, stuck his index finger down the back of his underpants and, after a few seconds of rootling, plunged it into my flopping mound of reconstituted potato, where it left a brown smudge.

Cheers.

So it was packed lunches for me and Stan (chess maestro) and Gonad (small ears) and Smurf (big lips), eaten in the same place every day – a kind of crinkle in the outside wall of the school library, out of the way of the wind, and, as it was partially hidden by a ragged line of dying rose bushes, easily missed by passing psychos.

To begin with, today, there was just me and Smurf. Like I said before, Smurf had 'nice' written all the way through him like rock. He usually joined in the piss-taking and banter when we were all together, but when it was just the two of us he became more serious. And the thing he was most serious about was girls.

As a gang we didn't talk much about girls – I mean, real girls as opposed to, for example, Hawkgirls. It wasn't that we didn't think about them, but just that, well, too much was at stake. You couldn't say that you fancied so and so, because it was pathetic, given that we were all no-hopers, and our chance of being fancied back was as close to zero as you can get without actually dipping into the negative numbers. A few of the other boys in the year – the cool, the bold, the persevering – had girlfriends, but that wasn't for us, and we coped with the fact in our own different ways. Stan clammed up. Gonad lusted graphically. I joked. But I think the one who suffered the most was Smurf, partly because he was such a romantic, which meant that he was usually in some kind of love with a girl. I mean the whole girl, too, and not just some bit of her like, for example, her breasts, and partly because of all of us, he was the one most subjected to ridicule, on account of the lips. It was a tragic combination.

And right now I could tell that not everything was well in the gentle heart of Simon Murphy. He was slumped in the corner, staring at his trainers. Smurf was a very bendy person, and sometimes looked like he had no bones at all.

ME: Whassup, Smurf?

SMURF: [He looks up, his big brown eyes full of love-misery. He shakes his head.] Nothing. Nah, nothing.

ME: Who is it this time?

SMURF: No one.

ME: Come on. It's either some girl, or you've just heard that an asteroid is going to vaporize us in ten minutes.

SMURF: [Pause. Then another pause.] Yeah, well. I was just thinking. So who do you think is the most . . . the one with the best . . . the . . . I mean, who do you fancy?

ME: You mean, Hawkgirl or Buffy?

SMURF: You know I don't mean that. I mean, just in general. In our year.

ME: Look, Smurf, just tell me who you're talking about.

SMURF: [Mumbling.] It's mad. I haven't got a chance.

HENRY: *He's right there, whoever it is. Unless it's Monga from Planet Ugly.*

ME: Shss— I mean, do you want me to guess? Is it that little rodenty thing in chemistry? The one who asked you if she could share your test tube? I'm sure she stores food in cheek pouches, like a gerbil.

SMURF: No, it's not her. And it was my burner, not my test tube.

ME: Aha! So you admit it's someone in particular, and not someone in general?

SMURF: [Non-committal shrug.]

HENRY: *It's probably an Internet porn star. I bet he's getting through ten packs of computer-screen wipes a night.*

ME: Dawn Elkington, then? She's not bad. You know. For a girl. I suppose it depends on where you stand on the issue of verrucas.

SMURF: How do you know she's got verrucas?

ME: Keeps her socks on for gymnastics.

SMURF: Oh yeah. Good deduction. No, not her. But not 'cause of the verrucas. I wouldn't let verrucas stand in the way. Not on their own. I'm not that superficial.

ME: Moira Pennington?

SMURF: No, not her either. Look, do you swear you won't tell the others?

ME: Of course I won't.

SMURF: Oh, Jesus, I can't even say it. Have another guess.

ME: I'm getting bored now. OK, Uma Upshaw, then.

I said it without thinking, not supposing for a second that Smurf would be mad enough to fancy someone like her. It was like the story of the mouse who lusts after a she-elephant. One day, when the elephant is having a drink in the river, the mouse sees his chance and leaps on her back and starts to, er, make passionate love to her. At that moment a crocodile grabs hold of the elephant's trunk, and the elephant starts thrashing around and trumpeting, and the mouse thinks that she's having a big elephanty orgasm and he squeaks out, 'Oh yeah, baby.' Well, OK, so it's not much like that, except in the way the elephant doesn't even know the mouse is there.

And then I saw from Smurf's face that I'd hit the mark.

ME: But she's a cow. And she used to go out with Tierney, you know.

SMURF: I know. But she's . . . she's beautiful. And she chucked Tierney, I heard.

HENRY: *Slap this joker down.*

ME: Bloody hell, Smurf. I mean, what do you plan to do? You can't ask her out, can you?

SMURF: Why not? No, I can't. Do you think I'd have a chance? Could you maybe ask one of her friends? I mean, ask them if she likes me?

ME: Are you kidding? Those girls are like African hunting dogs. Is there no one else? You know, someone more . . . someone nicer? The gerbil girl? If she didn't like you she wouldn't have shared your test tube.

SMURF: Bunsen burner.

He filled the words 'Bunsen' and 'burner' with a level of anguish that the great Otto Bunsen could never have imagined would be associated with his epoch-making invention. (I know, by the way, that the Bunsen burner was really developed by Robert Bunsen, but as he was a German and Robert sounds about as German as Seamus, I think he ought to be renamed Otto. Plus Otto is a slightly funny name, and Robert isn't funny at all.)

But I understood what Smurf meant. It didn't seem fair that the best we could hope for was a timid girl with nuts in her cheeks and a furry tail. And yeah, I realize it was just as bad for her, with her hopes set no higher than a big-lipped bendy boffin like Smurf, even if he would probably make the world's greatest boyfriend in terms of being nice to you and not messing about behind your back.

And those were the kind of thoughts we were both still lost in when Gonad and Stan joined us. Well, with me there was one other thought, but it didn't really belong to me. It came in the voice of Henry Tumour, and it said:

She's mine.

CHAPTER 9
THE NAKED LUNCH

Gonad peeled back the white bread from his sandwich.

'Mmm, chopped pork,' he said. 'I'm partial to chopped pork.'

It was what he always said. A kind of catchphrase, except not funny. Except that it had become kind of funny because he said it so much and because it wasn't really funny.

'What you got, Stan?'

'Soup.'

Stan often brought in a flask of soup. It was usually chicken noodle, but not often enough to make it funny, and sometimes he had oxtail, and sometimes it wasn't soup at all but a shock cheese roll or a surprise sausage bap.

Smurf opened his Tupperware and wordlessly showed off a slice of quiche with a dainty little garnish of lettuce, ruffled like a lace collar. There was no spirit of triumphalism in this. Simon's mother loved him. Perhaps too much. On the upside you could be pretty sure that Smurf's loving mother had secreted a tasty treat – a Wagon Wheel, say, or a Cadbury's Chocolate Roll – somewhere about his person. Today he had a Snickers, which was top of the range, but not, obviously, of interest to me.

Stan had been right about my nut allergy. I hadn't always had it, and I blame it on the fact that, because of Mum, nuts were about the commonest thing in my diet throughout my formative years. Nut roasts, nut cutlets; nuts fried, nuts boiled, nuts mashed. Brazil, cashew, pea, hazel, almond, macadamia, wal, you name it. Then, in Year Seven, I was eating a dry-roasted peanut when my throat started to itch, and then my eyes watered, and people started to stare at me, and Stan said that I'd gone a funny colour, and I coughed up the fatal peanut and loads of kids were around me laughing and pointing, and I had to go to the sick bay, and from then on nuts were out and I envied Simon his Snickers bar not one bit.

They all looked towards me. *My* lunchbox was feared among the cognoscenti. For lunch I always had whatever we'd eaten the night before, sometimes in sandwich form (sliced lentil bake on wholemeal, anyone?), sometimes neat (e.g. cold alfalfa pizza). Of course, there was always plenty left over from last night, because it was horrible even then. Served frigid and desiccated, calcified into strange shapes, it took some swallowing.

And then I realized that, in fact, today I had nothing. Not a rissole, not a falafel, not a chickpea. I had completely forgotten to scrape out last night's slop. For no good reason I found this shaming.

'Ate it already,' I said.

Stan looked at me strangely, his eyes growing narrow. And then I said something else. It came out in a mumbling sort of way, but with an edge that made it completely understandable.

I said: 'Losers.'

'What?' Smurf was chewing. Unlike Gonad, he was a polite chewer and you hardly ever saw what was in there.

I looked back at them, stuck again for words.

'Nothing.'

'You said something.'

That was Gonad. He sounded a bit touchy.

ME: I just said 'loofahs'.

GONAD: What's a loofah?

ME: For shitting in.

No one laughed. I don't know why. We laughed at stuff every day that wasn't funny.

SMURF: It's one of those long scratchy things for washing your back. I think it's the inside of something. My mum uses one for exfoliating.

GONAD: Isn't that what you do to trees? You know, Agent Orange and all that. The Americans in Vietnam. So the geeks had nowhere to hide.

ME: *Gooks*. They called them gooks.

GONAD: Whatever.

SMURF: Yeah, but girls do it too.

ME: What?

SMURF: Exfoliating.

GONAD: So what have girls and trees got in common? I mean, so the same thing can happen to them?

ME: Well, if it's a melon tree, they both have melons.

STAN	Melons don't grow on trees.
GONAD:	Course they do. All fruit grows on trees.
SMURF:	Strawberries don't. Nor melons.
GONAD:	So where do they grow?
STAN:	Just sort of on the floor, kind of lying there.
GONAD:	Doesn't seem very likely.
STAN:	I think we're drifting off the point.
SMURF:	Which was?
ME:	What it is that girls and trees both have in common so that they can both do this 'exfoliating' thing?
STAN:	Actually, that wasn't the point.
SMURF:	What was it then?
STAN:	The point was why Hector called us a bunch of losers.

And suddenly our little alcove, our refuge, our safe haven, had become a fraction colder. They were all looking at me strangely now.

Never seen such a whey-faced crowd of misbegotten lollards.

This time it didn't come out. This time it was all safely inside. But that didn't mean that I was comfortable with it.

Ditch them.

I blinked, trying to concentrate on the three on the outside, closing off the one within.

'I wasn't talking about you. I meant Tierney and that lot. I was – what do you call it? – musing.'

There was a little pause while the four of us all sort of mused together, but then in an entirely new tone,

Gonad said, 'Talk of the devil,' and I looked where he had glanced and saw Tierney and three others coming our way.

CHAPTER 10
THE RAID

One was Johnson; one was a hollow-eyed lanky kid called Murdo, who had always scared the shit out of me on the solid enough grounds that he was shit scary; and the other one didn't have a name or at least not one that I knew. He was a skinhead, so pale he looked albino, and you could see the veins underneath his skin, and he had the festering scabs of a glue-sniffer around his mouth and nose.

A good rule of thumb is: don't mess with glue-sniffers.

There were sores and scabs all over his ears as well, where his attempts at home piercing had gone wrong.

Another good rule of thumb is: don't mess with people who do their own body-piercing.

Now all this meant that this No-Name character should have been as scary as Murdo, but for some reason he wasn't. He was pathetic.

He's the one.

Uh?

He's the one.

What?

The one to target.

Target?

This time.

Time?

Always find the weak one. Oh yes.

Gonad, Stan and Smurf were hunkering down, trying to sink into the concrete. In fact, it was more telescopic than that, because their heads had sunk into their necks and their necks into their shoulders and their shoulders into their chests and their chests into their arses and their arses into the hard world.

This kind of thing happened about one in every six lunchtimes, or slightly over fifteen per cent of the time, which may not sound much, but it was enough to take any fun out of it. They'd find us here, steal our food, slap our heads, take the piss.

Sometimes they'd almost act as if we were just messing about together, having a laugh. But then it would turn, just as you found yourself smiling at some dumb thing Johnson had said, or at one of Tierney's sly put downs. And then you'd get stamped on. And that made it worse, because they'd managed to suck you in, so you felt dirty as well as sore (and hungry).

I don't know why, but this time I didn't join my friends in shrinking into the concrete. Something to do with what was happening inside my head, I expect. I wasn't looking at Tierney, but at the no-name scab boy. I felt kind of funny. Kind of tingly.

No, should try harder than that.

What I felt was a faint pinpricking across my shoulders, as if sharp claws were delicately running over my skin, and there was a tension at the base of my skull, and a humming in my ears like the sound you hear from power lines, and a smell like bitter almonds, not unlike the smell I'd got before I fainted, I mean passed out. These were all new sensations to me and I think that overall I'd have to say that they were pleasant, that they were exciting.

'Hey, it's bummers' corner,' said Tierney.

'Gis a sarnie,' said Johnson, wading in, all elbows and ammonia.

'And I'll have that,' said Murdo, taking a Wagon Wheel from Gonad.

Smurf had dropped his Snickers bar in the middle of us. Instead of taking it, Tierney pushed through and stamped on it, grinding the chocolate, caramel, nougat and nuts into the concrete.

And then the one without a name leaned across me, stretching out his hand to reach for Stan's thermos of soup.

Now, said Henry, and I don't know if he was saying it to me or to himself. I didn't have any control over what came next. I grabbed No-Name's wrist with my right hand, and stood up, twisting his arm as I rose. With my left hand I took the thermos from Stan's unresisting fingers. I wrenched No-Name's arm behind his back, and then I forced him down onto his knees, right in the middle of the half-circle formed by our group.

I couldn't see Johnson, Tierney or Murdo, but somehow I knew that they were too stunned to do anything, for now at least. Stunned, I mean, because this sort of thing never happened. Not even nearly. The No-Name kid was sort of mumbling and murmuring, coming out with the half-formed cries of anguish that I'd got used to hearing from us lot.

I still didn't have any control over what was going on, but something in me was liking this, even if in another part of my brain I knew I was going to pay for it when the rest of Tierney's mob got over their surprise. But now I was pushing No-Name's head forwards, and I was pouring the hot chicken-noodle soup down the back of his neck. I could see the black ring of grime around the inside of his collar, and I got a smell of sweat and piss before it was drowned out by the soup smell.

And now No-Name was crying and squirming, but he couldn't squirm too much because I had his arm twisted behind his back. The soup was hot but not scalding, so I knew I wasn't going to burn him badly or do any serious damage, but anyway, like I said, it wasn't up to me. Stopping, I mean.

And then I looked at the faces of my friends. Gonad was blank, with his mouth open. Smurf looked frightened, as if he was next, as if I was going to go and twist his arm behind his back and then pour soup down *his* neck.

But Stan.

Stan looked at me like I was something he'd found stuck to his shoe.

And then I heard a sound from behind me, and I thought I was going to get it from the others, but when I looked round at them, I saw that Tierney had this kind of smirk on his face, and he was giggling, and then the others joined in with the giggling, which soon turned into full-on laughter, and then suddenly Tierney's face went hard again and you could see the line of his jaw emerging out from the smooth skin, and I thought, right, now this really is it, because that

was a pattern we all knew, the laughter turning hard,
I mean. And Tierney moved to one side and pulled back
his leg and let fly with a kick, but it wasn't aimed at me,
or any of us, but at No-Name, and he took it in the guts,
and that made me let go of his arm, and he sank down to
the cold concrete and looked at me, and the look wasn't
what I expected, some sort of mixture of hate and fear,
but it was a look of betrayal, as though I'd failed in some
duty that I owed him. And then Tierney kicked him again
in the guts and he rolled into a ball. Then Tierney said,
'C'mon,' and walked away, and Johnson and Murdo
followed him.

Bye-bye.

Now this all got a bit embarrassing. No-Name was on
the floor, and I think he was crying, but without any sound
coming out. I didn't know where to look, or what to do
with my face. Whenever one of us took a spanking, there
were established policies in place. You didn't make a big
fuss about it, because that made them feel worse. You'd
usually settle on saying what a bunch of Cnuts they were,
and a quick 'You all right, Smurf?' or whatever. But that
didn't seem right in these circumstances. After all, I'd been
the one handing out the spanking. (By the way, for those of
you who don't know the term, Cnuts was our version of the
useful, ever popular, but boringly over-used c**t. One of
our greatest innovations in the heroic search for real
swearing.)

It was Stan who put his hand on the boy's shoulder, and
said, 'Are you OK, Neil?'

So that was his name. There seemed to be no end to the

stuff Stan knew. Not that Neil appreciated Stan's concern. He gave a violent shrug, made some kind of animal noise, and got up and scuttled away, like a wounded beast escaping into the undergrowth.

'Have you been going to judo lessons or something?' asked Smurf.

There was a kind of admiration in his voice, but it was mixed up with something else.

'No. But when I saw his arm stretching out like that, it just seemed like the thing to do.'

'You didn't have to pour my soup down his back.' That was Stan, of course.

'Fuck it, Stan, I was trying to help. If I hadn't grabbed him he'd have had your soup, and probably spat it out in your face. Look,' I continued, taking a handful of change out of my blazer pocket, 'here's some cash. Go and buy something at the tuck shop.'

'I don't care about the soup,' he said, and all of his twitches were up and running together. 'There's something different . . . something's got into you.'

The other two were looking at us, not knowing what to think. Hell, I didn't know what to think. But I did know I was annoyed at Stan, and I still had a sort of afterglow from that pleasant tingle, and a layer of something else – the feeling you get when you hurt someone, and they haven't hurt you – and I'm sorry to say that it wasn't at all a bad feeling, although I knew it should have been.

And then some other kids came over – the other nerds and half-nerds and quarter-nerds with whom we sometimes spoke, kids who had their own sandwich nooks and niches around the playground – and there was much back slapping, and, 'Well done, Brunty,' and that sort of thing, and Gonad and Smurf got caught up with that, because I'd become a bit of a hero and everyone wants to be on the side of the hero. But I kept looking at Stan, who wasn't getting involved at all, and the last I saw of him was his back as he went off to the lunchtime chess club, and his back spoke louder than all the slaps and smiles and compliments of the kids around me.

CHAPTER 11
AN ACT OF GALLANTRY

The second period that afternoon was physics. There were four science labs on the third floor, two for chemistry and two for physics, and you sat on high stools at benches, and there were Bunsen burners on the benches, but that was about it for equipment. With chemistry we sometimes got to make stuff, mixing up chemicals in test tubes, but physics was all chalk and talk, not that I minded, because I was good at it, and I could take it all in and I liked the equations.

Physics was taught by Mr Curlew, who was neither nice nor nasty, giving the impression that all he wanted was to get through each day with as little damage as possible. He wasn't a bad teacher, but he'd given up hope, probably back sometime in the seventies. I only ever once saw him animated, and that was when he was showing us some mercury he kept in a vial in his pocket. He poured it out into his leathery old palm and then let it run from one hand to the other like a living thing. Suddenly his face, usually a motionless collection of folds and flaps, caught the flame of life from the darting, flowing mercury, and his yellow eyes filled with delight. But then the mercury was put away, and with it the light in his eyes, and out came the chalk.

So, anyway, the two physics labs are at the end of the corridor, and I was lining up outside one ready to go in when things started to happen. The kids began to file out of the other room, with the usual bustle, and then Mr McHale began to shout.

Mr McHale was one of the popular teachers. He was a fierce-looking red-faced Scotsman who wore a very odd safari suit every day to school and was sometimes known to smell of drink in the afternoons, but unlike Curlew, he hadn't lost his will to live, and so he still fought to get knowledge into us, and was exasperated when he failed and genuinely exultant when he succeeded. But all this was at a price, hence the smelling of drink and the occasional fits of madness.

Like now.

BANG!

We all jumped. The door to McHale's room had been slammed shut with a noise like a detonating shell. The kids who'd just come out span round, and those of us waiting to go in all leaped into the air.

'What the hell did you think you were playing at?'

The closed door did little to muffle McHale's rage, and his words came through loud and clear.

We clustered around the little safety-glass window in the door. McHale was looming over Flaherty, his beige safari suit flapping about him like the wings of a very un-fashionable bat.

I don't know what Flaherty said next, but whatever it was it tipped McHale over the edge. He made a grab for Flaherty, but the boy was too quick for him, and he ducked under the lunging arms and raced towards the door. He reached it a millisecond before McHale, pulled it open and burst out like a ball of phlegm shot from a footballer's nose. McHale was right behind him, a red-faced avenging angel. *Whoosh* went Flaherty, and *whoosh* went McHale, scattering the kids in the corridor.

It was fantastic, the sort of scene that gets talked about for years afterwards.

Only one kid hadn't been watching what was going on. She was lining up for another room on the floor, and she had her back to the excitement, her straight, strawberry-blonde hair reaching down almost to the waistband of her skirt. I don't know if she had deliberately turned her back to the action in a not-wanting-to-follow-the-herd kind of way, or if she was simply lost in her thoughts. But as the two figures raced down the corridor towards her she began to turn, stepping further from the wall to do so.

Agile little Flaherty easily swerved round her, his feet dancer-quick. But McHale caught her with his hip and spun her backwards onto the floor. Her school bag skittered away behind her and, as it went, it spilled one item of its cargo: a small box.

McHale was so focused on his target that he didn't notice what he'd done, and carried on after Flaherty. The two of them disappeared down the stairs, the teacher still shouting and straining to lay hands on the imp. And as the shouts and footsteps from the stairwell grew faint, so attention shifted to the girl.

Someone, a little Year Six brat, shouted out, 'Jamrags! She's got jamrags!' and then there was a general jeering and cruel laughter, as if having a period was some terrible mistake she'd made that ought to be punished.

Amanda Something was still on her back, but now she turned onto all fours, and I was glad that I could not see her face, because even having to imagine it caused me pain.

Over the past few days I'd found myself doing things without meaning to, without trying to, without wanting to. But now the opposite was happening. I made myself walk, made myself act against some knotty internal resistance.

What the hell are you doing?

I walked, slowly at first, between the lines of jeering kids; walked past Amanda, who was still on the floor, her face in her hands. The little brat and his mates had begun kicking the box of tampons about like a football.

Stop!

I went up to the one in possession and pushed him back out of the way. I felt the corridor become quiet.

'Hey!' said the kid. He looked about six years old, but he must have been twelve or thirteen.

'Back off,' I said, and I guess I must have sounded pretty mean, because he did.

Henry had been trying to stop me from moving, but he couldn't, and now he was talking rapidly.

Don't ignore me. This is a big mistake. There's a time to stand out, and a time to tuck in. You're going to taint yourself. Don't help this one. She's weak. She's one of the damned. Stay away. Steer clear. Sometimes the mob understands best. You'll be dragged back into them. The stink will never leave you. Her touch is death. Burn the witch.

Henry had become shrill and birdlike. He was

squawking, his rage making him incoherent. And that made it not harder, but easier, to ignore him.

I bent and picked up the box, resisting the urge to look at it. A gasp came from the corridor – and that's how it felt, as if it were the walls and floor that were shocked. I walked back to Amanda, and then I got a bit stuck. She looked up at me, still helpless. It was one of the days when she had make-up over her birthmark, but it had become flaky and worn.

I'd never been this close to her. Her eyes were a green so pale they seemed almost colourless. There was a little mole no bigger than a full stop above her lip. Should I give her my hand to help her up?

It would mean touching her.

I think I wanted to touch her.

Touching wasn't the right thing to do.

I held the box out to her. She was kneeling. She took the box, her eyes on mine, and put it back in her bag. Her lips formed a 'thank you' but I don't think any noise came out.

'Hey, Brunty's got a bird!'

I'm not sure who shouted it out, but it should have been the beginning of a raucous jabber. There must have been forty kids in the corridor, and I expected to get some grief. Grief was a given.

But the cry was not taken up. No one joined in or added anything or came up and slapped me on the head. I was lucky in that there weren't any of my enemies around, just the younger kids and a load of others who didn't care about me one way or the other. But there was more to it than that; some weird . . . I don't know, *spell* or something that stopped them taking the piss. Maybe it was that the thing I'd done – picking up the girl's box of tampons and giving them back to her – was so transgressive it had sailed clear out of their gunsights. Or maybe they all felt a bit sorry for laughing at the girl with the birthmark, guilty about her loneliness, guilty about the years of pain they had done nothing to assuage, and this gave them a chance to redeem themselves. Redeem themselves above all for the fear and disgust her face brought them.

Maybe not.

And then McHale was back, without the wretched Flaherty, growling and muttering, and Mrs Plenty, who teaches biology, appeared from another room, looking suspiciously about her. Mr Curlew beckoned us in, we all started to move to our desks, and when I looked round Amanda Something wasn't there.

CHAPTER 12
SOME ART HISTORY

I was walking out of the gates that afternoon with Gonad, and although we were talking about who'd be better at blow-jobs, Hawkgirl or Catwoman, I was really thinking about Amanda Something, but not in a blow-job way, more just having her face hover around in my head. I was trying to work out what I thought about the whole thing, but this was a problem that you couldn't fix with thought. The thought couldn't get at it. It was like trying to get full on soup. Then I noticed the little crowd, maybe twenty or twenty-five kids, clustered around the social club wall.

I'd forgotten about the strange fresco.

When we got closer I saw that there was a teacher at the front of the crowd. It was the deputy head, Mr Mordred. Mordred had only just taken over from Mr Kerr, who was an old-fashioned psychopath, an ogre with the traditional ogre's job of frightening children – a job he had accomplished with, if not finesse, then at least a certain brutal efficiency. In his later years, however, Kerr had become a bit of a joke. He had an artificial leg that creaked when he walked, and he was known to pine unrequitedly for Mrs Eldridge, the French teacher. He was given early retirement after an incident in the school tuck shop, although no one knew what happened, only that a packet of pickled-onion-flavour Monster Munch was involved, and that it wasn't pretty.

Mordred was brought in from a reform school or quasi-borstal in Doncaster or Halifax or somewhere exotic like that, and tried to introduce an element of science to the job of intimidating the kids, and he soon succeeded in making himself the most feared and hated of all the members of staff. Unlike Mr Kerr, he possessed all his limbs, but he was short and bald and spoke with supernatural clarity, and he had these creepy rimless glasses, which made him look like a concentration-camp doctor, the sort that did experiments on twins, and you just knew that for him humiliating kids was a poor substitute for applying electrodes to their genitals or pulling out their toenails with hot tongs.

Me and Smurf came late into a school assembly once – late only because we were carrying the overhead projector – and Mordred said with that voice of his that cut like a Stanley knife, 'When you and your *girlfriend* have finished discussing your *make-up*, we'd like to get on with the assembly.'

Of course the whole school exploded into laughter. It wasn't witty, but it was brilliantly designed to whip the mob into a frenzy, and we were still feeling the heat from it a month later, and for us heat took the form of being spat on, thumped, dead-legged, and hunted down with the dreaded shit stick. And if you don't know what one of those is, then you've never been to a school like The Body . . .

So, as you gather, I had no very high regard for Mr Mordred.

I could hear his voice now – high-pitched, cruel, the hint of barely suppressed hysteria – passing through the crowd as easily as a neutrino slides through matter (and that's actually very easily, in case you aren't good at physics).

'This will *not* be tolerated. I want to know who did this. I want *names*. I want to tear the entrails from whoever was responsible and eat them raw, and then defecate in the cavity.'

Well, not the last bit.

The trouble was that, despite the natural fear that Mordred could generate, there were two major factors working to undermine his authority. The first was that he was outside the school gates, and as the darkness was to orcs, so the school grounds were to Mordred.

The second was that he was standing in front of what could now without equivocation, doubt or uncertainty be described as a Colossal Knob.

Yes, the shape emerging from the wall had now clarified itself into the unmistakable outline of a ginormous willy. It was like when you see someone coming towards you from miles off, and at first they're just a smudge, but then they become human, and then you begin to recognize them, or at least begin to find something familiar, even if you can't say for sure who they are, and then you think you know who they are, and then you definitely know them. And OK, so sometimes *then* you realize that it's not who you thought it was, and you have to take the stupid grin off your face, or freeze that wave halfway through, or pretend you were looking at someone else behind the baffled stranger who's now staring back at you, or perhaps you try to pass off the gesture as something else altogether, say maybe that you're cleaning a huge sheet of glass which happens to be propped across the footpath, or you pretend that you're just doing a bit of stretching, that's it, *reach* to the left and *reach* to the right, one two, one two.

Where was I? Yeah, the knob. We were all used to seeing them scattered around the place: kids would scrawl them on your exercise books or etch them with compasses onto the cubicles in the bogs. They would turn up in odd places, like on the ceiling in the library or drawn in lipstick on the security-glass panel in the headmaster's office door.

And the interesting thing about all of these cocks – well, actually the *boring* thing about them – is that they all looked exactly the same. Short stubby cylinders aimed upwards at the stars like a 1940s comic-book vision of a rocket, complete with the two side boosters.

But this one was different. It was, in all, about two metres long, and painted about three metres from the ground, so whoever it was must have had a stepladder. Or a brush on a stick. Or very long arms. The medium would appear to be white emulsion, although the delicacy of the shading created the illusion that other colours had been used. The most striking aspect was the clever employment of perspective to give a lifelike three-dimensionality to the phallus. It seemed to curve out at an angle from the wall, as if its owner had half turned to face the viewer.

And rather than the cold, metallic lines of the traditional knob, this one was soft and yielding and organic. Almost vulnerable, in fact, despite its heroic dimensions. So in a world filled with pricks (and I don't just mean of the illustrated variety), this one truly stood out.

Yes, it was a masterpiece.

CHAPTER 13
MORDRED, THE
GLASSES, THE GIRL

And it was this masterpiece that confronted Mordred now, making his usual Nazi act entirely ineffective.

Someone started to giggle. There was some jeering, which gathered force as it turned into a cascade of laughter and jokes, and then the pushing started, but not in a vicious way, more a way of getting someone else to lurch into Mordred, and then suddenly all you had was a mass ruck with everyone diving on top of each other, and I saw Mordred crawling away, but without his rimless specs. And then he stopped crawling and turned round to look for them, feeling about like some kind of cave creature because he was blind without them.

That's when Henry Tumour said,

Now,

and I knew what he meant, and I started to move.

Somehow I'd already made my way to the front of the crowd, where Mordred was crawling and feeling. I saw the glasses there, just out of his reach. And then, without pausing, I walked up to them and . . .

crunched.

It was a satisfying feeling, and a satisfying sound. It felt like a large bit of machinery sliding into place, notch clunking into groove.

Instantly Mordred froze, and the noise of the crunching glasses even penetrated the mind of the mob, and a silence fell.

'What was that? You, boy!'

I wasn't really in charge of any of this. I should have been shitting myself, but all I felt was mildly perturbed, but also interested about what would happen. It was as if I was a spectator on my own life.

'Oh, I'm sorry, sir,' I said dreamily. 'I was trying to help . . . with your glasses, and I . . . I seem to have stepped on them.'

'Give them here.' He held out his hand. There was the tiniest hint of a tremble.

I stooped, scooped the broken bits and passed them to him. Mordred tried to fit the mangled specs on his face. It was a pleasingly *Lord of the Flies* moment.

I guess that Mordred felt that his authority had been diluted down to school-canteen-orange-squash levels, or else he'd surely have dragged me back into school where he could devise some form of torture for me, but all he said then was, 'My office. Tomorrow morning.'

There was something deeply wonderful about his helplessness. Like I said, this wasn't a nice man, or a well-meaning one, or even a rough diamond.

'Sir,' I said, non-committally.

He peered through the cracked lenses. He was probably

seeing about seven of me. I, on the other hand, was seeing him with a weird clarity. I could see the dry skin on his thin lips. I could see his tiny white teeth, like the ones you see when there's a whole fish, head and all, in the fish bit of the supermarket. I could see the dimple on top of his baldy head. It looked like someone had dropped a ball bearing on him from an upstairs window. I could see the signet ring on his little finger, and I could see two black hairs peeping out from the space between the buttons of his crisp white shirt.

'Name, boy.'

'Ness, sir.'

He changed the angle of his head, trying to see me through a bigger segment of the broken lens.

'Initials.'

'A. P., sir.'

'Remember then, my office, before registration.'

The threat was there, but it was a feeble one. The roar of a toothless lion, a eunuch's come-hither. And by now one or two of the bright sparks had got my little joke, which isn't surprising as it was as old as language itself.

Mordred had begun to walk primly back towards the school when the first voice shouted out: 'Mordred wants to see A. P. Ness.'

'Another one. He can't get enough of them.'

By the time he'd spun back, the crowd had started to scatter. His mouth opened. A kind of hi-pitched wail came out. *Aieeeeaillah*. Something like that. More despair than rage. Oh, it was good, it was very *very* good.

I ran too. There were bodies around me, and my back

was clapped, and my hair was ruffled, and voices said 'nice one' and 'genius' and other things I never expected to hear. And then I stopped and there was a little group around me, and Gonad was there, puffed and flushed and happy.

But someone else too.

It was Uma Upshaw. The love of Smurf's life.

'That was good,' she said. 'Really good.'

I hadn't noticed her before in the crowd.

You're in, old son.

'Ah, it was nothing.'

I was worried I was going to blush. Blushing would probably have been bad.

I'm working here for you, boy, said Henry, straining. *Got a grip on those facial arteries, holding back the blood. Teamwork.*

'Something,' said Uma.

'OK. Maybe something.'

She was smiling at me. Right at me. I thought of Smurf. I tried not to think of Smurf. I succeeded.

And then she walked away with a couple of her hand-maidens. After a few steps she half turned, and smiled again. I went weak at the knees. Going weak at the knees is one of those clichés based on the truth – it's exactly what happens to you. But this time there was more – hell, I went weak at the *everythings*.

CHAPTER 14
A PARTING SHOT

So that was all great, or I should say, really great, but with a bit of mild panic about what tomorrow might bring. And then, as I was heading home, still with Gonad and a couple of other kids from my year, I felt a hot pain as someone grabbed the hair at the back of my neck.

I thought for a second that Mordred had come to wreak his revenge, and I turned, expecting the worst, cringing and twisting with the pain.

It wasn't the worst, but it wasn't good either. Tierney was behind me. He let go of my hair.

'Funny boy,' he said. 'Think you're clever?'

Bit hard answering that. So I didn't say anything.

'Fancy Uma Upshaw, don't you?'

'What's it to you?'

I knew what it was to him. Like I'd said to Smurf, he'd gone out with Uma a couple of times, before she dumped him for an older boy who had a moped. We weren't really supposed to know all that, but nothing stays a secret for long at The Body.

'She's my bird,' he said, jutting his chin out.

Big mistake.

'No she isn't.'

Tierney looked confused, as well he might. It had been worth him attempting to state an obvious untruth as long as no one had the guts to contradict him. He'd look stupid now if he kept on lamely saying he was going out with someone when he wasn't.

So he changed tack.

'You're dead, you know.'

'He looks pretty alive to me.'

It was some big kid from Year Eleven who'd been part of the gang around the fresco. He was with a couple of his buddies. Tierney looked at them, then started to slope off. But just like Uma, he had a parting shot.

'You're dead,' he said again.

CHAPTER 15
EROS, THANATOS AND
THE BORG QUEEN

I was one majorly confused kid that evening.

On the way home, buoyed up by all that hero worship, I felt like I was walking on marshmallows. OK, so maybe it wasn't hero worship. Maybe it was more just not getting kicked and spat on, but you know what I mean. And one of the weird things is that the person I wanted to talk it over with most – and I accept that 'person' here may not be the conventional way to put it – was Henry, my personal tumour. The trouble is that once you start thinking about your brain tumour, then it's hard to stay buoyed up by the fickle adulation of the mob.

So that was the first up-and-down combo.

And then there was the whole death-threat thing from Tierney. That wasn't nice. I'd done a bit of acting tough lately, but acting was all it was. I wasn't tough. I was a fraidy girly coward, and I didn't know how to fight, because I'd never had one, except in the slightly one-sided sense of having been punched quite a lot.

And then the smile from Uma. All mixed up with poor old Smurf's hopeless infatuation.

Up-and-down combo number two.

'Any advice, here, Henry?' I said to myself. Sort of.

HENRY: *What about – death or girls?*

It was still a shock when he actually answered back like that.

ME: Well, I can't imagine that you've got anything constructive to say about death. Unless you're going to tell me that you're moving out. That'd help.

HENRY: *I wish I could oblige you there, my friend. But we are bound together in this, like body and soul. Like Romeo and Juliet.*

ME: No way I'm Juliet.

HENRY: *If it's any consolation, the thought of personal extinction doesn't exactly fill me with joy either, you know. That's why we've got to get on with it.*

ME: On with what?

HENRY: *It.*

ME: I wish you wouldn't talk in riddles.

A gap. I sensed Henry thinking. We were getting near to our road.

HENRY: *Eros and Thanatos.*

ME: Eros and tomatoes?

HENRY: *Eros and Thanatos, dummy. Sex and death. The two great drives.*

ME: Bullshit. I haven't got a death drive. I don't want to be driving anywhere near death. I've got the opposite.

HENRY: *Eros is the opposite of Thanatos. The sex drive and the life drive are the same thing. But think about it. Don't you sometimes crave peace? Rest? Tranquillity? An end to the striving? Sleep? Have you not desired to be where no storms come, where the green swell is in the havens dumb, and out of the swing of the sea?*

ME: Yes, well, apart from the last bit, which means absolutely sweet f.a. to me, but . . .

HENRY: *Yes but nothing. That's the death drive revealing itself. And perhaps it's your friend. Those are good things, after all. Perhaps I'm your friend.*

ME: You sound like you're trying to convince yourself.

HENRY: *Naturally.*

ME: So, advice then. I could use it.

HENRY: *Don't run with scissors.*

ME: Funny.

HENRY: *Don't worry about the seduction side of things. That's my territory.*

ME: Seduction? Territory? What are you . . . ? I hope you don't mean Uma. I can't. Not just that she wouldn't even think about it, with me, I mean. But Smurf . . . if she did, then he'd . . .

HENRY: *You have to forget about him. He's not in the race.*

ME: But he's my friend.

HENRY: *In love and death there are no friends.*

ME: You said you were my friend.

HENRY: *And I am. But you must see, for once the rational and the carnal speak with one voice here. You cannot help Murphy. But you can help yourself. And I can help you to help yourself.*

ME: And when you help me to help myself, that helps you?

It seemed that was all I was getting out of Henry Tumour, for now. But I sensed that he was uneasy about this – I mean us, about what we were and how we'd end up. And he was certainly right about our fates being bound together. Until something, or someone, tore us apart.

Mum wasn't in when I got back. She worked in the Oxfam shop. She was a bit too dreamy for the till so they usually got her to sort out and price the smelly clothes at the back, where it was hard to see how even a spacer like Mum could screw it up.

I sometimes used to imagine her there. Oh, old lady knickers. Faint smell of urine, mild discoloration, might only be a coffee stain, 10p. Tramp's vest. Stench of sweat, piss, blood, vomit, death, 5p.

I think she was hoping they'd let her move on to the books, which would be good as she loves books and knows lots about them, and I suppose that's something she passed on to me, because I read a lot, and not just fact stuff but novels as well, although having a crap telly helps with that. But I suppose if Mum was put on the books in the Oxfam shop, she'd only start reading something and end up weeping in the corner because someone died, or some man didn't love a woman enough, or Earth got assimilated by the Borg.

Well maybe *that* wouldn't worry her so much, but *I* used to lie awake at night thinking about it. Borg assimilation, I mean. I remember a couple of years ago talking about it with Gonad and Smurf and Stan. We all thought that the Borg were a major contribution to the Star Trek world, which had pretty well used up its store of goodwill by then. There was no denying that the Borg were both scary and cool. Stan made the useful criticism that with the Borg you have that whole problem-of-origins thing. You know, the Borg assimilate other races and thereby spread throughout the galaxy. But Stan wanted to know how the first Borg was made. Classic chicken-and-egg. But there was a general agreement that we really didn't want to be part of the Borg collective, even if they did bring a kind of peace and order to the universe, because you could see the bad effect it had had on Captain Picarde, who was never quite the same man after they got him.

And then Gonad said, 'I wouldn't mind being assimilated by that Borg queen,' and we all just looked at him. We were curiously troubled by this statement. You see, the Borg queen only really exists as a head and spinal column, which gets plugged into various transport and maintenance pods, usually in the form of kinky leatherette. And, while even her face is indisputably Borgesian, she still has a queasy sexiness, that vague look of being up for anything. Not that we were consciously aware of it back then.

So we all had these murky feelings which we couldn't understand, mixed up with the knowledge that somehow we were polluting and contaminating sci-fi by so much as entertaining these thoughts. And this is before we even get onto the subject of Seven of Nine, although now she's come up I may as well give vent to my theory that Seven's undoubted hubbability is given a dark and wondrous twist by the fact of her being still part-Borg, and that is only possibly because the Borg queen has already trailblazed that whole territory (I mean the territory of being a sexy lady Borg, almost certainly into the kind of stuff you'd need a credit card to access on the Internet).

And, now I think about it, the Borg queen herself, well, what is she but sex and death, Eros and Thanatos? Oh, Henry Tumour, you have a lot to answer for.

Anyway, so Mum wasn't in. I went and stood in front of the bathroom mirror, which I'd come to associate with Henry T., although he was just as likely to start jabbering anywhere else. He was right on it.

HENRY: *OK, let's start with the hair.*

ME: I know, it's a joke. Bog brush. Tell me something I don't know.

HENRY: *Let's go get a cut.*

ME: It doesn't help.

HENRY: *That's because you go to an Albanian butcher down a stinking alleyway.*

ME: He only charges a fiver.

HENRY: *And look what he does to you.*

ME: I feel sorry for him. He's a refugee.

91

HENRY: *He's going to slit your throat, steal your bus pass, feed your corpse to his pit bull.*

ME: It's not a pit bull. It's a Staffordshire bull terrier.

HENRY: *And they don't eat?*

ME: Not humans, no. Other dogs, mainly.

HENRY: *Back to hair. If you're gonna score, and boy are you gonna score, we have to do something about it. And then there're the clothes.*

ME: You don't have to tell me my clothes are crap.

HENRY: *So I'm not telling you. What I am telling you is that we have to do something about it.*

ME: What makes you the expert?

HENRY: *I know stuff.*

ME: How do you know? How can you know things that I don't?

HENRY: *Look, I've already explained. There are things that you know that you don't know that you know. Everything you've ever seen or heard or sniffed is stored back here somewhere. And I have an access-all-areas pass. So trust me.*

ME: OK, fine, if you say so. But where am I going to get the money?

HENRY: *Your savings. That deposit at the Halifax. Two hundred quid.*

ME: That's my life savings!

HENRY: *Yeah, and this is your life. You want to spend it on your funeral?*

ME: Funeral? What do you . . . ? What are you saying?

HENRY: *Calm down, kid. I'm not saying anything. All I mean is that it's time to live a little. We've got some wild oats to sow, but first we need to get ourselves some of that wild-oat-sowing equipment. And if you're too tight to spend money, well then there are other ways and means. Other options. We just have to employ a little lateral thinking.*

I went to sleep that night thinking about many things. I thought quite a lot about Henry Tumour. I'd gone past the point of being gobsmacked by the mere fact of having a dirty-minded brain tumour that chatted away to me like he was some kind of friend or brother, or even sometimes in a kind of warped-dad way. Now I was more thinking about the content, if you see what I mean, mulling over what he was saying, not just the fact that he was saying anything at all. And that led me on to thinking about Uma Upshaw. She was a stunner, and she had smiled upon me. I fixed on her for a while, but another, less-glamorous face was there too: a face with a red birthmark, a face framed with strawberry-blonde hair, straight as railway tracks.

And then, heading backwards and downwards, I thought about Mr Mordred and what he was going to do to me the next day if he recognized me.

CHAPTER 16
THE THOUGHT
EXPERIMENT

It was morning break. Nothing so far had gone wrong, meaning I hadn't been hauled out of registration to be sent for interrogation by Mordred. Nor had there been any incidents involving girls' sanitary stuff or being smiled at. We were by the fence that separates the Body of Christ High School from the Body of Christ Junior School. The junior school was a squat, brooding, red-brick building that looked like it had been converted from some kind of Victorian correctional institution, maybe for fallen women or men with unsightly facial hair. The kids there had somehow bypassed any kind of cute stage, and were basically miniature versions of the thugs in the high school. There'd sometimes be spitting contests between the two schools, the outcome decided more by wind direction than superior technique or catarrhal output. But this place by the fence was one of our regular morning-break hangouts. We could gather round and talk about our stuff without having to worry too much about errant footballs or fists. We were all there, though Stan still wasn't looking me in the eye.

ME:	Face.
GONAD:	Body. Definitely body. No contest. There's more you can do with a body.
ME:	Yeah, but a beautiful face makes up for anything. What about you, Stan?
STAN:	Dunno.
SMURF:	It's a stupid question. It doesn't make sense to split them up.
GONAD:	It's not stupid. It's a – what-do-you-call-it? – thought experiment.
SMURF:	It's not a 'what-do-you-call-it thought experiment', because it hasn't been within a million miles of a brain. You don't love, I mean go out with a face floating in mid-air, or a body without a head on it. You go out with a whole person.
GONAD:	Bullshit. It's a perfectly reasonable question. Given that a girl has a body and a face, what's more important?
SMURF:	Both, obviously.
GONAD:	That's cheating. You've got to decide.
SMURF:	Why have I got to decide? It's a free country. I don't have to do anything.
ME:	No, Smurf, it's a fair point. The rule is, that when one person says which is best, x or y, you have to give an answer. It's an absolutely basic principle. If you can't say to someone, 'Would you rather eat a teaspoon of poo or drink a gallon of horse piss?' or, 'Who would you rather snog, Anne Widdecombe or Mother Theresa,

when she was alive?' or, 'Would you rather wipe your bum on a hedgehog or a jellyfish?' and expect an answer, then what have we come to? All the laws of civil society would break down. You as well, Stan. You know the rules.

STAN: Well then, I'll say they're both equally important.

ME: That's impossible, Stan. How could they both be *exactly the same* in importance, like to the *millionth* decimal place? It's a mathematical impossibility. One must be a tiny bit more important. It's like God.

HENRY: *Oh, here we go.*

ME: I mean, being an agnostic. You're saying that you've looked at all the evidence, and it's exactly as likely that He exists as that He doesn't exist. That just can't be true, and it means you haven't looked at all the evidence, or you haven't understood it, and so you're not an agnostic at all, but just a know-nothing.

GONAD: Don't ruin this, Heck, by bringing God into it. We're talking about girls.

ME: Sorry. Go on then, Stan. You too, Smurf. They can't be exactly the same. Face or body?

HENRY: *This is absurd. It's like four bald men arguing over a comb. Face or body! Their only chance of a grope is buying a shovel and heading down to the graveyard.*

SMURF: I don't think the question makes sense. A face and a body are different things. You like them for different reasons. It's like saying, 'What do you prefer, crisps or chips?' Crisps are a snack. Chips are a meal. In the crisp world, you could say if you like cheese and onion more than salt and vinegar, but you can't say you like crisps more than chips.

GONAD: All right then, would you rather have a bird with a fit body and an ugly face, or a fit face and an ugly body? And don't try to wriggle out of this one. It's a real-world example. Happens all the time.

SMURF: Why can't I have one with both? I mean, a nice face and a nice body?

HENRY: *Both, ha! You mean neither.*

Smurf spoke with a faraway look in his eyes, and I knew who he was thinking about, and that made me think about her too, and yes, she seemed to be a best-of-both-worlds option. But not, as Henry suggested, one open to us.

STAN: This is definitely a thought experiment.

Then we were all quiet for a minute, until I thought of a knock-down argument.

ME: You're all missing the— OW!

CHAPTER 17
A KICK, A PUNCH, A SPIT IN THE EAR, KEEP MOVING

I was face down. I was hurting. I couldn't understand why. For a few blurry seconds I thought it was to do with Henry T. To do with what was happening in my head. But then the generalized all-body pain began to focus, and it wasn't in my head, but on my back. And then I heard laughter, the cackling, spluttering glee of kids who take their joy from hurting.

As I reconstructed it afterwards, what happened was that Tierney, Johnson and a couple of other droogs came bombing in from behind us, feet first. I took most of the impact and now I was down on the concrete with Tierney standing on my back like I was a board and he was surfing me.

And then he dropped his knee into my spine, and I twisted and writhed like he'd hit me with electrodes wired up to the grid. There was no getting up from this, no smart move, no grabbing wrists. I was helpless. I craned up to try to find my friends, but they'd been blown away by the first assault. And then I felt Tierney's breath on my cheek.

'Not so clever now, are you? What, can't speak? Beg me for mercy, or you're dead. Beg, you poof, beg.'

I'd have begged, but I couldn't find any words. I hoped that Henry T. might chip in, but he was silent too.

'Nothing? Nothing to say? Have some of that then,' and Tierney punched me twice on the side of my face. It didn't hurt that much, as I don't think he could get an angle for leverage, but it added to the humiliation, that feeling that he could do whatever he wanted to me. And then, because that probably wasn't quite humiliating enough, he spat in my ear. Then he got up.

It was good having him off my back. I turned and watched him stroll away, swaggering with his mates. There hadn't been enough time for a decent crowd to gather, but there were still a dozen people standing about, watching, in little clumps. One of them was Uma Upshaw. She had her hands on her hips, and she stepped in front of Tierney.

'That *was* brave,' she said.

Subtlety wasn't one of Uma's virtues, and the sarcasm dripped like pus from a festering boil.

'What?'

Tierney sounded perplexed. He probably thought he had been brave. There was always the chance he might have scuffed his shoes on the back of my neck.

'Sneaking up like that. Brave. You should get a medal.'

'What you talking about?'

If Tierney had left it there, with the 'about' and the question mark and the closing speech marks, he might still have been able to walk away with some dignity left intact.

But no, he had to say it. And the fact that he mumbled it under his breath didn't help him one little bit.

What he said was: 'bitch'.

And now there *had* been time for a crowd to gather, and collectively it drew its breath. Uma Upshaw wasn't the kind of girl you called a bitch, not in that insultingly half-arsed way. In fact, there was always the chance that if he'd hollered it out loud like a gangsta rapper he might have got away with it. But to mumble it was to commit the twin peaks of folly: it showed both a lack of respect *and* a lack of guts.

Uma's face – that thing of hard chiselled near-beauty – became more hard and chiselled but I'd estimate about eight per cent less beautiful. It took on the look of some warrior queen, or maybe a death goddess, or even a warrior queen death goddess.

Quite horny really, in a way that could only truly be described as kinky. Despite the eight per cent decline in beauty.

Shut it with the eight per cent, Einstein. Let's just sit back and watch this baby work.

Now, as I've said before, Tierney wasn't exactly one of the great hulking bullies, the knuckle-dragging, feel-no-pain, heavy-browed, bruising, biffing, blustering, lobotomized thugs, and we had plenty of those for the sake of comparison. No, Tierney was of the snide, manipulating variety, the evil-mastermind type, although in truth he was not especially bright, as evil masterminds, or even as ordinary kids, go. But my point is that raw physical courage wasn't quite Tierney's bag of chips. And, as I've also said, Uma Upshaw was a big girl. Not big in the compacted lard-and-muscle way like some of the other girls, but strapping and lissom, with long levers and hard cogs.

Levers and cogs? What are you talking about? That isn't a steam engine – that's a fine young woman you're discussing there. Levers and cogs!

Shut up, Henry. I'm telling this story. This bit doesn't concern you.

It all concerns me.

Don't be such an egotist.

Don't you be such a prick then. If you cut out the levers and cogs stuff I'll let you tell it your way. Deal?

Deal.

So, Uma steps towards Tierney with her warrior-goddess head on, and she clouts him across the face so hard that he staggers sideways, and it looks like he's actually going to take a tumble, fall right down on his evil arse. And if he had, the whole world would have been a very different place. No gang leader could survive being sent flying by a mere girl, even if she is some hybrid of Boudicca and Buffy the Vampire Slayer. The fall (in both senses) of Tierney would have created a power vacuum at the top, and who knows what might happen then. A new benevolent regime bringing justice and happiness for all? Or a new tyranny, more crushing than the last? Or maybe a nothing, just a sort of happy anarchy, with each kid allowed to eat his Wagon Wheels in peace, and talk about whatever shit he wanted to talk about, and the only oppression the shared oppression of the teachers?

The teachers.

The teacher.

Oh balls.

Mr Mordred.

In all the excitement of Tierney and the immortal death goddess Uma Upshaw, I had entirely forgotten about the balls.

And the willy.

And what I'd said. To Mr Mordred.

He'd probably been surveying the playground from his office. I bet he had a telescope up there. Or a pair of binoculars, at the least. I could imagine him, peering down, getting himself worked up by minor acts of mischief – nose picking, greeny-spitting, insufficient reverence for the badge on the school blazer (Motto: 'I think therefore I am', universally rendered by us as: 'I'm pink, therefore I'm spam'. Coat of arms: a cross with a weird sort of eye thing in the middle, a bit like the Red Eye of Mordor, or, for that matter, the bloodshot eye of Mr Mordred, peering down through his pervy telescope). And he'd seen me, and now he was marching across the playground, although it might be more accurate to describe his tiny, tiptoe steps as mincing more than marching. Yes, he looked like a mincing little fascist, confident only because he had the armed might of the Waffen SS behind him. He was wearing a pair of reserve spectacles, big brown plastic jobs that carried none of the evil menace of his old pair.

'You, boy!'

Up to that point none of the crowd had noticed his approach, because they were all focused on the

Upshaw–Tierney confrontation. I could see him because I was facing his way. But now, with that voice, all attention spun towards the feared deputy head.

And Tierney hadn't fallen. His low centre of gravity bailed him out, and he recovered his balance, and now even the humiliation of the slap was lost, blown away on the wind of this new drama. Still half crouching, he turned to me and spat: 'I told you you was dead.'

I looked back at Mordred. He seemed momentarily distracted by the crowd. He must have seen me before Tierney's attack and started on his way down during the action, expecting to find me still in my little huddled gang, only to emerge into what was obviously an interesting spectacle, rife with possibilities for administering punishment. But he wasn't going to be diverted. He was definitely verted, and verted right on me.

Everything else blurred. All that existed in the world was me and Mordred. Before he reached me he stretched out his arm. It seemed to be about eight metres long and when I felt his hand on my shoulder it pierced like talons. He pulled me towards him, and his face came to meet mine. He was centimetres away. I could smell mint on his breath, but it covered something darker, something rotten. I could see his teeth, small, white, but with brown stains in the gaps. He was smiling now, the sort of smile a vampire gives when it sees the naked bosom of a sleeping girl heaving before him.

Mmm, bosoms.

Henry!

Sorry.

And all this is happening which, on its own, is quite enough to make me feel a bit, well, strange, but then there's something else going on as well. He's pushing me ahead of him now, but my legs aren't working the way they should, and I'm stumbling a bit and Mordred's getting annoyed at this, and he's shouting something at me and I want to tell him that I'm feeling funny but I can't get it out, and then I feel him shaking me and half dragging me up the steps into the school, and I know this shaking is the best he can do because he's not allowed to actually hit us, and maybe even shaking is against the rules but he can always say he was just holding me so that I didn't run away.

And now we're inside the school, on the smooth hard tiles of the foyer, and all of a sudden it's very bright in there, and the foyer has big windows and a glass roof, but even so it's brighter than it should be, and suddenly I become aware of the pattern in the tiles, and I know that they mean something, something important, something profound, and then a voice inside me, the voice of Henry Tumour, but far away, even though he's inside, says *here we go* and then there is nothing.

CHAPTER 18
A SHORT CHAPTER, CONCERNING MAINLY VOMIT

'I had nothing to do with it. The boy just fainted.'

There was panic in the voice – the harsh, cracked sound of a man under knacker-clacking stress.

I opened my eyes.

I shut them again.

I was in the sick bay with the grisly-head-and-torso resuscitation dummy and the two sick buckets, but also, evidently, Mr Mordred and, dismayingly, my mother.

'I've told you, he has a medical condition. The doctors don't know what it is. He's having a scan tomorrow. A brain scan.'

And then some crying. Not from Mr Mordred, yet.

'Mrs Brunty . . .'

'Ms,' she managed to sob.

'Ms Brunty, I . . . Hector, yesterday, made comments. Said things of a nature . . . of a . . . of a *sexual* nature. About me. In front of . . . there were several . . . of an intimate nature. Not acceptable in any way, shape or . . .'

It was good hearing Mordred flustered. I'd have enjoyed it more in other circumstances.

'Well, what did he say?'

'He, er, ah, suggested his name, when I asked him . . . he said he was called . . . it was of a *sexual*, ah, *nature*. As I said.'

It sounded pretty feeble.

'And what exactly did you do to him?'

Mum was getting angry now, which got rid of the tears, for the time being.

'Nothing . . . I was simply asking him to come up to my . . . and he . . . well, *slumped*, but not in any way that I could have . . . and I thought he was playing the fool again, and I wasn't going to be humiliated in front of . . . every intention of suspending the . . . but when it became clear that, that . . . we naturally phoned the, ah, ambulance. Immediately. And you, of course. Er, naturally. And immediately. Even more immediately.'

'Mum,' I said, to let her know that I was awake.

And then I was sick.

More than you'd have expected.

I mean more than you'd have expected even if you'd guessed that I was going to be sick, which would have been clever of you.

Now, whatever else you say about vomit, it's always interesting, from the point of view of what's in it. That is to say from a scientific point of view. In fact, you might say that science began when people started to look at stuff like vomit and point at it and say, 'Look at what's in there! Amazing!'

Obviously (back to *my* vomit rather than vomit *in general*) there was some of my breakfast in the mix, breakfast being muesli, a special kind my mum gets from the health-food shop, consisting mainly of some kind of fibrous material made out of sacks or something, without the dreaded nuts but with a few raisins, and they were pretty easy to spot, both in the muesli and in the vomit. And some mashed-up crisps and a brown smear of the Twix I'd had at break, bought from the school tuck shop.

It was fun buying things from the school tuck shop because it was run by Mr Churl, and he had these sausage fingers, and if you put your money down on the counter he couldn't pick it up, but sort of chased it around like an imbecile after the last pea on his plate, and it was pleasant to generate frustration for Mr Churl because he was a very shouty man who liked to scare the smaller children.

And (back to the vomit) there was also, more surprisingly, some of last night's brown rice salad, which was made from brown rice served cold, which turned it into a salad, mixed in with some real salad ingredients like spring onions and peppers, which all sounds quite nice, but you have to remember that the rice was cooked by Mum, and so emerged as a big blob of beige goo, like something you'd use to plaster a wattle-and-daub outhouse. But now it was much runnier, and would never work in a wattle-and-daub context or, for that matter, pass the pencil test.

Oh, have I mentioned the pencil test yet? We first came across it in Citizenship, when the teacher told us that in South Africa during the apartheid years, one of the ways they decided if you were coloured (meaning mixed race) or black (meaning black) was whether or not a pencil would stand up if thrust into your hair. Now, this was stupid, horrific, sick, etc., etc., but also quite funny, as long as you remember that you're laughing at the idiots who came up with the test rather than the poor sods having pencils stuck into their heads, so we adopted the pencil test for other circumstances. Like phlegm, crap, rice pudding and, of course, vomit.

It – the rice salad, I mean – and the other products of my activities in the field of digestion, splashed over the floor and up the walls, and ran in complex river systems until they reached Mordred's feet, and then he had to do a little dance to try to escape the flow, but there was nowhere really for him to dance to, because I'd kind of cut him off from the door, and so he got my sick on his shoes, and that would have been satisfying if it wasn't for the fact that I felt like my head was going to explode, and I was still retching and there was sick caught in the back of my throat, which is never a nice place to have sick caught, and the whole room stank of puke, which is one of the things guaranteed to make you want to upchuck more than ever (that's what I call ironic).

My mum dived and got the empty sick bucket and held it under my chin, but that was completely closing the stable door after the horse had vomited. I took over the holding, and Mum turned back to Mordred and said: 'Perhaps now you can see that my son is seriously ill.'

And the tears were rolling again, although of course that could have been something to do with the stink.

Mordred was trying to look concerned about me, but it

was plain that he was much more concerned about the puke on his grey slip-on shoes, and he made a little leap, like a ballet dancer, to get over the main flow, but that was a disaster, a serious error of judgment, because he landed with his heel in one of the tributaries and the heel shot from under him and he ended up flopping back flat on his arse in the sick. Oh yes indeedy, about as much in the sick as he could have been if he'd set out with the deliberate intention of having a good old wallow in it.

Then the school secretary, Miss Bush, who had blue hair and brown teeth and wore her glasses on a chain around her wattled neck, opened the door and sort of shoed in two men in green overalls who looked like QuickFit fitters, but who I knew were really paramedics. One of them had a moustache and the other one didn't, although he might as well have done for all the difference it made.

They took in the situation: me, Mum, Mordred sitting in sick, and for a second I thought they were going to run for it, despite the fire-and-vomit-repelling suits and their belts adorned with hi-tech weaponry. But then they got their courage back, and the next thing I knew I was being wheeled away, dimly aware of the eyes of the school upon me.

CHAPTER 19
CASUALTY

So I went back to the hospital, this time with a bit more style and drama about the whole business, riding in the back of the ambulance like a genuine emergency. The paramedics turned out to be pretty funny, in a slightly forced, double-acty kind of way.

Sample joke: Paramedic A (the one without the moustache) is sitting beside me (I'm still lying down at this stage, although I feel OK, maybe about eighty-two per cent normal) and he has a clipboard. He looks for a pen, then takes out something from his top pocket and sort of goes through a little mime of writing with it before he looks at it in disgust. Paramedic B (moustachioed) says, 'What's that?' and Paramedic A replies, 'My rectal thermometer.' And then together they say, 'Oh no! Some arsehole's got my pen,' and then they laugh at their own routine, and I smile as well, because it's obviously the sort of thing they do all the time.

But Mum isn't really listening, and just carries on looking like it's *her* with the brain tumour.

Yes, Mum rode in the ambulance too, which put the dampers on things, in the way that being punched in the head and collapsing in the foyer and the fountains of spew never really had. She insisted on holding my hand.

I suppose if I was being honest I'd have to admit that I didn't mind, really, this once.

The ambulance dumped us at casualty, and the men said goodbye like we were old friends, but I guess they forgot about us the second we were somebody else's business.

There was a brief conference with some hospital people of indeterminate function, and I was moved from a trolley to a wheelchair, but not one of the cool ones – a brown spazzy job with little wheels. Then there was a wait to get seen by the big-haired receptionist, and then another wait to see the nurse who finds out if you're about to keel over or not (pretty, in a uniformed kind of way, which, all kinkiness aside, is one of the best ways, and I'm really sorry if that's offensive to nurses and policewomen), and then another wait, the *real* wait, before you get to see the doctor. Mum went and told the big-haired woman on reception about my scan, and she went on in a boring way about how they had to tell Doctor Jones that I was here.

The waiting room was about the most depressing spot in the universe, the kind of place they stick you in after you die and before they let you into Hell. It was full of people with dirty bandages and crying kids, and it was hard to know if it was the kids who were sick or their mothers, who were all tired and grey and greasy-haired, and you could see them itching for a fag. The mothers, I mean, but maybe the kids as well, who were probably passively smoking about forty a day.

No one here looked at all healthy to me.

After about an hour I got wheeled through a doorway

and into a cubicle, with Mum still holding onto my hand like she thought I was going to make a break for freedom. After another ten minutes Doctor Jones appeared, along with a couple of other doctors – unless they were impostors disguised as doctors, which happens more often than you'd think, according to the papers, at least, but probably not in this case.

'Well, well,' said Doc Jones, 'what have we been up to?'

I didn't really mind his patronizing tone. As long as people are trying to save me from deadly cancers, etc., they can patronize me as much as they like. What I object to are people who patronize me either before or after beating me up in that overly literal way of adding insult to injury.

'I think I, er, fainted.'

'Think?'

'Well, I was unconscious at the time.'

My mum pinched me.

'That's good,' said Doc Jones, peering into my eyes through a reasonably cool gadget with a lens and a red light.

After a bit more general-purpose examining ('Tongue out . . . Please cough . . . How many fingers?' . . . etc., etc.), Doc Jones said to my mum: 'I think we'll keep him in tonight. Just to be on the safe side. And, anyway, he's scheduled for his scan tomorrow afternoon, so it'll save you both the journey.'

He smiled, and when he smiled his eyes disappeared, to show that his whole face was getting in on the act.

So that was that. I hung around for another hour while they tried to find a bed for me, and Mum seemed to cheer up a bit now she knew that the burden of keeping me alive wasn't solely on her back, and I quite liked that feeling too – the feeling, I mean, that the professionals had taken over. Most of the time what you do, how you get by, how you survive, is down to you. But when you're in hospital, that's all for someone else to worry about, and so you can think about other stuff, if you want to.

I was looking forward to Mum leaving, so I could do just that. But she hung on in there until I was finally pushed up to a ward, when she said, 'I'll nip home and bring you back some pyjamas, and some clean clothes for tomorrow.'

Henry Tumour, you'll have noticed, kept his mouth shut through all of this. Worn out, no doubt, by all that collapsing and spewing. And then I don't suppose he liked hospitals much. But I knew he'd be back.

CHAPTER 20
THE MEANING OF LIFE

I was wheeled up to the ward by a tiny man who, when I asked him, said he was from Mauritius. I told him that that was where dodos were from, and he pretended to be interested, but I'm sure he knew it already, because even I knew it, and I wasn't from anywhere near Mauritius.

He left me with a nurse who took me to my bed. She said I could lie down on top of it until my mum came back with my pyjamas. Then she bustled off and I looked around at the ward.

Like most hospital wards, this one was full of sick people.

Sick old people.

Sunken faces, sparse grey hair, bits of flesh the colour of putty.

About half of the old geezers had drips coming in or going out. One man was sleeping with his mouth open, gums all over the place. There was a tube coming out from under his bedclothes. It was blood red and ran into a jar. The jar was half full.

Or half empty.

Not the cheeriest place on God's earth.

What a bunch of derelicts. And that smell. Someone has

*definitely had an accident around here. Will someone
please tell me exactly what the arguments are* against
euthanasia?

Yep, there he was again, with his first contribution since
I'd passed out. I thought about ignoring him, but I wanted
to know what had happened to me.

'Was that you?'

A couple of the old guys swivelled round towards me.
The sleeper briefly awoke, closed his mouth, and then fell
asleep again.

*You don't have to shout. One of these poor old sods'll
have a heart attack if you keep up with that. Just think it.
But think it clearly, think it in words.*

*No, not like that, I said in words. As if you're speaking,
but then don't move your lips. You'll find you attract less
attention. Was what me?*

As if you don't know. Was it you that made me pass out?

*Oh, that. Well, you can't make an omelette without
breaking eggs.*

What have omelettes got to do with it?

*The omelette is a metaphor. You know, when one thing
is described in the terms of another for the purposes of
amusement, education or—*

I know what a metaphor is. Me brainy, remember. But
what exactly is it a metaphor for?

Metaphor for for for, said Henry in a mocking voice.
*I've been working back here, behind the scenes. Stretching
my wings. Learning how to soar.*

Well, I wish you hadn't made me faint.

Look, it could have been a lot worse.

How?

Think sphincters. Think losing control of them. A notch or two lower down on the old consciousness settings, and you'd have beshat and pissed your pants. Which might have made you more at home here with the fossils, but not necessarily what you'd want the fragrant Uma to see. Or sniff.

So I'm supposed to be grateful that you didn't make me crap myself? Well, thank you sooooo much.

Or you could have had an eppie. Think about that one. You could have been flipping and jigging like a guppy in a bucket. I could have made you look like you need horse-pill medication just to get you back to the level of a straight-forward epileptic fit. But I didn't. I had to close you down to do a little maintenance work, run a couple of level-one diagnostics. I kept it all as low key as possible. We're working together on this, remember.

And what is it, exactly, that we're working on? Death?

Don't be so morbid.

MORBID? Christ, you're the cancer, you're the killer here, and *you're* calling *me* morbid. If it's not death that's your game, then what is it?

Life, said Henry Tumour, with such seriousness it had to be a joke.

I spat out the appropriate response of bitter laughter. Heads turned to me again. I guess I wasn't looking too sane to the crumblies.

Actually, crumblies gets them exactly wrong. Age and illness weren't drying these people up: their decay was moist and wet. They were rotting down to a pulp.

And soon I'd be joining them.

I thought of a sick joke, told months ago by that psycho Flaherty. Not very funny, but apt.

A leper comes running up to Jesus in a state of obvious distress.

'What is it, my son?'

'It's him, master,' says the leper, pointing at another beggar. 'He dipped his bread in me neck.'

Blood, mucus, pus, lymph. We die wetly. We die in the damp.

I'm not getting all that, said Henry T, *but I don't like the look of it. I'm seeing some unpleasant things here. You should never have spent so much time thumbing the medical encyclopaedia in the library. Let's accentuate the positive. Which takes us back to what I was saying. Not death but life. Love. And I'm not talking any of that love-thy-neighbour shit either.*

Henry's voice had taken on a new quality: panting, primeval, not very appealing.

What do you mean?

Look, Heck, what's life all about, what's it all for?

How the hell should I know? I haven't had enough of it yet.

No need to be so modest. I don't need a philosophical answer. We're in the sciences, not the humanities. We're in biology. We're making babies, that's where we are.

I know what you're getting at. You're saying the only point to life is reproduction.

Hey, don't make it sound so dull. No wonder you haven't exactly been fighting them off with a sharp stick.

You don't have to get personal. Anyway, I seem to be doing all right with Uma Upshaw.

And who have you got to thank for that?

Oh, well, maybe . . . but that's not the point. I don't believe what you're saying, that the only point to life is to screw. What about art and poetry and—?

Listen to yourself, boy. Art and poetry? What do you think they're for?

They're for . . .

And what are they about?

They're about . . .

Not got an answer? Let me give you one. Or two. Second first. What they are about is sex. What do you think a love poem is? And how many millions of pictures are there of women WITH NO CLOTHES ON? Take the sex out of art, and you haven't got much art left.

Music. That's not about sex.

Have you ever listened? Have you ever danced? No need to answer that, I know you can't dance, but we can fix that. Music is about dancing. Dancing is just sex standing up, and sex is dancing lying down.

What about symphonies? You don't dance to Beethoven. And not all paintings are paintings of nude girls. Landscapes. Pictures of the sea. Abstract art, lumps of wood, and stuffed sharks and all that.

Even if I accept your point, which I don't, I've still got my other answer, which is what art is for. Artists are all show-offs. They want attention and they want money. They want attention from girls and they want money so that they can impress them so that they can have it away with them. Sex, sex, sex.

I thought they were all gay.

Not all of them, as you well know. But the point remains. Making the beast with two backs, performing the deed of darkness, sheathing the beef dagger, playtime for Percy. Let's get it on.

You're disgusting. And plain wrong. There's more to life than that.

Yes, but the more is all a means to an end.

And what if you kill me? Not much chance for . . . anything then, is there? I'm not stupid. I know what you are, and what you might do to me.

Heck, Heck, Heck, how can you say that? How can you even think it? Why would I want to hurt you? Don't you see, we're in this together. Divided we . . . I mean together we stand, divided we fall. Hey, cool it. Here comes that creepy doctor. I don't like him, don't like him one bit.

Yeah, and I know why, because he's got your number, because—

'Hector?'

'Oh, hello, Doctor Jones.'

'Are you OK . . . ? You seemed a bit, ah, distracted.'

'Been a funny old day, so far.'

'Yes, of course. I'm just here to tell you what to expect tomorrow.'

'The scan.'

'Precisely. They'll come for you at about ten to eleven. You'll be taken down to radiography, and they'll give you the CAT scan.'

'How long does it take?'

'About half an hour. Perhaps three quarters. They'll play music. You get a choice. Bring your own, if you like.'

'And after that you'll know what it is?'

'What it . . . ?'

'This,' I said, pointing at my head. 'The thing in there.'

Doc Jones paused. And then cleared his throat. And then paused again.

'It should give us a good idea, yes,' he managed finally.

'I think I already know.'

'You do?' Doc Jones looked amused, but not in a snidey way. 'You're a better doctor than me, in that case.'

'Let's just say I have a . . . different perspective.'

'And what do you suppose you've got?'

'A brain tumour.'

Jones looked startled, but then got a grip on his face and went back to neutral.

'Well, that's not necessarily the case. Very rare in boys of your age. Plenty of other things it could be.'

'But it *could* be cancer, right?'

'Well, we can't rule that out. But, you know, just because there's . . . I mean, even if we find a little something in there, that doesn't mean it has to be what you might call cancer. For every malignant brain tumour we find . . . well . . . several non-malignant growths. Harmless little chaps, mostly. Relatively harmless, that is.'

'What do you do if it's one of those?'

'Oh, I don't want to go too deeply into the options now, before we even know what, if anything, we're dealing with.'

'But roughly, what can you do?'

Jones looked at me seriously. I think he'd got the message that I wasn't just some kid who wanted re-assurance. I think he understood that I needed the truth, the way some other people need lies.

'There are various ways we can attack it. Shrink it down to, ah, manageable proportions. And then, if necessary, we can, ah, remove it.'

'An operation?'

'Yes, an operation.'

Don't listen to him, he's a maniac.

'Shut up!'

'OK, I know that must be worrying, but we're a long way from there . . .'

'Sorry, no, not you . . .'

And Doctor Jones left me, looking thoughtful. Or worried. Or like he'd just heard some kid jabbering to him-self like a nutter.

A little later Mum came back with my pyjamas and things, and she'd brought a CD with some songs on it. I groaned when I saw what it was: *Puff the Magic Dragon and Other Nursery Favourites.*

'You always used to love it, when you were small. If you were frightened or if things happened that you didn't like, you used to put it on. I thought you might like it now.'

'Mum, you're mad. I haven't listened to it for ten years. It's baby music.'

'I just thought . . .'

I should have been angry or at least annoyed, but I was too tired for that. I drifted towards sleep, and I saw Mum wandering off to some of the other patients, chatting with them, pouring out niceness and sympathy. And I thought about Puff the magic dragon, who lived by the sea, and who, if I remembered correctly, frolicked in the autumn mist in a land that, if I wasn't mistaken, was called Honah Lee.

CHAPTER 21
A SISTER OF MERCY

Wakey wakey.

There are dreams and then there are weird dreams and then there are the kind of dreams I was just in the middle of. It began with me being chased, which isn't really weird at all, it being a pretty accurate reflection of real life. The thing that was chasing me was not, surprisingly, Puff the magic dragon, but some big blobby thing like a globule of phlegm, but with spikes in it. I suppose that was probably my visualisation of my brain tumour, although of course it could just have represented my fear of being chased by giant globules of phlegm.

Hey, I'm nothing like that. I'm more of a Brad Pitt kind of brain tumour. Phlegm! You know you aren't exactly the young Adonis.

'Shut it.'

But instead of the normal chase-dream thing where you're about to be caught by the monster and then you wake up, I fell right into the arms of Uma Upshaw. And my face was right in between those magnificent bazookas of hers, and that should have been fun, but I had the unpleasant feeling of being smothered, so maybe in real life the pillow was on my head or something like that. And I was kind of stuck there, as if my nose was embedded in the space between her wondrous orbs, you know, like when Pinocchio is in his big-nose phase and keeps getting it stuck places.

And then it became really unpleasant, because I couldn't breathe, and I still thought that the giant bogey/tumour thing was coming up behind me, and I could almost feel its hot foul breath . . .

Hey!

. . . hot foul breath on me, and so I sort of flapped away blindly to fend the thing off, but then something grabbed my hand, and at first I thought, right, that's it, I'm gonna get chomped, I am soooo cancer food, but then I realized that it wasn't a, like, *tumoury* hand, but a real one, I mean a human one, and it wasn't all slimy, but dry and warm, and it tugged me gently away, easing me out of the booby nose trap, and when I was free (*POP!*) I turned, and I had no idea who it was going to be, thinking it would probably be Mum, or maybe the Virgin Mary or someone like that, but it wasn't someone like that. And so for a second I didn't recognize her, and she was a bit hazy, a bit fluid, the way things are in dreams, but then she became clear to me, and it was her, the girl with the strawberry hair and the port-wine birthmark on her face, and that's when Henry T. shouted: *Wakey wakey.*

'What?' Or rather, 'Whaugh?' I wasn't in a coherent state to internalize my thoughts.

A bright new day.

'Yeah.'

Don't sound so glum. You know it's me who shouldn't

be happy about being here. All these people want to do me harm. They hate me. But I stay cheerful.

'Aren't you the plucky tumour.'

And then a huge black nurse appeared, pushing a trolley with stuff in it. She must have been two metres wide. Her uniform was stretched tightly across her front like a big blue sail in a hurricane.

'Now then, darlin',' she said in a Jamaican accent as rich as Bill Gates, 'are you feeling good?'

She was wearing big glasses which kept sliding down her face, but unlike most of the doctors and nurses she looked me right in the eye.

'Not too bad.'

She rolled closer to me, and put her hand on my forehead.

Ow! Get her off me.

Henry sounded as if he was in real pain, and I found myself flinching, although I liked the feel of the nurse's leathery hand on my head. Her face changed, her smile turning slowly, almost mechanically, into a frown.

'Things not all good either. Not in there. Me takin' your blood pressure now. Don't be lookin' worried. Don't hurt a bit.'

She was right. Having your blood pressure taken doesn't hurt a bit. Then she reached into that trolley and pulled out a plastic bag. A plastic bag containing, I could see, a syringe.

Keep that thing away from me.

Henry sounded on the edge of panic. I was perfectly happy about that – he was such a smug tumour that a bit of panic had to do him some good. But I'd noticed before that there were links between us, and what he felt I would feel, or at least an echo of it, a ripple, and the ripples reached me now, and I found myself flinching, and I couldn't honestly swear that I didn't do a bit of trembling too.

'Now, darlin', Sister Winifred's done more of these things than you've had hot dinners.'

'Well you'd better go and get her then.'

The nurse leaned towards me, with just the tiniest hint of looming threat.

'Oh, are you having a little laugh at my expense?' Suddenly the Jamaican accent was gone and she sounded like a BBC radio announcer. 'Don't you know I only talk like that to make you poor lambs feel cosy?' And then she was back in her old voice. 'And you don't want one o' dem junior doctors learning on you and stabbin' and jabbin' at you like they want to chop off you arm. I been doing dis for thirty-five years and I know how to make it nice.'

And then she was swabbing my arm with alcohol and the needle was in, and it didn't hurt much, but when she pulled at the plunger and the barrel filled with my blood, so dark it seemed almost brown (that's because when they take blood they take it from a vein, not an artery, and it's been all the way round the body and given up its oxygen), well, anyone who says they'd enjoy that is some kind of freak.

I think that was when it first really hit me. Stupid, I know, after what I'd been experiencing over the past couple of weeks. But blood is such a . . . thing.

Thing? You can do better than that.

Oh, God, I don't know.

Symbol.

I mean it's a bit of you that should be inside you, and there it is, outside you. Slopping about. In a syringe. On its way to a lab where they test it to see if you've got CANCER OF THE BRAIN.

Blood.

A symbol for love and friendship.

A symbol for family.

A symbol for life.

A symbol for death.

That do?

Do just fine.

It was seeing my blood in the syringe that did it. I can't remember if the tears came first or the shaking. Let's be neat and say that they came together, although if we get down to hundredths or even tenths of a second, that becomes unlikely. And I felt my face sort of collapsing in on itself, and then the nurse, I mean Winifred, was holding me, saying, 'There there, there there,' like I was a toddler with a bashed knee, and she was pressing me into that enormous bosom of hers, but I can honestly say that, despite the whole uniform thing I touched on earlier, this was not what you would call an erotic moment, and nor was Winifred the kind of person you'd be having erotic thoughts about. And I could feel my shaking going into her, I mean sort of absorbing into her flesh, the trembles lessening as they penetrated her soft tissue, until they were finally lost there, somewhere in the middle of her, and I kind of imagined that there was a place there where hurt and pain got dealt with, like spent nuclear-fuel rods getting reprocessed.

After a while, and it could have been one minute or twenty, because time stood still with me clamped to that healing chest, I stopped the crying and the shaking, although I thought there might still be some little echoes and aftershocks travelling through Winifred, and maybe they're still travelling now, the way the songs of whales are supposed to carry on travelling around the world under water for months.

But there was something I wanted to say to Winifred.

'It wasn't the needle.'

I didn't want her to think I was crying just because of the syringe.

'I know it wasn't,' she said, in that voice of hers, half fierce, half melting. 'I come with you down to radiography, if you like. They find that fellow in there,' she said, tapping my head with a fat finger. 'They find him, then they sort him out.'

Noooooooooooooooooooooooooooooooooooooooooooo.

CHAPTER 22
THE GIANT POLO

The room had nothing much in it apart from the CAT scanner, but that was enough, really. Quite an impressive piece of kit, all things told. It looked a bit like a giant Polo mint, except its inner surface was sort of funnelly, you know, bigger at one end than the other.

Which makes me wonder: why is a funnel, like on a ship, called a funnel when it isn't funnel-shaped, but just a normal tube? Which is pretty well the opposite of a funnel. Why . . . ?

Shut up – no one cares – get on with my story.

OK, sorry.

Where was I? Giant Polo. Yes, and a Polo doesn't usually have a table going through the middle of it.

Winifred had said I could ride down in my chair, but I walked, still wearing my pyjamas and dressing gown, and carrying my clothes in a carrier bag. It was a bit embarrassing, after the hugging and crying business. The old people on the ward either looked at me with sympathy or tactfully scrutinized their bed sheets. I guess that old guys dying in hospitals don't usually take the piss.

There was a man in the room with the CAT-scan machine. He had on a white coat with about twenty pens crammed into the breast pocket. He was shy and nerdy and didn't look me in the eye, and his hair was tufty and orange and he had red blotches on his face, as if he'd just been slapped or had tried to shave himself with a bread knife.

'I'll be in there,' he said, pointing at a big window with another room behind it and some equipment in there, monitors and stuff. Not quite starship standard, unless it was one of those films where they try to make the vessel look all beat-up and old-fashioned, kept running by improvizations with string. And when something goes wrong, the stardrive or whatever, they just hit it with a wrench.

Which reminds me. Submarine films. The submarine is being depth-charged. The first thing that happens, after a few explosions, is that they lose the lights, and then they come on again, but red.

Why?

I know it's supposed to be back-up lighting, but why put in special red bulbs? But then the next thing is that, after a *really* close explosion, a pipe bursts and water sprays out, and then an engineer comes along with a big wrench and he hits the pipe with the wrench until it's fixed. Can that really be a good way to fix a burst pipe? Doesn't seem very likely to me.

For Christ's sake, boy, I've told you before, you're losing them. Hell, you're losing me and I'm right here with you and losing me is like losing—

My mind.

You said it.

'You put this gown on,' said Winifred, handing me what looked suspiciously like a nightie.

'Over my pyjamas?' I asked hopefully.

'No, darlin', you have to be taking all your pyjamas off. In the corner. I not looking. You tink I haven't seen it all before? I got two boys o' my own. One he work with computers now, the other one useless except at making babies. So I seen everyting.'

While she was talking I put on the white gown, first taking off my top, and then putting the gown on and only then taking my pyjama trousers off, so even if Winifred had seen everything, she wasn't going to be seeing any more of me than she had to.

But still, it wasn't the most macho of garments, and something about the fact that it did up at the back made it seem more like a dress, because there aren't really any clothes for boys that you have to tie at the back, and I suppose there's a reason for it, maybe something to do with the olden days and ladies having servants to get them dressed, or something like that.

Then the nerdy technician got me to lie on the table thing, and he positioned me just so, and my head went into a kind of rack, which I guessed was to keep me still so the pictures didn't come out all blurry.

As he was bending over me I saw he had a name badge on his white lab coat. Barry Cunliffe. Cunliffe. It sounded like an Anglo Saxon name for a lady's you-know-what.

'Thanks, Barry,' I said.

He looked at me, blinking.

'Oh, the coat. No. It's not mine,' he said.

But he didn't tell me what his name was, so in my head I still called him Barry.

I felt very helpless lying there in my white cotton nightie. It was cold, and I began to shiver, and then a beeper went off in Winifred's pocket and she looked at it and said, 'Sorry, darlin', but I got to go,' and I said that of course she could go and I was fine, but I didn't feel fine.

Then Barry the scanman said: 'Just going next door. You'll hear me through the speaker, and there's a mic so I can hear you. Just shout if . . . Well, once we start, you have to stay still, very still, so don't, er, shout. I mean because I can hear you even if you talk quietly. But don't talk too quietly in case I, er, can't hear you. Just talk normally.'

'Like this?'

'Er?'

'Or *more* normally?'

'That's about the right level of, er, normalcy.'

And then he was gone, instantly happier to be among machines and consoles and monitors than facing a real person.

That could be you, you know, said Henry sulkily.

He *really* didn't like hospitals.

That's what happens to you when you hang out with nerds. You become one.

Maybe I'm one to begin with.

If you are, then I am, but I'm not, so you aren't. Not deep down. We'll get you loose, don't worry. Oh shit, what's happening?

There was a humming noise and I started to move, or rather the bench I was lying on started to move, or rather the giant Polo started to move, which made it seem as if I was moving, all motion being relative, according to Einstein.

'Ah, oh, sorry. Meant to say we've begun.' So said the voice in the speaker. 'That is, we've begun.'

That's it, I'm hiding, said Henry T.

And he did, or at least he shut up.

For the next forty minutes I lay there as the Polo inched its way across my head and down as far as my shoulders. After the first ten minutes Barry remembered that he was supposed to play music to keep me calm, and because I'd kept 'Puff the Magic Dragon' very much to myself he put on a tape of Kylie Minogue, which made me want to stand up and hurl the two tonnes of CAT scanner through the window at him, even if she is, well, gorgeous.

And then it was all over. Barry opened the door and said, 'That's it, fine.'

I felt a surge of elation.

Fine.

He said I was fine.

There was nothing in my head. No cancer, no brain tumour. Just a voice. I was mad, not dying, yippee!

And then – maybe because he realized what I was thinking – Barry said, 'Nice clear scan. We'll send these up to Doctor Jones. He'll, ah, let you know. About what . . . I mean, he'll be in touch.'

It took a couple of seconds for that to sink in, and then I understood. No, of course this spoddy dweeb couldn't just tell me I was in the clear. All he meant was that the scans were OK, not that my brain was.

'Can I go then?'

'Oh, ah, yes. Put your clothes on, though.'

I think he was trying to be helpful.

CHAPTER 23
THE HOXTON FIN

I was out of there by midday. No one came to see me off, no one came to meet me. All a bit anticlimactic, really.

Like I always said, it's just you and me, buddy.

You never said that.

I'm saying it now.

I thought about going to see Mum at the charity shop, but I wasn't sure if I could take the smell – you know, the tang of old clothes and lost hope and stale piss, and somehow the way they try to cover it up with air freshener just makes it worse. So that left roaming the streets, or school, or home. I still didn't feel quite myself after the collapse of the day before, so I got the bus home and went to bed with my clothes on. Even Henry seemed tired, and we both fell asleep in the time it takes to think about the bits of Uma Upshaw between her hair and her chin, which is as far as I got, missing out on the good stuff. I think Mum came in later, and I remember the feel of her lips on my cheek, and when I woke up the next morning I was in my T-shirt and underpants, which must have been her doing, and I was very glad she stopped there, rather than trying to go full pyjamas.

She brought me breakfast in bed. Toast and proper tea, meaning not ginseng-and-buttercup flavour.

'No school for you today,' she said.

I could feel the effort she was making to be normal. It was like watching a drunk person try to walk in a straight line.

'What day is it?'

'Friday.'

I was going to object. I like Fridays. Double maths. But I felt Henry's presence, felt that he wanted me to keep quiet. To stay put.

We had a little chat about the scan – me and Mum, not me and Henry. I reassured her that I didn't feel too bad, and when she offered to come back to give me lunch I told her not to be silly. Yes, she was acting pretty normal, but it was still a relief when she left for work. Henry felt it too.

'Sblood, but I thought that was never going to end. And now it's time to go shopping.

But, but . . .

But me, no buts. We're going to get you properly attired in good green buckram.

In what?

A figure of speech.

You know, Henry, I don't understand you.

Hey, I'm a complex guy.

But I should. I mean, if you only know what I know, even if I've forgotten what I know and you can remember it, then it should be familiar when you say it. But some of the time you could be speaking Greek.

I am alpha and omega.

Yeah, funny, even I know that much Greek. First and last letter of the Greek alphabet. And also God, which is a bit big-headed of you, when you think about it.

Oh, I didn't mean to play Lucifer and unseat Jehovah. Alpha and omega, beginning and the end. Did I mean that I was here before you? I think that I may. Did I mean that I would be here after you? We all know the past, but the future is a place of shadow. We go through life facing backwards, our eyes on our memories, our now an instant. How fine must you slice time to find the present moment? Alpha and omega. Strange that they should choose to translate the Hebrew thus. Emeth. Truth. Made from three letters: Aleph, Mem and Thaw. Aleph and Thaw are the first and last letters in the Hebrew alphabet. So truth is the first and last. A pleasing coincidence, or a mystical sign? Who can say?

That's exactly what I mean! I don't know that. I don't know Hebrew.

I'm sorry, I was showing off. C'mon, let's shop.

I still don't feel great. In fact your Hebrew's made me feel worse.

OK, Let's have a little look from in here.

Weird feeling of rummaging again.

Da-da-dum-dee-daa-daa-dum.

Please don't hum while you're in my brain. It's very irritating.

You're the boss.

He didn't sound like he meant it. For some reason that unnerved me, as if he'd stopped caring much what I thought, but still felt he had to go through the motions.

Anyway, no, looks fine back here to me. Just need some fresh air. And time flies. There's a lot to do.

I didn't have the strength to argue. We got the bus into town. Henry was in a good mood, obviously happy to be out and about.

So, we've got to plan this like a military campaign.

What, shopping?

Not just the shopping. Styling you up is just the opening move. Then we make our play for Uma Upshaw. We got to get ourselves some of them jeans.

Levi's?

You are trying to be funny, aren't you? No, G-E-N-E-S.

Oh. And what am I going to do with her genes? And what about Smurf? I've only got three friends in the world, and he's one of them, and he's really into her, and he'd never forgive me if . . .

But then I felt myself trail off, the way you do when you know your words are empty. Henry was doing things to me. Some of the things were dramatic, and some were subtle, and one of these subtle things was happening now, and it took the form of not really caring about what other people thought or felt if it got in the way of what I wanted, or what Henry wanted. I knew that this was a bad thing and I tried to fight it, but it was strong as well as subtle.

We've been there, said Henry, *and you know the truth of this, and what must be done*, and then he looked at me. Of course, Henry didn't really have what it takes to look – you know, eyes, etc. – but I still got the feeling he was giving me one. A look, I mean. A hard one.

After a while of the looking thing, he said, *How much we got?*

I took out my wallet. Well, it was a bit more like a purse than a wallet, so I tended to hide it at school. It had beads on it. In a pattern like this:

which to me looked like a really depressed bloke but which, to Mum, used to be about the most important thing in the world, because it's the sign for CND, the Campaign for Nuclear Disarmament.

Five pounds.

And a cashpoint card.

Yes, I replied uncertainly.

Look, chill out. I've had an idea for the hair. At Vidal Sassoon you can have a trainee do your hair for free.

A trainee – you mean let someone who doesn't know how to cut hair cut my hair? Great idea.

I said it was free.

Mmmm . . .

And they're good. Well, better than the Albanian butcher.

So we went to the Vidal Sassoon's on Cross Street.

I'd never been into a proper hairdressers before, and I felt self-conscious and stupid standing there by the counter, with posh ladies everywhere. There was an atmosphere of restless activity, with people darting around and carrying things and doing stuff to people's hair. It was a bit like the bridge on the *Enterprise*, but with less of an alien presence and more ladies with towels on their heads.

Finally a man looked at me and said, 'Can I help you?'

He was young – I find it a bit hard to tell how old people are, but I'd guess he was in his early twenties. He had on a black T-shirt made from some kind of stretchy stuff with the word CUM printed upside down in little white letters on the front, and a pair of black jeans with a chain going from the back pocket to the zip at the front, a bit like the good old days of punk, except he was no more a punk than he was a pelican. But it was his hair that I noticed. He had a sort of band of it going diagonally across the top of his head, standing up about five centimetres from the rest of his hair.

That's the one. The Hoxton Fin. Get one of those.

'Can you cut my hair?' I said in a small voice, adding, 'For free?'

The young man smiled at me.

'You want to be a guinea pig? We usually do that in the evening. And shouldn't you be in school?'

Tell him you're a student.

'I'm a student.'

Show him your bus pass, tell him it's a student ID card.

I waved my bus pass vaguely at the man. Let's call him Hoxton. Well, Hoxton didn't seem very interested in my card, but his face went all twinkly as if he was finding something irresistibly amusing in my being there.

'We're not busy. I'll see if one of the girls can do you.'

He paused before he said 'do you', which made it seem mucky. 'If anyone asks,' he went on, 'remember to tell them that you're a . . . *student*.'

'But I *am* a—'

I had to wait around for twenty minutes. I spent the time reading magazines. They had loads of them. Mostly for ladies, but some for men too. The ones for men had mainly pictures of women about to burst out of their bras, and then articles about how to get a six pack, and how it was now OK to use stuff to make your face soft, and what clothes you should wear, and I read those, but I only enjoyed the sections about gadgets, like iPods and plasma-screen TVs and satellite navigation systems.

Henry was taking it all in, getting excited about the ladies coming out of their bras, but he was not very interested in the satellite navigation systems, which is probably because he already knew where he was and where he was going.

And then a girl was sort of bowing in front of me, although it looked more like she was ducking projectiles being fired at her. She was Japanese, but I only found that out later, and at first I only knew that she was Chinesey. She was taller than you'd expect, and did a lot of stooping as if she was ashamed of it. In her land she was probably a giant, and that was why she had come here so she could look more normal. Funny that, how sometimes you have to go somewhere else to be more yourself.

That's not profound.

I'm only fourteen. Make allowances.

I don't care how old you are. I've scraped better wisdom than that off my shoe.

You don't have shoes.

Get on with the story.

She took me by the arm over to a row of sinks. I'd never had a haircut where they washed your hair first.

The Japanese lady was actually pretty cool-looking, in a manga kind of way. She had on this sort of bandolier across her front with her scissors and combs in it, which gave her a martial-arts look, and the sound of her voice was like a bird chirping, and about as meaningful. Sometimes she'd say one of her chirruping things and then look at me as if I was supposed to answer, and so I'd say yes or no, or sometimes just laugh, and everyone seemed happy with the arrangement.

She may or may not have said that her name was Miko.

Once I'd got over the embarrassment and weirdness of having a girl person who wasn't my mum messing about on top of my head, I began to quite like having my hair washed. I had to lie back, and there was a semi-circle cut out of the sink for your neck to go in, and it all meant that I was looking up at Miko as she looked down at my hair. She was putting a lot of concentration into it, as if she had to work out exactly how much cleaning each individual hair needed. Henry was liking it too, and kept up a distracting commentary, along the lines of: *That's it, baby, squeeeeeeeze, yeah, one more time, squeeeeeeeeeeeeze.*

And then Miko was towelling me, and moving me to another chair in front of a mirror, and I'm pretty sure she said, 'What we do here?' sort of holding up two bits of hair like horns.

For about seven seconds I couldn't think of anything to

say. And then I saw the Hoxton man, and I pointed at him and said, 'I want one of those,' and he stopped and pulled a little face and wiggled his hips. 'A Hoxton Fin,' I declared loudly. Miko giggled, putting her hand over her mouth. All the other hairdressers within earshot looked round, some with shocked expressions, some with wry amusement. Hoxton himself shimmied off.

Well, to cut (some kind of pun in there, but I can't quite pull it out) a long story short, I was out of there two hours later with the sort of haircut you might see on a pop star or trendy hairdresser but not, usually, on a nerdy kid.

I felt different.

Different good?

Yes, different good.

I kept checking myself out in shop windows. I liked what I saw. And so did Henry.

Cool.

People don't say cool any more. It's not cool.

God's teeth, you speak some errant scut. Cool has become a classic word. It can never go out of fashion. Anyway, you say cool all the time.

Well the cool kids in my school don't say cool. They say 'hectic', or 'cushie', or 'boo'.

Mere ephemera.

Mere what?

Ephemera. Here today, gone tomorrow. 'Boo', 'cushie', 'hectic', shall pass; they shall vanish. There will come a day when no living person can even begin to recreate the time when such words had a meaning. But cool is cool is cool. We look cool, and that's an end to it. But our work here continues – hair maketh the man, but clothes getteth the girl: we must completeth the image.

CHAPTER 24
FREE MARKET
ECONOMICS

So, we went shopping. And real shopping. Not Primark, not M&S, but what could only be described with a shiver of fear and trepidation as *boutiques*, the places where not so much the cool shopped, as the rich.

It wasn't my choice: Henry was in charge.

I'd seen some of these places before as I mooched around town. I'd even been into a couple of them at sale time, looking for a T-shirt or a pair of socks. But I'd never lingered long. I didn't know how to behave in them, how to move, what to do with my face. And I'm not saying that the sales assistants actually sneered at me, but, well, if they didn't it was because their expressions were set permanently in a state of bored condescension. Let's say at least that they knew I wasn't about to flourish my gold Amex card and start buying racks of silk-and-cashmere suits, and so they didn't spend a lot of time helping me out. Which was good, because that would have set me off sweating and panicking, like a scared bunny about to be squashed by a truck.

Well, I don't know if it was the new haircut or having

Henry on board to steer me, but today I just seemed to glide through the fashionable boutiques as if I'd been doing it all my life. I knew where to go and what to get, and I tried on things and experienced a Zen-like calm.

In fact, there was unquestionably a weirdness about the whole thing, a dreamy quality. I couldn't feel my legs moving, or the coldness of the air, but I was definitely going from shop to shop.

And then suddenly I was myself again.

Run, you bozo, run!

What?

Panic. Heartbeat like a bongo drum.

Run!

And I looked down, and saw that my arms were full of trousers, shirts, tops, and there were new trainers on my feet. And then I was running, running like I'd never run before. And running was something I was good at, from all the practice. Yeah, I could run all right.

And curse.

What the bollocking pissing arsing hell have you done?

Hey, I didn't do anything. I'm just a passenger here.

If Henry had had shoulders, he'd have shrugged them.

You've stolen these clothes. We're a shoplifter.

We just liberated them.

You shit. You've turned me into a thief. I'm taking them back.

Back to the shops?

Yes.

But I was still running.

And what will you say?

146

I'll say it was a mistake.

What, you grabbed a load of stylish clothes from the most expensive shop in town by accident?

I'll say it was you.

You'll say your tumour stole them?

I'll say you made me do it.

So, you'd rather go to the loony bin than the young-offenders unit? Touch and go, if you ask me. Is it better to be knifed by a jabbering psychotic who thinks the Teletubbies are sending him messages to kill, kill, kill, or humped in the shower by a two-hundred-kilo football hooligan with swastikas tattooed on his schlong?

They won't send me anywhere. I'm sick.

You said it.

I hate you. I hate thieves. They . . . they . . . steal things.

I was still running. People were staring at me as I flashed by, but I was gone before what had happened registered. I didn't know if anyone was behind me, chasing me, and I wasn't stopping to look.

That's a tautology, and beneath you. Listen, these were fancy shops with big profits. The benefit to you from this is massive. We get to look good. We get to pull. We find immortality through the joys of reproduction. All the shop loses is a few quid's worth of gear that their insurance covers anyway. You're making the world a happier place. You know it's the right thing to do. The moral thing.

I don't care what the effect is, I just don't want to be a thief. It's not about what happens in the world, it's about what I think of myself.

Thinking? You're not thinking. You're reasoning

147

without reasons, and that's just another word for prejudice. What you have is a slave morality, and that's not the one for us. We've moved beyond good and evil, into the realm of the Übermensch. Anyway, it's too late. Oh, and we're safe now. You can stop running.

I looked around me. I was in an alleyway near the bus station. There were bins and filth and me and my stolen clothes.

I suggest you change.

What, here?

Yes, here. Then dump your old rags.

It made sense. I wasn't exactly inconspicuous with my piles of designer clothes, labels flapping in the breeze. So there and then in the dingy alleyway I changed myself and threw what I'd been wearing into one of the big wheelie bins and put all the spare new stuff in my rucksack.

When I came out blinking into the cold light I felt as though more than my clothes had changed. I was wearing a black top and a black jacket and black jeans. And, what with my hair, I looked like a mini version of the Hoxton guy in the hairdressers. I felt sick, but also excited. And sordid. I'd never stolen anything before in my life.

Until the bus actually got going I was convinced that a posse of store detectives and armed police would come galloping up to cart me off to gaol. Of course, no posse came, and nor were we stopped by a frantically nee-nawing pursuit car, or strafed by the RAF.

In fact, nothing happened. I got a funny look from the bus driver, but then you expect that.

CHAPTER 25
NOT STINKING

I was desperate to get home before Mum so she didn't think I'd been up to no good. No good like the Genghis Khan-scale pillaging I'd been doing. She usually got back at five, and I made it by four thirty. I rushed straight upstairs and looked in the mirrored door of the bathroom cabinet.

What had I done?

You look like a prince.

Who wants to look like a prince?

A figure of speech.

I look like a twat.

The girls'll love it.

I'm going to be a laughing stock, a figure of fun. And that's the good part.

And the bad part?

I'm going to get punched to the ground and then stamped on, and then spat at. And that's going to be my life until my hair grows normal again. You don't understand. Hair is a battleground at our school. Like the Somme. It's a great way to get yourself slaughtered.

I've told you – your days of getting slaughtered are behind you. From now on it's all champagne and roses.

But—

Enough! Now, unless I'm mistaken, the delectable Miss Upshaw works at her father's fish and chip shop on Preston Street after school.

Yeah, I think she does . . . Why? What are you thinking?

That we should go a-courting.

No way. You are simply out of your mind, and I wish you were out of mine. I can't believe you want me to go and chat her up. Smurf! I won't. I can't. I don't know how.

Let me take care of that. It's what I do.

What's what you do?

Reproduction. It's my middle name.

OK then, Henry Reproduction Tumour, just how do you think she's going to feel about me turning up while she's battering the haddock . . . ?

That's one way to put it.

Stop, for Christ's sake. Look, working in a chip shop isn't exactly the coolest job in the world, and she isn't going to be best pleased when I turn up to see her in her shame. I thought you were supposed to be a *brain* tumour, as in intelligent.

I quite take your point, said Henry in a prim and precise voice, *that, in general, to be observed in a moment of embarrassment breeds hatred for the observer in the observed, but I think you are underestimating the resilience of Uma's ego. She is not some fragile girl whose self respect crumbles at the first challenge. She's made of sterner stuff, Uma Upshaw. Blood and iron.*

I'll bow to your greater knowledge, I retorted sarcastically, but I had to admit, for internal consumption

150

only, that Henry really did seem to have greater knowledge when it came to girls. And blood and iron.

Anyway, I replied feebly, I probably stink.

As I've said, my concerns with not stinking had led me to rebel against Mum's policy on hair washing, but I still worried quite a lot about stinking, although I knew it was irrational, as I had a bath every other day, which made me a bit of a hygiene freak at my school.

Easily fixed. Look in the cabinet.

Mechanically, I opened the mirrored door to the bathroom cabinet. It was full of the usual things: ancient toothbrushes, their bristles splayed like a chorus line doing the splits; various tubs of potions employed by Mum for some unfathomable lady-purpose; the Bic razor that Mum used guiltily to shave her legs, thereby cruelly betraying the whole feminist movement. And, dusty with age and neglect, two bottles.

One was a white bottle of Old Spice aftershave with a picture of a sailing ship. It had been there since we moved into the house. Sometimes, if there was a bad smell in the bathroom, I sprinkled it around the toilet, to help freshen things up a bit. It definitely smelled better than poo.

Splash it on.

But I don't shave.

Doesn't matter, just pour some out onto your hands and hit yourself.

I did so.

I don't know if the Old Spice was supposed to smell this bad, or if it had been in the cabinet so long it had gone off, but either way I felt as if I'd walked into a cloud of ammonia. My eyes began to water and I went briefly deaf.

Phew, big mistake.

What? It was your idea.

Every great enterprise has its reversals. Read any epic poem: there's always the section where the hero has to go backwards before he can go forwards. It's how you deal with them that counts. All we have to do is to block this out, somehow. Try the other bottle.

The other bottle was perfume, given to Mum years before by someone who couldn't have known what she was like. She didn't use products that might have been tested on animals, although putting perfume on a rabbit and sending it out to a nightclub in a slinky dress to see if it pulls doesn't seem too cruel to me. Only kidding. I know they pour it in their eyes. When I was little Mum used to make me say prayers for them. It was called Tramp – the perfume, I mean, not the rabbit, although now I think about it, Tramp would be quite a good name for a rabbit.

But it's for girls.

Yes, but the other bottle was for boys. The two smells will exactly cancel each other out. It's basic science – I thought that was your field.

It is, but . . .

Well, I wasn't thinking too clearly, you know, brain tumour, etc., etc., and that was why I opened the top and dabbed a helping of the perfume on my face in the hope it would counteract the cold pissy smell of the aftershave.

It didn't work.

That's better.

'ARE YOU MAD?' I yelled, out loud this time, choking

and gagging. It was horrible. I'd learned that Old Spice +
Tramp = Old Tramp.

*Calm down, calm down. I'm sorry, but I haven't quite
got a grip on your olfactory area yet, so I accept that maybe
smell isn't my strong point. But it's not that bad. It can't
be. And it's probably better than you smelled before.
Anyway, if I'm not mistaken that's Mum coming in, which
I say means it's time to get your arse in gear.*

I quickly tried to wipe off the Old Tramp with a manky
sponge. It seemed to help. I smeared some extra gel in my
hair, trying to bring my Hoxton Fin into a state of
perfection, and then I had a last check to make sure there
weren't any bogey stalactites working their way out of my
nose, or any obvious food deposits in my teeth, and down
I went.

CHAPTER 26
CLYTEMNESTRA AND
OTHER HEROINES

Mum was in the kitchen. She'd been to Sainsbury's, and the bags were on the table, but she wasn't doing anything with them.

'Help you unpack, Mum?' I asked.

She turned slowly to face me. She looked about a hundred years older than usual.

'Yes,' she said slowly. 'Yes, that would be nice.'

'And I'll make you some mint tea.'

'Tea. Yes.'

She hadn't noticed my hair.

Or the stench.

As I was putting things away (and it was odd, because Mum had bought things that we never had but I'd always wanted – things like Pop-Tarts and Coco Pops and Pot Noodles; the good stuff where they actually go to the effort of jazzing them up with nice colours and chemicals to stop them going off, unlike the things that Mum usually buys, where they can't be bothered putting any extra stuff in at all, the cheapskates), I heard a noise and I looked at Mum and saw that she was crying, which was hardly unusual, but this seemed like a different sort of crying. I gave her a hug. She just sat there and didn't hug back with her arms, but I felt her fingers grip me and her nails dig in.

'It's all right, Mum,' I said, although I don't know what I was reassuring her about.

Me, I suppose.

Me and my head.

Her fingers were hurting me, so I pulled away as gently as I could, and I went and put the kettle on and got the mint tea bags from the cupboard, and while I was doing that Mum started talking.

'There are some things I need to tell you,' she said.

From the sound of it she didn't mean a new type of organic shoe polish she'd discovered that actually made your shoes *less* shiny whilst simultaneously helping out with the world's ozone problem.

Hurry her up, can't you? We've work to do. Important work. The work of life.

I ignored him, but I could feel a little surge of impatience, which was Henry doing his thing to my brain chemicals.

'OK, Mum.'

'You know for a long time I haven't been myself.'

I moved my head in a sort of non-committal way, so it didn't look like I was agreeing that she was crazy as a loon. And the truth was that she'd never been herself, as far as I was concerned. At least not if herself was someone different to the person I'd always known. Unless . . . perhaps if I thought back really hard, there might have been a time when she was, I don't know, more together. A bit. I had a half-memory of a trip to a park, and I was sitting on a big stone lion, and she was tickling me, and whenever I laughed so much that I slipped off she caught me and put me back and began tickling me again, and I was laughing so much I thought I would wet myself, but I don't think I did. She seemed more normal then.

But memory is deceptive, and I don't even know if the lion was real. Well, I know it wasn't a real lion, of the eating-you variety, but I mean a real stone lion, and not an imagined stone lion.

'Well, there's a reason for that,' she continued. 'It goes back a long time, back to when I was at the peace camp . . .'

Here we go. I can't listen to any more of this. I'm off to do some tinkering back here. Let me know when she's shut her hole.

There was almost a click as Henry closed himself down. Good riddance.

'. . . back to when, to when I had you. Well, things didn't go the way I hoped. I mean for me, and for peace, and for the world. And I became depressed. In those days they didn't know the dangers of giving you things. I mean the tablets they give you. I went to the doctor, and he prescribed Valium. Do you know what Valium is?'

I nodded. Course I knew what Valium was. I'd seen the pills on her bedside table when I was looking for stuff. And one of the kids at school once brought some in from *his* mum's stash to sell, saying it was better than dope, but nobody believed him.

'Well, that's what he gave me, and I'll never forgive him. But it seemed to help for a while. Helped me to cope with some of the things . . . the things I had to cope with. And it was quite nice. It makes you feel . . . better. Less angry. Less sad. And you don't notice what's happening to you. What's happening to the people around you.'

'But, Mum . . .'

This kind of thing was always embarrassing. You don't want your mum or dad talking like that. It's not fair.

Plus I was all jittery about what I was going to have to do next with Henry and Uma, and I wanted to get it out of the way, because I always find that humiliation is less daunting when you're safely on the far side and all you have to do is cringe and whimper at it, than when it's lying before you, a big mouth of shame waiting to eat you up and you have to gird your loins and walk into it.

'Let me finish, Hector. I got hooked on the stuff. More than ten years of my life. Just a mist. Gone. *Your* life. I wasn't there for it. I'm so sorry.'

'It's all right, Mum. You didn't miss much.'

And Mum laughed at that, a sort of choking, snorting laugh, and some stuff came out of her nose, so I got her a tissue and put my arm round her.

'But now you're . . . ill . . . I don't mean ill, I mean, whatever it is you've got . . . I know I can't be in a fog any more, I have to be here. So I've thrown them away. I went to see the doctor, the new doctor, the lady one that you went to see when you first started to feel ill . . .'

'Yeah, she was nice.'

Doctor Merchant, she was called. I was worried about the possibility of a rectal probe as soon as I saw her, but luckily it never materialized. Some people might say I have an irrational fear of rectal probes, but I'd say that fear is entirely justified, and that anyone who isn't afraid of an attractive lady doctor sticking her fingers up their bum needs their head examining. Or their rectums. Suppose that should be rectum, really. Unless you happen to be one of the fortunate few polyrectals.

Hector!

'And she told me that it was going to be hard, and that I'd get worse before I got better, and that I'd be anxious and snappy, and that I'd need help.'

I wasn't sure what to do with my face during this, so I left it vacant.

'And so I've asked Aunty Clytemnestra to come and stay.'

That got rid of the vacancy and replaced it with (although, of course, I couldn't see my own face and I have to speculate here somewhat) a mixture of dismay and rage.

'No!'

'Look, I know Clyte can be a bit—'

Mental, unbalanced, deranged, unstable. I didn't say that, but it's what I thought. What I said was: 'Mum, does she have to come?'

'Yes, she does,' replied Mum, in a way you'd have to describe as snappy. Then she took a couple of deep breaths and continued in a calmer voice. 'She's the last friend I have left from the old days, from before . . . She can help us. She'll help around the place, help me to help you. Help me get through this. If I'm to be a real mother to you again . . . if I'm to become myself again . . . then, yes, she has to come.'

Clytemnestra was no more my aunt than she was my

uncle. And she wasn't even called Clytemnestra. Mum told me that she changed her name at the peace camp and picked a famous ancient Greek heroine. It was years later when I was reading my book of Greek myths retold for children that I found out that Clytemnestra was only a heroine in the sense of having murdered her husband, which I always think of as one of the weaker senses of being a heroine. Not exactly Hawkgirl. She was probably called Wendy or something like that before. Actually, Mum said they all took special names at the camp, and hers had been Gaia, who was an earth goddess, but that name had been very popular among the peace-camp women, so they had a Gaia 1, Gaia 2, etc., but then they decided that that was too hierarchical, so they became things like Gaia Moon and Gaia Oak Tree, but by then it had turned silly, and in the end Mum just went back to being Mum. Or rather Christabel, which is her name.

That's enough. We've work to do. The work of Life.

'Yeah, you said.'

'What was that, Hector?'

'Nothing. Just . . . I'm going out, Mum.'

She looked up at me through the green haze from her mint tea.

'But you're not well. You shouldn't go out. You might—'

'The doctor said it was all right. And, well, I'm seeing someone and, I don't know . . .'

I left it hovering there – the idea that there might not be too many more chances for me to do this: to go out, to see people.

'Oh, OK, it was just that I thought we could be together tonight. Have something to eat. Talk . . .'

'I won't be late. And I'll grab some chips while I'm out.'

Yeah, chips.

'OK.' And then she focused, and smiled. 'Who are you seeing? Is it a . . . ? I like your hair. It looks cool.'

She smiled some more, and it was a nice smile, but as I left I heard her sniff, and I'm not sure if it meant she had started to cry again, or if it was that she'd just noticed the heady aroma of Old Tramp and thought there was a gas leak or trouble with the drains.

CHAPTER 27
THE CHIP WARS

I don't know if I looked any good as I walked the scruffy streets of our estate on the way to the Upshaw's chippie. I was wearing all my new stuff and I was conscious of my gelled hair cutting through the atmosphere, more shark than Hoxton Fin. My honest guess is that I looked pretty fine, by my standards, but then my standards were undeniably low.

Some people were definitely staring: a man washing the thirty-year-old Ford Capri he never drove, a lady at her net curtains, some shaven children picking their scabs and eating chewing gum off the pavement.

I remember reading a poem in school – I can't remember who wrote it – but it was called 'The Donkey', I think, and it was certainly about one, and this donkey was despised for having the usual donkey bits – big ears, ugly voice, all that – but then suddenly all these people were cheering it and laying down palm leaves for it to walk on. And, in case you haven't got it, they weren't really cheering the donkey, but Jesus who was riding into town, but the donkey thought it was all for him. And my point is that so maybe I was just the donkey.

I'm now going to have to tell you the story of the two

161

fish and chip shops. If you live around here you either go to Upshaw's or to what people still call 'the new place', although it's really called Fry Me to the Moon (or at least that's what the sign outside says) and has been there for years, although not as long as Upshaw's.

Upshaw's has always been Upshaw's, but there was a time when Fry Me to the Moon was a cake shop, and then after that it was a Chinese takeaway. Then it became a chippie, run by two men who called it Fry Me to the Moon. Because the two men lived together over the chippie, they were generally taken to be gay, even though they didn't seem very gay, and nobody went there because they sold *gay* fish and chips and if you ate them it meant that you were *gay* too, or might become *gay*, so the men sold it to a hard-faced couple called Doyle, who kept the name and some of the fancy gay things, like frying in sunflower oil rather than lard, but they brought back the traditional jar of pickled eggs and otherwise ran it like a standard, non-gay chippie.

The Doyles may or may not have been of traveller stock, so Fry Me To The Moon was also sometimes called the 'gyppo chippo', or sometimes the 'gyppy chippie', as well as 'the new place'.

When it was a Chinese, and when the fish and chips were gay, there was no proper competition and the Upshaws could revel in the luxury of knowing they were the only real option if fried seafood and chipped root vegetable was what you were after. But the Doyles knew their chips, and soon they were winning custom from Upshaw's, and that's when it all turned nasty. About once a fortnight the window of FMTTM would be bricked, and that happened about six times before they put in special glass. Then burning paper was put in through the letterbox, but that just melted a patch on the lino. Then the black propaganda campaign kicked in, and rumours were spread about people finding rats, bats and bits of cats in the frying vats.

Things became nastier and nastier until finally there was a brawl, with the supporters of the two fish and chip empires slugging it out with baseball bats and chip scoops and pickled eggs that had overstayed their welcome.

Now it's well-known that if you get in a scrap with traveller folk, then you're gonna get wupped, but Mr Upshaw, who's first name was Les, was not someone to be trifled with. He was at least three metres tall and as wide as a bin lorry, and he often rested his huge beer belly on the top of the metal counter in the chip shop, despite the fact that it was hot enough to melt lead. In the end the field of battle (the car park at the Spleen and Marrow pub) was strewn with bodies and dismembered pickled eggs, and only Mr Doyle and Les Upshaw were left standing, swaying and panting, but still resolute, like two champions from the days of yore. After an age, something unspoken passed between them, and they turned slowly away.

After that, Upshaw's opened on Mondays, Wednesdays and Saturdays, and FMTTM on Tuesdays, Thursdays and Sundays, and they both opened on Fridays, when there was enough custom to go round.

So, you see that Les Upshaw was a thug, but no mug. The fish and chip business had treated him well and he drove around in a BMW with a personalized number plate that read CHIP1, although he still lived on the estate so that he could keep in touch with his roots, or rather rub in the fact that he was the richest man around.

Uma's mother, Eve Upshaw, was superficially as formidable as her husband. Her fingers were heavy with enormous rings and she was always perfectly, or at least heavily, made-up, with her hair frozen in a state of lacquered shock even when she was behind the counter. She was sharp-tongued and intolerant of those who wavered in their orders, uncertain perhaps whether to plump for the haddock or the cod, or whether tonight was the night to try a black-pudding fritter. And she'd been known to go for any floozy she caught casting a randy glance on Les's magnificent beer gut. But undermining all that, there was something desperate and fragile about Eve. Halfway into a busy shift her make-up would begin to run, showing through to the orange perma-tan beneath, and her hair would collapse into a greasemire and her whole body would seem to sink in on itself, like a star caught in the act of collapsing into a black hole.

Despite that you could still see that she had once been a nice-looking woman, and what most helped you to see that was Uma.

CHAPTER 28
SMOKE AND MIRRORS

OK, so now the panic was rising like tsunami flood waters. Suddenly the twitching curtains seemed to indicate not admiration for my new look, but rather the fact everyone inside knew that I was on a lurve mission, and that I'd had a silly haircut in a vain attempt to impress my girl, and that I was going to be rejected like one of Les Upshaw's mouldy spuds.

And maybe people were also staring because I was sort of flapping and flailing around, trying to get the air to carry away the stench of Old Tramp.

Tactics.

What?

I said 'tactics'.

Yeah, that's what I need, tactics. Um, what do you mean?

A plan.

Plan. That's it. Tell me what to do. And don't just say 'be yourself'. Be yourself is rubbish advice. Myself is a useless nerd who's afraid of girls. I need to be someone else.

First of all, cool it, chillax, as I believe you crazy kids say. Screw your courage to the sticking place, as I'd prefer to put it. Faint heart never won fair maid, and winning fair

165

*maid is what we're all about. And I wasn't going to say 'be
yourself'. What kind of cliché spouter do you take me for?
Who would you like to be?*

The Flash was always good with girls, in a slightly
cheesy way.

The Flash was regularly mocked by the other Justice
Leaguers for his frivolity. Too often he'd be chatting up a
couple of girls in a bar when he should be saving the
universe. But he usually got there in the end, saving-the-
universe-wise.

*So, think like The Flash. Remember, girls love
confidence. They want to feel that they've landed a big fish,
that they've got the guy all the other girls want. You're
God's gift, and you know it.*

So much for his avoidance of cliché. But I didn't say anything about it. No sense hurting his feelings. Not now, at
least, when I needed him on my team. If I was going to be
The Flash, he was J'Onn J'Onzz, great in both age and
wisdom, a mind-reader, oozing empathy, but powerful also
in attack and resolute in defence. And, er, green.

But that's just what I don't know. Nobody wants me.
And Uma knows that. I mean, she knows that I don't know
that I'm God's gift. If you follow me.

Smoke and mirrors.

What?

*It's all smoke and mirrors. Illusion. Create the
impression that you're a sex god, and she'll see you as a sex
god.*

And how do I do that?

By believing it.

But I told you, I don't believe it. I don't believe it because it's not true.

Pause. Tumour thinking.

Well, I can fix that.

How?

Give me a second.

Another pause, and then it all went a bit mental. I felt Henry T. begin to rummage around. It was almost as if he was looking for a magazine or a book left in an untidy bedroom. I even heard him curse to himself, as if he'd stubbed his toe or barked his shins.

Whatever it was he was looking for, he found it.

Oh yes. Yes indeedy-do.

With a jolt like a slap in the face, the world came into sharper focus. Colours were brighter, the air clearer. I could hear things that I shouldn't have been able to hear – far-off things, silent things. Ideas came into my head, calculations, equations, bits of poetry. Things I'd learned and forgotten years ago all ran together in a mass like a dream or a nightmare: **toseetheuniverseinagrainofsandontogenyrecapitulatesphylogenyaspectreishauntingeuropeifihaveseenfurtherthanyouitisbystandingontheshouldersofgiantsobravenewworldthathassuchpeopleinit**negativenumbershavenosquarerootbecauseifyoumultiplytwonegativenumbersyougetapositive.

I tried to slow the thoughtstream, but it kept coming, kept fizzing, so then I tried to put it back, hiding it, covering it, and that worked, sort of, and the thought became a hum, like electric wires.

I was walking more quickly, almost skipping (but not

skipping – that wouldn't have done at all), and I sniffed, and my fingers drummed, and I ground my teeth together to some mad rhythm, maybe a rumba or a salsa or something from the jazz age or from the future. And if all that sounds bad, then it shouldn't because I felt great; great isn't the word, the word should be, well there isn't a word, so I'll call it `ofdnz;cljkf9eklgh'dpigfoijfl` and you can make your own mind up about it.

But the best thing was that I knew that it was all going to be fine with Uma Upshaw. How could it not be? Wasn't I gorgeous? Wasn't I as cool as a human boy could be, cool as a penguin sucking an ice pop? And wouldn't Uma melt into my arms like caramel on a tongue? But melt isn't right because I was cool, like the penguin, remember, but it doesn't matter because you understand. Up until this point I'd still kept alive the idea that I might maybe just perhaps be going to Uma's to tell her that Smurf fancied her. Well now that idea died. Now I had but one idea.

What have you done? I asked wonderingly, fizzingly, frantically.

Like it?

Yeah, it's fantastic, it's `ofdnz;cljkf9eklgh'dpig-foijfl`. But what is it? What have you done done done done?

Dopamine.

Dopamine . . . ? That's a . . . brain . . . thing, right?

Oh yes.

What does it do?

Well, all the things you're feeling now. It makes you feel confident and happy, and gives you an energy hit.

It makes everything connect. It's absolutely my favourite brain chemical.

And you just told my brain to make some?

Sort of. Your brain makes it all the time. But it also sucks it back in again. I blocked the sucking-back-in bit, so you've got more of it sloshing around. Cool, eh?

Pretty cool, yeah.

And are you ready to rock?

You bet. Rock. Yes, let's rock.

Good, because we're here.

CHAPTER 29
THERE'S A GIRL
WORKS DOWN THE
CHIP SHOP

And so we were. Right outside Upshaw's. I could see three or four people in there, queuing, big coats hunched along the counter. And behind the counter were Mrs Upshaw and, Holy of Holies, Uma. She was wearing a pale green-and-white-checked coat-thing that entirely concealed the wondrous spread of her bosombas, and a little paper hat not unlike a nurse's hat. She was shovelling chips into a bag. Two full scoops, then a flick. Nice action. Then she put a battered fillet of what deduction told me was likely to be cod on top of the chips and dextrously wrapped the combo in white paper. She worked neatly, quickly, but with a hint of anger in the whiteness of her knuckles, and the grim set of her mouth.

Watching her work, I felt some of the chemical effervescence begin to fizzle out.

Now or never.

What's the downside of never?

Just move it.

So I opened the door and went in. I was dazzled by the

harsh neon light, fugged by the smell of old chip fat. The blessed chip fat – surely, if anything could, that would block out the Old Tramp.

Almost straight away, Uma looked up. Her eyes sharpened and then went vague, as though she were trying to hide whatever it was she was feeling. Annoyance, perhaps. Or embarrassment. Unlikely to be lust.

'Hey,' I said, from the back of the queue.

An old man in a heavy coat that looked like it was made from the dead remains of many other coats, turned and huffed at me. He had enough hair coming out of his ears to thatch a dozen gonks.

'Some of us are waiting,' he said gruffly, taking me for a pusher-in. His false teeth clacked like he was simultaneously sending out a message in Morse code. I was going to say something back, but then I noticed the pink hearing aid and the coiling wire, and I instantly saw all the possibilities for looking like an idiot if I tried to talk to the deaf old geezer. 'What? Eh? You said my hovercraft is full of eels? I'll give you hovercraft!' That sort of thing. And looking up I saw that Uma was smiling.

'Hair,' she said, and my fizzing mind decoded it, working as fast as the people in Bletchley Park who decoded the German Ultra transcripts and won the war for us.

I-L-I-K-E-Y-O-U-R-H-A-I-R.

Could that be it? I ran it through again.

I-L-I-K-E-Y-O-U-R-H-A-I-R.

Yes!

Please let it not just be the dopamine playing havoc with my judgment.

'I thought you always went to the gyppy chippie,' she said, without breaking her rhythm of two scoops and a shake.

It was definitely quite a promising start. She could easily have accused me of being an Eater of the Gay Chip. The very fact that she knew what my usual chip shop was suggested that she had some kind of interest in me. Either that or her concern for local chip-eating trends was purely scientific and business-oriented, which seemed unlikely.

'It's closer,' I said, 'but . . .'

'But what?'

Uma was looking deep into the fryer, as if there was something especially interesting about the fat. Maybe it contained a piece of batter shaped like Mother Theresa.

'But . . .' But what? I had to think of something good. C'mon, Henry, c'mon, dopamine, this is where I need you.

But your cod fillets are a bit thicker?

But you use a better quality of vinegar?

But . . . help! My brain was spinning and whirring but going nowhere.

'But . . . *you don't work there.*'

It was Henry. He'd taken over for a moment, done my talking for me. I should have been annoyed, but this wasn't the time. And I'm not saying it was necessarily in the top one hundred all-time great chip shop chat-up lines, but it was a hell of a lot better than silence. I think Henry even managed to get a little extra something into my voice, a certain . . . *swagger*, which meant that the words punched above their weight.

And then the unthinkable happened.

Uma Upshaw, the unflappable, imperturbable, iron-clad

Uma Upshaw blushed. I saw it. She really did. It began somewhere beneath the green nylon collar of her coat and carried right up until it hit her hairline, where, for all I knew, it continued till it met at a point right beneath the centre of her little paper hat. It was the world turned upside down. I didn't make people blush. I was the blusher. I think a little natural dopamine got injected into my system with that minor triumph.

Oh boy, said Henry.

Without quite understanding how, I found that I was at the front of the queue, and Mrs Upshaw was looking at me. I don't think she'd taken in the juddering import of what had just occurred: the chat-up, the blushing, the glory.

'What can I get you, love?' she asked mechanically. I guess that if I'd have been a slavering werewolf she'd have said the same thing.

'I'm here for Uma,' I said.

'Chips with that?'

No, Eve Upshaw didn't seem to be quite all there tonight.

'No, er, I said Uma, I've come for Uma.'

Before Mrs Upshaw had time to respond, a shadow loomed over the counter. Uma's dad had appeared from the kitchen. He was wearing a white apron and carrying a bucket of raw chips as big as a beer barrel.

'Who's this?' he said, aiming at me, but speaking to God knows who.

'I'm here for Uma,' I managed to say, and I don't think it came out as a squeak, but you never know.

Les dropped his bucket of chips. His face was a solid

slab of meat, and it seemed to sort of flow into his bald head, so you couldn't really say where face stopped and scalp began. I noticed for the first time that he had a very small mouth. It wasn't a pretty face, but it was an impressive one.

And now it was making a growling noise.

'I've come to ask her out. On a walk.'

'You what?'

He sounded like I'd said, 'to the nearest dung heap, on which I plan to ravish her with the aid of a selection of large, misshapen root vegetables, including, but not limited to, turnip, swede, beetroot and kohlrabi.'

'For a walk, Mr Upshaw. Now.'

Blustering outrage took over from puzzled anger.

'She . . . *not a chance* . . . work to do . . . walking the streets with the likes of . . . ought to come round there and—'

'Go and get ready, Uma, love.'

This was, unexpectedly, Eve Upshaw speaking.

'What you on about? I just said—'

'Lesley, this is Hector Brunty. He's a nice lad. His mother works at the charity shop.'

'But there's chips to—'

'Don't make a bother. We're quiet. You can see we are.'

And it was then that I noticed that we were alone in the shop – no one had come in after me. But Les Upshaw wasn't beaten yet.

'Aye, but the rush'll be on soon.'

'We'll cope.'

Without saying anything, Uma dashed past her parents

and out the back. Rationally, of course, I had no way of knowing if this just meant that she had cleared off to catch *EastEnders* – after all, she hadn't said yes to going on a walk with me, let alone the ravishing on the dung heap with the vegetables. But the dopamine permitted no pessimism and I knew she'd return to me.

But for now I was on my own with Les and Eve.

Ugh.

Les was looking vaguely stunned now, as if he'd just woken up during an operation. An anal probe, perhaps. His inappropriately petite mouth was hanging open. And, now I looked more closely, I could see that his lips were of normal proportions, and it was the side-to-side measurement of the mouth opening that was unusually restricted. It made his lips protrude somewhat, giving him a guppy-like appearance. A fucking big guppy, mind you.

Eve was smiling at me.

'And how's your mother?' she asked.

'Fine.'

I thought maybe they had counselling together. Something like that.

'Want some chips, while you wait?'

'Er, no thanks, Mrs Upshaw.'

'Summat up wi' my chips?' That was Les, of course, prickling for a fight.

'No! Your chips are great. And your fish. And your, er, pickled eggs.'

'Battered sausage?'

'Oh, they're the best.'

'Ha, got you! We don't do a battered sausage. That's the other place what does them.'

'Les! It's not fair to trick the boy. You got him flustered, that's all, with your battered sausages. Who can think straight when there's a battered sausage at stake? It's no wonder he got a bit confused. Battered sausage indeed!'

Then there was a couple of minutes silence as Les faffed about with the fryer settings and Eve smiled and the dopamine drained out of me like air from a punctured bicycle, and I began to hope for one of those tears in the fabric of space and time to open up so I could pop into a different dimension for a few minutes. Henry made unpleasant remarks which I tried really hard not to listen to, along the lines of suggesting what Les might want to do with his battered sausage, i.e. stick it up his sole. As in a kind of fish. This being a fish and chip shop, and 'sole' being the last syllable of arsehole, the whole thing therefore being a joke.

You've killed it dead. Too much explication. Thanks a bundle.

Sorry, Henry. It's the tension getting to me.

And then Les stopped what he was doing and sniffed the air.

'What's that smell?'

Oh shit. I mean, Old Tramp.

Les scanned the room nasally, trying to track down the source of the stench. He began to focus on me. I was doomed. Not only was I going to ravish his daughter, but I was going to do it smelling like a gay hobo.

My panicked eyes met Mrs Upshaw. She returned my

stare for a second. I think she understood. Understood everything. And then she galloped to the rescue.

'It's my new perfume,' she said. 'Do you like it?'

I loved Eve Upshaw in that moment. If the afore-mentioned rent in time/space was really available, I'd have gone back to when Eve was a teenager and taken her away from all this – from Les, from the chips, from her nylon overall – found an island somewhere with goats and coconuts, and we'd have been happy together, Eve and I.

'What?' said Les, his smooth meaty face registering surprise. 'Oh, aye. Nice.' And then his tiny little mouth went into a spasm, which I was forced to interpret as a smile. I suppose he thought that this unprecedented use of scent in the chip shop meant that Mrs U. was in the mood for love. 'Very nice.'

Very nice for him, perhaps, but bloody unpleasant for me to think about, and a nasty intrusion to our island with the goats and coconuts, and the grass skirt, and nothing to do but find new ways to pleasurize each other. It's her wearing the grass skirt, by the way, not me. Just wanted to clear that up. In case you were wondering.

And then Uma was there to banish such thoughts (I mean the thoughts of Eve on the island, and Les with Eve), and I'd swear that when she appeared in the doorway the whole chip shop filled with light, as if she was being illuminated by the flashbulbs of a thousand paparazzi.

CHAPTER 30
AN INTERLUDE AT THE
SPLEEN AND MARROW

'C'mon then,' she said.

Oh boy.

      Oh boy.

           Oh boy.

Couldn't have put it better myself.

Oh boy.

'You're not going out like that.'

Les, of course. And he had a point. Except that she *was* going out like that.

'You look lovely, dear,' said Mrs Upshaw, which was also true.

Uma was wearing a top that rippled with iridescence like a mermaid's scales, and a black skirt so short you'd think there was some world material crisis and they'd brought in rationing.

'She'll catch her death. Or worse.'

Brave words, but there was little defiance left in Big Les now. He knew he was defeated.

'It's warm out,' said Mrs Upshaw, and Les was out of the ring.

Uma lifted the counter and floated past. I tried to say

goodbye to Mr and Mrs Upshaw, but I'd lost my voice and I didn't find it until we were out in the street.

'Where do you want to go?'

'Isn't that your job? Deciding things and stuff?'

The words may have sounded stroppy, but the tone was flirtatious.

I ran through the possibilities, in table form.

	Advantages	Disadvantages
The Odeon	1. Wouldn't have to think of anything to say to her during the film. 2. Could snog her in the back row.	1. Cost more money than I had. 2. Would have to snog her in the back row, and I didn't think I knew how to snog people, in the back row or anywhere else.
McDonald's	1. Cheap – the whole date might well come in under a fiver. 2. Limited snogging, and therefore snogging-related embarrassment opportunities.	1. Disgusting and, like, Uma would really want to go to a smelly fast-food outlet when she's just escaped from a smelly fast-food outlet? 2. What I said about snogging, only the other way round.

This is already decided – tell her we're just going for a walk. Try to sound mysterious, without being creepy if you can manage that. I'll take care of the rest.

So I told her, cranking up the mystery quotient, then easing off on the lever before we reached creepy, just like Henry told me, and she seemed OK with it all, although she didn't appear much mystified in either a good or bad way.

It was seven o'clock now, and the streets were emptyish, as most people were at home, having their teas or watching telly. I thought how nice it would be to be sitting at home watching telly, not having to think of things to say to pretty girls who knew much more about life than you did.

'So what's with the new image then?'

'Oh, my hair and that? Just sort of felt like a change,' I said as casually as I could.

'Suits you. You don't look like such a saddo any more.'

'Thanks.'

You're easily pleased.

The first thirty seconds were going well. Obviously the dopamine had helped. The last drops were still in there, but it wouldn't last much longer. I hoped Henry would give me another spurt.

Uma was looking at me. I was expected to say something.

Tell her she looks like a rare orchid; like a young faun; like a still-unravished Danae, awaiting the shower of gold; like Leda supine beneath the beating wings.

'Oh, er, you look . . .' What? I didn't just want to be Henry's mouthpiece, I wanted to find my own words. Nice?

Scrumptious? Intelligent? Worthy of a place as sexy alien on board the *Enterprise*?

Like Artemis, hot with pursuit; like Psyche, tender in the darkness.

'Gorgeous.'

Ugh!

'Ta.' She looked quite pleased, but she was probably used to being called things like gorgeous. 'Why are we going in the direction of the graveyard?'

'Are we?' I noticed that we were, in fact, heading towards the old graveyard of St Arsenius, the local posh C of E church. I detected Henry's subtle hand at work on my legs. 'Er, we are. Yes. For a walk. Nice and quiet. With the graves and everything. Flowers.'

'OK, but not yet. Let's go somewhere else first.'

Bum. Odeon or McDonald's? Time to decide.

'Like the pub.'

'The pub . . . but I've never . . . OK, yeah, the pub. I was going to say that. Always a good idea to go to the pub. First. Pub . . . drink . . . good.'

'Liar. You've never been, have you?'

She said it with a laugh in her voice. Couldn't quite tell if it was laughing-with or laughing-at. Probably at. It was usually at.

'Yes. A few times.' Pause. 'No, not really.'

I hung my head in shame, but Uma didn't seem bothered.

'Have you got any money?'

I took out my wallet.

'Nice purse.'

'It's a wallet.'

'Touchy.'

'No, it's just that . . . well, it's a wallet.'

There was five pounds in my purse, I mean wallet. I felt deep into my pockets, and scraped together another two-fifty.

I held it all out to show her: 'Is that enough?'

'Yeah, it'll do,' said Uma, not really trying to hide her disappointment. It was the first proper setback in my hot date with Uma Upshaw. Would it be the last? Only time would—

Get on with it.

So we diverted from our path to the graveyard and walked the couple of streets to the Spleen and Marrow. I tried to get really close to Uma to show that I liked her, without actually touching, which she might think was me trying to grope her. As we walked we kept bumping together in a random way that wasn't one thing or the other, and I learned the interesting fact that boys and girls walk to a different rhythm.

Conversation came in fits and starts, and got stuck for a while on chips, and why you don't get a free bag of scraps (that's bits of loose batter from the fryer, in case you've never had them) any more. I was relieved when we arrived.

And it *was* my first time in a pub. I'd never been with Mum, of course, because she didn't go out. I'd seen pubs and bars on the telly, so I roughly knew what to expect, but telly doesn't prepare you fully for reality. If it did, then there'd be a lot more pretty girls in the world, because nearly all the girls on the telly are pretty.

There was one of those doors where you don't know if you should push or pull, but I finally managed to get the better of it and entered with a sort of falling motion.

First pub impressions: warm and smoky.

The place was sparsely populated, with just a few yellow-eyed old geezers dotted about at the tables, most of them smoking, all of them looking pretty glum. They could have been the same gang from the hospital ward, but with their coats on. Perhaps their lives consisted only of this constant shuttling between the hospital and the pub.

Everything inside the Spleen and Marrow was brown, although I don't know if that was deliberate, meaning someone had painted it all brown, or if it was just stained brown with brown stuff that people brought with them, like smoke and mud and grime and grease.

'Get us a Campari and lemonade, will you?' said Uma, sounding the cheeriest thing in there by a factor of a million. 'And,' she added decisively, 'some crisps.'

She took off her jacket and sat down on a chair. The seat of the chair was made of red plastic which had split, and the foam bulged out like a hairy beer belly bulging through the gaps in a shirt.

'Yeah, sure, I'll just, er . . .' and I shuffled off towards the bar. Campari. I'd heard of Campari. I'd get one of those too.

No you don't.

Why?

Lady's drink.

Oh.

A lady's drink. No, I couldn't get one of those. Because I wasn't a lady. OK, what did I want?

Hello, Henry, come in please. Need some help here. What do I want?

A cup of sack, or glass of malmsey. Yes, that would do the trick. But I don't suppose we've much hope here. It hardly matters, so long as you drink deep, and drink long.

No use at all, which meant it was down to me. Beer would be the manly thing, but I'd tasted beer a few times and it was horrible. About the only alcoholic thing I'd ever tasted that I liked was martini and lemonade at our next-door-neighbour's New Year's Eve party, but I had a nasty feeling that if Campari was a lady's drink, then Martini and lemonade might be a gay one.

And then an inspiration.

Alcopop!

They tasted like pop, but they were made of alcohol! They were invented to get children drunk. Genius.

I reached the bar. The man behind it looked a bit like Les Upshaw but without his twinkling, happy-go-lucky side.

I'm being sarcastic.

This one looked like he'd been hacked out of a quarry and towed here by truck.

'A Campari and lemonade and a Tangerine Tosshead, please,' I said, in a gruff, lumberjack kind of voice.

The barman stared at me. You'd have to call it a withering stare. Anyway, I withered.

'Age?'

I thought about confusing him by claiming to be seventy-two. Some sort of freak of nature, eternal youth, monkey-gland treatment.

'Eighteen.'

He carried on withering me for a while and then, greed overcoming his belief that under-age children shouldn't be served alcohol, he turned and did his thing with glasses and bottles and coolers and came back with what I'd asked for.

'Four ninety-eight.'

I gave him the five pounds and said loudly, 'Keep the change,' because that seemed the thing to do – open-handed and grown-up. Very Ernest Hemingway. And then I remembered the crisps.

'And some crisps, please.'

The barman breathed heavily, like it – the breathing, I mean – was something he was still getting to grips with.

'Flavour?'

I couldn't think of any flavours. Not one.

'Er, what have you got?'

His eyes rolled slowly upwards, and for a moment I thought he was in the middle of dying, but then he said, counting off with his huge, calloused fingers like jumbo sausage rolls: 'Whale and bacon, lemur, veal calf, cheese and cucumber, squid . . .' and I think he would probably have gone on for another half an hour or so.

'Plain,' I said, to stop him.

Long pause.

'You mean ready-salted?'

'Yes.'

'Sea salt or rock?'

'Erm . . . just the normal, whatever that is.'

'What kept you?' said Uma, when I finally got back to her.

'Crisps,' I replied, laying before her the drinks and three

packets, one sea salt, one rock salt, and one whale and bacon (to be on the safe side).

'Oh,' she said distantly. 'Don't really fancy them now.'

That was annoying. Never mind, her loss, my gain. I was about to open up the whale and bacon when I heard a warning voice.

No! Can't eat strong-flavoured snack products if you're going to snog her. Don't you know anything? Why do you think she changed her mind? She thought it through while you were at the bar. Nothing worse than coming across a mashed morsel of cheesy mush when you're tongue-surfing.

'When I'm what?'

'When you're what what?' said Uma.

'Oh, sorry. Nothing. How's your Campari?'

'Nice.'

She sipped her drink and a little line of pale red moisture formed itself around her lips. And, now I was looking lip-ward, I saw that whatever stuff she had put on them, lipgloss or lipstick, had bits of sparkle in it. I couldn't decide if this was babyish or slutty. Well, my head couldn't decide, but elsewhere decisions were being made.

I took a gulp of my Tangerine Tosshead. There was a slight mechanical problem as my lips got sucked into the neck of the bottle and I had to pull them out with a loud smacking noise. Uma turned away courteously. The stuff was as sickly sweet as a Mr Kipling's French Fancy dissolved in Vimto. Which was fine, but then the alcohol felt its way blindly through the sugar and put its claws into my gullet, and I had to swallow a mini-retch, which left me with a big burp caught half in and half out. Finally the pain was so bad I had to release it, so I held the bottle up to my lips and tried to belch discreetly back into it, which seemed like the politest of the options I had before me. I don't know why, but the bottled burp made the drink fizz into a frenzy, and it bubbled and spilled out and down my front and onto the table.

Bravo, maestro.

It wasn't one of my best performances. And then I noticed that Uma was laughing.

'I'm sorry, Uma. I don't know what I'm doing here. I shouldn't have—'

'Oh shut up and neck your drink,' she said, her words breaking up under the pressure of her smile. 'I'm having a laugh. It's not every night you get to go out with the school weirdo, who suddenly turns out to be quite good-looking under all that hair.'

And with that she did something extraordinary.

She kissed me.

It was a light kiss, weighing about as much as a pencil or a jam-jar lid, i.e. something in the region of two grams, which may not sound like much to you, but to me was like having a tank run over my lips, but in a good way, by which I'm trying to say that it was nice. Short, but nice. Probably less than a second in duration, but, of course, time goes funny when you have someone attached to your lips.

Wa-haaaaay! Told you we were in. In like Flynn! In like Flynn!

I restrained myself from saying 'shut up'.

'Let's finish our drinks and go down the graveyard,' said Uma.

It was the best offer I'd had all day, for which read 'in my entire life'.

CHAPTER 31
ELEGY IN A CITY
CHURCHYARD

The next thing I knew we were walking down the lane to the church, and Uma had taken my arm. I don't know if it was Henry T. on the case, or just the natural result of having the prettiest girl in the school holding onto me, and us about to enter the dark verdant world of the graveyard, but I felt dopamine drench my brain, spurting like champagne at the end of a Grand Prix.

Doing what like champagne?

Spur— Shut up.

'Is this where you take all your girlfriends?'

She was being teasing and playful, and I didn't know if she was asking because she secretly hated the idea of me being here with other girls, or because she was actually excited by it, or if she really didn't give a toss and she was just winding me up. Or all of those things.

'I haven't been here before with a—'

Stop! Girls like boys with a bit of experience. Play up to it.

'I mean lately. Not for days now. With girls. Or a girl.'

Yes, whatever Henry said, I didn't want her to think I was having orgies down here with packs of nudie girls.

'Where do you usually go?'

'Go?'

Go to do it, dummy!

'Oh God. I mean, I go down here.'

I actually knew the old graveyard well. It was one of the better places to hang out.

Need to give you a quick picture of our part of town: there's the school and the social club and the Catholic church kind of at the epicentre of the estate, but the whole place is in this boggy mess, with these low, soggy fields where the gypsies come to camp. But it's only a ten-minute walk to an older part of town, where the houses are bigger, and no one has their windows boarded up and there's less general rubbish around like old prams and cars propped on piles of bricks because their wheels have been nicked. That's where St Arsenius is. And I suppose you'd have to call it kind of beautiful. The church is probably only a hundred years old, but it was made to look old even then, like some Gothic cathedral in miniature. And the churchyard is like a bit of the real countryside dumped in town. There are tall trees and low trees and a spreading yew and bushes and hidden corners and lots of gravestones and some mausoleums, like small palaces where the rich lie dead and the dead lie rich.

I used to come here when I was a kid to watch birds, but don't tell anyone because it's like train-spotting and making model aeroplanes, being one of the things to guarantee that nobody will ever fancy you. I never got good enough so that I could tell the little brown jobs apart – I mean, say, a willow warbler from a chiffchaff, or the drab female chaffinch from a female sparrow – but I could still tick off a good ten species while I sat on a bench or a grave. Blue tit, coal tit, great tit, male chaffinches with their pink breasts – *hey, that's a lot of tit action there* – shut up, and magpies and jays, and blackbirds, of course, and robins coming close in that not-giving-a-fuck way of theirs, and the rooks up high, and sometimes even the dark silhouette of a tawny owl.

For some reason the thugs hardly ever came to the graveyard, although you would have thought it was a good place to sniff glue and mug people. Maybe it was the ghosts of the place or the quietness of it that made them feel uncomfortable.

So yeah, I knew the graveyard quite well, and I knew where I was going to take Uma Upshaw, and I suppose at some level I knew what I was going to have to do when I got there.

'This way,' I said, and I was holding her hand.

The terrifying Uma Upshaw had become strangely meek, and as she grew more delicate, so I became more robust. I didn't feel fourteen any more. I felt more like fifteen. Maybe sixteen. The dopamine, good stuff. I felt close to her. Felt able to ask her the question that was pressing me.

'Uma,' I said, 'why did you agree to come out with me? I mean, you've never acted interested in me much. I mean before the other day, outside school.'

'Why did I come? Because you asked me. Lots of boys are afraid of me. Or too shy to ask. But you did. And I *had* noticed you before. I thought you sometimes said funny things. And you've got a cute smile. And you couldn't be worse than that little shit . . . you know who.'

I didn't want to think about Tierney. But the rest of that was good to hear. This didn't feel like my life any more, I mean my usual boring life. It felt like the life I wanted, a life where things happened.

I found the place I was looking for. It was a weeping willow at the edge of the graveyard. The ground beneath the drooping branches was always dry, and soft with the fallen leaves. It was a place where I came long ago on summer evenings to read comics and imagine myself a hero, and even before that I'd come here to play Top Trumps with Smurf and Phil, and we'd lie there and talk about nothing, and one of us would have brought a bottle of Tizer, and we'd have burping contests, or see if we could piss as far as the wall from within the shelter of the willow branches.

Once an old man parted the curtain and put his head through, and he sort of looked at us for a while and then he went away, half smiling, and I suppose he was the vicar.

Smurf. It was always his pack of Top Trumps we played with. His image began to form in my head, mournful, accusing. But then I felt Henry smother him before he had the chance to mess things up with Uma, and he disappeared with a faint 'pop', taking my guilt with him.

I held back the softly falling branches for Uma.

'I'm not going in there,' she said, poking her head through.

'It's really nice,' I said. 'It's my favourite place in the world. The ground's dry.'

That was all it took. She went into the space beneath the boughs.

'This is OK, actually,' she said, bumping herself down.

Action stations. Code yellow.

I sat down beside her. Three packets of crisps crunched in my pockets.

Nice move.

We still hadn't had anything resembling a conversation. I thought now might be as good a time as any to start.

'Which is your favourite *Star Wars* film?'

Noooooooooo!

'My what?'

'Er, favourite *Star Wars* film. I think mine's *The Empire Strikes Back.*'

Jeez.

'I haven't got one. I saw the last one, what was it called? Anyway, it was shit.'

'Yeah, a fiasco. But at least it didn't have Ja Ja Binks in it.'

'Hector—'

'You can call me Heck.'

'Heck—'

'Yeah?'

'Shut up and give me a kiss.'

Code red. I repeat, Code red.

The moment had come, the moment I had been dreading. I moved closer to her, and put my hand on her shoulder. She folded herself into me and I kissed her. I was leaning on my left arm and I then made the mistake of moving it before I'd readjusted my balance, and we fell back together, and my lips and teeth ground into her. She pushed me off.

'Ow! That really hurt.'

'Sorry.'

'It's all right. Am I bleeding?

'I don't think so.'

I touched her lips with my finger and then looked at it. There was a little spot of blood on it.

Lick it.

I put my finger to my mouth and kissed off the spot of blood. Then Uma's eyes went kind of bleary, and she half rose to meet me, and I stooped to her and we were kissing again and I could taste the salty blood.

Listen, Heck, you take care of the face, and I'll look after the rest, OK?

I wasn't listening to Henry by then. The kissing felt so nice, so warm. It was like finding something you didn't realize you had lost. But there was something else too. The feeling that perhaps this wasn't really the thing I'd lost, just something that looked like it, that the fit wasn't quite right.

And then I realized what my hands were doing.

Or rather undoing.

Her blouse.

It was Henry.

'No,' said Uma.

'Sorry.'

'You can stay outside, or forget it.'

I tried to wrench my hand out, but Henry resisted. Uma helped, pulling at my wrist. And then my hand was touching her breasts through her top, and she let out a little sort of half-moan, half-groan, and Henry did some more things with my hand.

There was an added complication here, in that a Saturn V rocket seemed to be trying to break out of the gravitational pull of my trousers. I don't know how it got there. The damn thing appeared to have nothing to do with the rest of me. Probably Henry in the pilot's seat. There was no way I could get Houston to abort the mission. The best I could do was to try to keep it in orbit, avoiding a splashdown.

At least I seemed to have got the hang of the kissing. I basically did what she did, only more so.

'No!'

Oh God. I looked down at my hand. It was lost somewhere under her skirt. I tried to pull it out, but Henry wouldn't let me.

Yes! We've got to do this.

'No, we don't,' I said, out loud.

'Don't what?' said Uma, still wrestling with my hand.

Must.

'Shut up.'

'Don't tell me to shut up.'

Uma had finally managed to remove my hand from her skirt.

'Not you, I mean—'

'You really are a psycho.' She stood up, pulling down her ruffled skirt. 'I'm off. I can't believe I came here with you. I didn't think you were like this . . . like all the others. After what you can get.'

'Wait, I wasn't—'

'What were you doing then? I told you to stop it and you kept on, and it was nice before that.'

I gave up.

'I'm really sorry, it wasn't meant to be like this.'

'Too right.' And she was out of there.

'I'll walk you home,' I called to her.

'Fuck off.'

CHAPTER 32
THE MUSIC OF THE SPHERES

I slumped back down.

'Nice work, Henry.'

Me? It was you who messed it up. That was our best chance. Our last best chance.

Henry sounded like a spoiled toddler surveying his ice cream lying cone-up in the mud.

'Best chance for what?'

You know what.

'I don't know what you mean. Don't know what you want. Don't know what you are. And I didn't even like her that much. Not as much as Smurf, anyway.'

She was perfect.

'But—' I hesitated here because, well, it's embarrassing 'I . . . I didn't, I don't love her.'

LOVE HER! What century are we in here? Stupid wanker.

'I don't want to hear this now, Henry. I don't feel too good. I have a brain tumour, remember.'

And I did suddenly feel pretty low. There was a weight on my forehead, pressing me down. I was trying not to think about the horror of what I'd just been through with

Uma. And sure, she was magnificent, but I really *didn't* love her. Or even fancy her that much. You can sometimes accept that someone is perfect, physically, but nothing happens; no bells, no music, no *twang*. OK, maybe a bit of a twang, what with the Saturn V rocket. I'm fourteen, remember, and all kinds of things can make you go twang. But all I'd done with Uma was humiliate myself. And worse, because I tried to force her to do things she didn't want to do.

Oh God. I was as bad as Tierney and his droogs.

What had Uma called me? A psycho – yes, exactly what we called *them*.

It was like the bit at the end of *Animal Farm*, when the horse, or whichever animal it is, looks through the farm-house window from the pigs to the humans and back again and he can't tell which is the pig and which the human.

That's why we can't mess about. We might not have enough time.

Henry was sounding different now. The petulance had gone, replaced by an awkward, jarring urgency.

'Time . . . what do you—?'

But I knew what he meant, and now I had something else to feel shit about. Henry meant that I was going to die, and die soon. He meant that I was going to stop being a thing made of soft, warm, breathing, living stuff, and become a thing made of cold, dead stuff, and I'd never see my friends again, or be able to help my mum when she got older, and nor would I ever have sex with another of those soft, breathing, warm, living things.

I haven't got for ever. Remember when Smurf went on

that last-minute bargain to Egypt?

'Yeah, some bargain. He said he hardly ever climbed off the bog. Said he had to stuff tissues in his undies to make a sort of nappy.'

But do you remember the postcard he sent you? The one with the pyramids in the background, and the big sign saying: CAMEL RIDE TO THE TOMB?

'Yeah, but—'

Well that's what we're all on. You, me, everyone. A lurching, comic, absurd camel ride to the tomb. And we have to make the most of it.

'Here we go again. What did you call it before? Thanatos and Eros. Bollocks and bullshit.'

Hector, please, this is too important. The ride to the tomb, the ride to the tomb only matters if your line ends. Genetic death is the only death. We have within us the capacity for immortality. There are genes within you that are a hundred million years old. Look forwards another hundred million. You can be there too. We both can. You don't matter. What matters is the code you carry.

'But I don't care about the code. I'm more than the code. I don't care if bits of me are alive in a billion years inside somebody else. I want them alive inside me – now.'

But your genes . . .

'I don't give a fuck about my genes. My genes might have made me, but I'm more than they are. I've escaped from them. And if my genes made you as well, then I hate them.'

OK, so I was losing it a bit. It had been a tough day.

Look, I'm sorry, I'm really sorry. And now even the

urgency had gone from Henry's voice, leaving only sadness in its wake, and so we were one, in our sadness at least.

I didn't mean to ... Come on, cheer up. We'll have another go with Uma – nothing's as bad as it seems.

But I was lost to such platitudes. I was lying here in this ancient quiet space, a space I'd always seen as a refuge, but now it was like a prison, and it might as well have been another of the graves looming and crowding around us.

'Why me?' It was the obvious question. Why you? Why us?

You mean why have you got a brain tumour?

'Did I do something wrong? Am I being punished?'

That's not the way to look at it. No one gets handed out tumours because they've done something bad or stupid.

'Smokers?'

OK, I'll give you smokers. But you didn't do anything to deserve me.

'So why did you come?'

A bit of genetics. A smidge of environment. A roll of the old dice. That Lady Luck can be a sour-faced old bitch.

'I wish I could go back or stop time or something. I don't want ... I don't want to ...' I was beyond tears, past the point where crying could do anything for me.

We can do that.

'Do what?' I might have sniffed a bit.

Stop time. For a while.

'How?'

I was intrigued, but also sceptical. And there was something sloppy about saying you'd stop time 'for a while', because, well, 'a while' is a period of time, and if you've stopped time, then how can you have a period of time? But that only occurred to me later, and I never did bring it up with Henry.

We'll do it together. Put out your arms.

I was lying on my back, looking up into the darkening skies through the narrow gaps between the leaves and branches. I could see the first of the stars coming through the willow. I shrugged and put out my arms to the side like a crucified Jesus. I felt like an idiot. Not even a happy idiot. A depressed idiot.

'Now what?'

Stretch out your fingers.

I did.

Close your eyes. Can you feel it? We're moving. We're spinning through space: you, me, the Earth. You know how fast?

Of course I knew.

'Six thousand, six hundred and ninety kilometres an hour.'

And moving around the sun. How fast?

'Thirty kilometres a second.'

And the solar system, and the galaxy. All spinning, flying through space, exploding away from the beginning of things. And time was born then too, back at the beginning, and it's flying and spinning with us. Feel for it, feel the air, feel the time, feel it thickening in your hands.

And you know what? Mental as it sounds, I did think that I could feel the stuff of time thick in my hands; a liquid like mercury, cool and heavy. I felt as though I could have formed it into a ball, and eaten it like an apple.

Now hold onto the earth. Dig those fingers in, boy. Grip it. Hold it tight. You've got it. Give it everything now, everything you've got. This isn't easy, this is the hardest thing there's ever been. This is work for superheroes. Yes! It's slowing.

And as I gripped the earth I thought that I could feel it grinding, feel the spin of it slow, and it was like when Superman slows a train speeding towards the broken rails and the steepling drop, his heels driven back and throwing up sparks, but stop it he always would. But my train was the earth, and the universe, and time, and I stopped it, I really did.

It's stopping.

'No.'

Yes. It's stopped. That's my boy.

I opened my eyes and everything was still. There was no breeze to move the willow leaves, and the stars were silent and unmoving, and there was no traffic noise from the road, and I knew it was because the cars had all stopped, the drivers' mouths frozen midway into mobile calls, and the birds were suspended in the evening sky, and Uma Upshaw was a mannequin out there somewhere, her brave bold stride caught like a photograph. And all the clocks of the world had stopped, and the breath of every living thing, and the beating of every heart.

'Has it really stopped?'

Don't you feel it? Feel the stillness of everything?

'I can't move.'

But of course not, you're holding it all still. If you move, the spell is broken.

'Can we stay like this for ever?'

Do you want to?

'I don't want to have a brain tumour. I don't want to die.'

We all have to die.

'I don't want to die yet.'

We can stay this way for as long as you like. Calm, serene, unmoving. We are like gods, beyond the touch of pain. But also joy. But also life.

It was beautiful lying there with the world dead around me, and me immortal. But I also saw that everything I cared about was in that world I'd stopped and which was lost to me, beyond my reach. And I knew what Henry was doing, what he was saying. You can't step out of the stream of life and yet be part of life, and more than that, that somehow we must acknowledge the truth of our death to understand the truth of our life. The only way to stop death was to stop life.

Well, then it struck me as wise and profound, but now I think it's just lying hippy bullshit.

I could hear a sound. I couldn't call it beautiful, but it was . . . perfect: a long, slow, simple sound, like the sound of a finger circling a wine glass. Except a million of them, and heard from far away.

'What is it?'

The music?

'Yes, the music.'

The music of the spheres.

The music of the spheres.

'It's nice. Can I sleep now?'

And I felt that I could sleep for ever here in this willow bower, and I didn't mind so much that life was elsewhere, and that sleep is a little death.

I'm not sure it's such a good idea. No, Heck, wake up, now isn't the time. Oh, look who's here.

And I looked and I saw at the edge of my vision a face pale against the leaves, and then I sort of snapped out of my trance, and the music of the spheres turned out to be an ice-cream van playing the theme from Neighbours, and when I turned and focused I saw that it was Uma, and she was staring at me like I was a major freak. She might have been there for a while. She might have heard me talking to Henry. Talking about having cancer and dying.

Yeah, big turn-on.

I tried to say something, but my mouth felt all gummy. Then Uma stooped and picked up the little sequinned bag she must have left behind, and was gone in a shimmer of leaves and starlight and sequins.

CHAPTER 33
A LITTLE KNOWLEDGE

I got home at about nine. There was a note from Mum saying she'd gone to bed early, and that there was some lentil bake in the oven. I left it there and went to my room, where I ate the three packets of crisps, although by now they'd become a sort of savoury powder. Henry had clocked off, exhausted no doubt from stopping time, and I was on my own, even in front of the mirror.

The one good thing about the evening's fiasco was that it was Friday, so there was no school tomorrow. That gave me a couple of days respite from whatever grief Uma decided to inflict although, of course, I had all the fun of imagining it in advance. And then I remembered with a groan that Clytemnestra was coming. It never rains but it pours a bucket of cold shite over your head.

So I read to take my mind off things. I began with *Crime and Punishment*, which I'd been reading for the past two years, but I wasn't in the mood for heaviness, and the Russian names were all spinning round in my head, so I put it down after a couple of pages. I then went to the opposite extreme, and tried a *Buffy the Vampire Slayer* novelization that Gonad had given me, but it was piss poor. So I turned to some old friends; I skimmed through my favourite bits from Frank Miller's *The Dark Knight Returns*, but that was hardly going to cheer me up, and nor was Alan Moore's *Watchmen*. No, it had to be the Justice League, and that night I fell asleep nestling in the down-soft wings of Hawkgirl, watched over and protected by my friends The Flash, Martian Manhunter and Green Lantern.

Bit of a shock the next morning. Mum actually came in with a cup of tea for me. Almost as freaky as having a talking brain tumour or stopping time or going out on a date with Uma Upshaw. And yes, it was ordinary tea, none of your aardvark-spittle-and-lime-bark. She looked old and tired, but also better in some way I couldn't quite put my finger on.

'How you feeling, Heck?'

'Me? Oh, not too bad. You know, considering.'

'One of your friends called last night.'

'Which one?'

'The little one.'

'You could tell he was little over the phone?'

'Silly! I've met him before. Recognized his voice.'

'Stan.'

'Yes, Stan. He said he had some homework for you. He said you'd want it, which seemed a bit odd to me, but I said he should come over today and have lunch.'

'OK, thanks, Mum.'

Poor Stan. Still though, I was glad that he'd called. We didn't meet up at the weekends that often any more, not the whole gang of us. Stan's family had moved away from the estate, and Smurf had never lived that close, and Gonad was always doing other things at the weekends. I think he may have had special weekend friends, and he didn't like to mix and match. I didn't know if it was because they were the embarrassing lot, or we were.

'I said that I thought you'd gone to see him last night, but obviously you hadn't.'

'Yeah, well, I was just, er . . .' But nothing else came out, except a blush, and then Mum started to smile, and I think that she had an idea what was going on, although she couldn't have, not the whole thing.

'When's Clytemnestra getting here?' I said finally, trying to change the subject.

'Not until the evening. I'll leave you to your tea now. See you for breakfast later. Or I can bring it up, if you like?'

Things really had changed.

Stan came around in the middle of the morning.

Oh no, not that schmuck.

Hello, Henry, welcome back.

'What happened to your head?' he (Stan) asked, in that quiet voice of his, pointing at my hair. 'Looks like you got dive-bombed by some kind of bird of prey, and it got stuck on your head.'

ME: What sort of bird of prey? An eagle?
STAN: Nah, much smaller. How stupid would you look with an eagle on your head?
ME: Buzzard?
STAN: Smaller.
ME: Kestrel?
STAN: Now you've gone too far.

ME: Goshawk, then. Must be.

STAN: Goshawk, I think, yes.

HENRY: *Well, thank God that's all sorted.*

And from then on it was all OK, and the stuff from earlier in the week, the little misunderstandings, the awkwardness, was all gone. He'd brought some maths and physics, and we finished it together in half an hour in my room, and then we mooched about for a bit and he told me some things that happened at school, and then I told him about my hot date with Uma Upshaw. Luckily I didn't have to mention about the Smurf side of things as he'd sworn me to secrecy. So if I told Stan about betraying Smurf I'd have to tell him that Smurf fancied Uma, and that would have meant betraying Smurf. Which is ironic. I think. Or maybe just circular.

It was usually hard to work out what was going on inside Stanislaw's head, but not now. It was as if he was miming 'astonishment' as part of a course explaining Earth emotions to visiting extra-terrestrials.

'You went to see her at the chippie? Just like that? And she went out with you? And you went to the pub? And then you went to the churchyard? And then you snogged her? And then you tried to grope her and she dumped you?'

With each item in the list his voice went up an octave.

'That's about it.'

'That's like a whole adolescence in one evening. Or like when you're dying, and your life flashes before you . . . Oh, what's up, Heck?'

So I thought it was time to tell Stan about my head.

'The thing is, Stan, I didn't just faint the other day. I mean, I did, but it's happened before and there have been other things happening too. When I went to the doctor the other day, it was because they were worried that there was something serious up with my brain. I had a scan and they'll get the results soon, but it might be bad. It might be really bad.'

'Bad like what?'

'Bad like a brain tumour.'

There was quite a long silence. I was expecting Stan to come out with something sympathetic in the consoling line, but eventually what he said was: 'You haven't got broadband, have you?'

I scoffed: 'Broadband? You know very well we haven't even got a computer. We haven't got satellite telly, a DVD player. I haven't got a mobile and we don't have a microwave or a car or any of the equipment that makes life worth living. We have mung beans instead. Hell, if it was up to Mum, I wouldn't even have a toothbrush and I'd be cleaning my teeth with special twigs. Why?'

'To check out brain tumours on the Internet. Let's go to the library.'

Boring.

Which we did. We had to wait for twenty minutes for a free slot, which meant hanging about with the tramps and dossers sheltering from the rain, and the mums with crying babies here for the Saturday-morning sing-a-long, but then it was plain sailing.

Well, plain sailing INTO THE ABYSS.

I suppose Stan thought that a bit of knowledge would

help to banish any irrational fears I might be experiencing. What our Internet search mainly did was to reassure me that my fears were perfectly rational. All my symptoms pointed to a brain tumour, and I had over 160 different types to choose between, split up into half a dozen different groups. One site happily described these groups as 'families', but, frankly, any family that goes about eating people's brains is even more dysfunctional than mine. The different types were classified according to what kinds of cells they were derived from, but I found that a bit hard to take in. Some types picked on kids, some on adults, some on both. Some liked to eat particular bits of your brain, some chewed away contentedly on any old lobe. Strangely there didn't seem to be anything about the brain tumours that jabber at you or try to get you to grope girls or make you get your hair cut, but then even the Internet has its limits.

I found out that brain tumours are the biggest cause of death by cancer among teenagers and young adults (they only count as number two among actual kids, because of good ole leukaemia), and that, compared to lots of other cancers, treatment is still pretty hit and miss. Only a third of adults with brain tumours live for five years, although the picture was better for childhood brain tumours, in which case, assuming I still counted as a child, I had a two-thirds chance of making it, that's if I wasn't already riddled with the stuff. Of course, if Henry was one of the nastier types then I was well and truly shafted.

And maybe I was tumbling headlong into cliché, but the truth is that knowledge *did* make me feel a bit better about it all. It wasn't exactly that I'd had nothing to fear but fear itself, no not at all, I had plenty to fear, but at least now the fear had boundaries and didn't stretch away to infinity.

So then we left the library, and I asked Stan if he wanted to come back to ours for a bean something, and he declined on the grounds of not wanting to, and we wandered around for a while until we got near school, and the social club, and I remembered the huge knob on the wall, so we went for another look.

It was still there, although I thought that it appeared less distinct than the last time I'd seen it, as if maybe it was sinking back into the brickwork again.

'There's definitely something weird about it,' I said as we stood there.

'What do you mean?'

'I mean, like how it's just appeared, like it's a message.'

'Funny kind of message. Like, what? "Look at me, I'm a great big willy."'

'It's not just that. It's a . . . symbol. It's so, I don't know, human; kind of weak and magnificent at the same time. Or like the spirit of humanity, showing through the brutality around, triumphing over the system.'

'And who is the messenger supposed to be?'

'I've a feeling it was some lone rebel, a freedom fighter, sort of. Because he wasn't just putting two fingers up at the school, although he was doing that as well, but he was saying that if you try, you can make something special, something beautiful, and not just scrawl crappy cocks all over the place. He's saying you don't just revolt *against*, but that you revolt *into* something.'

Stan looked at me blankly. 'Heck, you've been thinking about it too much.'

'You're the deep one, Stan. You think about everything too much.'

Then there was a pause, and then he said, 'I'd better get home.' And he began to wander off, but then he turned.

'Something else I've got to tell you. About Tierney and his mob. He's really pissed off. He says he's going to . . . do stuff to you. He says he's going to kill you.'

Kill you. The kind of thing we said all the time. I'll kill you. Hadn't Tierney said it before? You're dead. Something like that. He didn't mean it. And anyway, there was a queue, right, Henry?

Whatever.

CHAPTER 34
STRAWBERRY GIRL

Stan went one way home, and I went another. I thought I'd take a shortcut across the low, damp, tussocky field by the side of the school – the gypsy field, it was usually called, because the gypsies turned up there sometimes, and stayed for a while, and then left. It was always worth having a look around after they'd gone. Not because there'd be anything valuable left behind, because that wasn't the gypsy way, but occasionally there would be something interesting. A dead animal, or a burned chair, or a fridge with its insides all gone.

That was all rubbish, you know. The Internet stuff.

Rubbish? Which bit? The bit that gave me a decent chance of living?

A little learning is a dangerous thing.

Dangerous to you.

I keep telling you, we're in this together, you have to trust me.

Yeah, one for all, all for one. Together we stand, divided we fall. Laugh and the world laughs with you, snore and you sleep alone. You're just scared because Doctor Jones is going to cut you out and slice you up and eat you with a fine Chianti.

I expected a quick comeback: mine wasn't the kind of tumour to take things lying down. But nothing.

Henry?

Still nothing.

Henry? C'mon.

Silence. Seemed like I'd really got to him.

OK, sorry. Didn't mean anything by it.

Finally, his tone one of wounded dignity, Henry managed to speak: *Are we not hurt with the same weapons, subject to the same diseases, healed by the same means? If you prick us do we not bleed? If you poison us do we not die?*

Like I said, I'm really sorry if I hurt your feelings. But you started it.

Did not.

Did too.

And that was that, but I could tell Henry was still stropping. Although, to be fair, that whole confronting-your-own-mortality thing can do that to a tumour. Or a boy.

I was trudging along, following the path by the beck, leaning into the fine rain, which was probably causing all kinds of grief to the goshawk on my head, when I saw someone coming in the opposite direction. I knew who it was straight away. Something about the way she looked like she wished that she wasn't there at all, as if she aspired to invisibility. And then there was that hair, finer than the fine rain, pale and lost and beautiful. And she saw me, and I felt her stiffen with surprise and shame and something else.

214

God's teeth, not her. Why does it have to be her?

Oh, welcome back. And shut up. I'm not in the mood for your noise.

But my heart was in my mouth, and I didn't know why.

Bloody obvious. Not that that makes it any less stupid.

I'd never seen Amanda Something out of school before, didn't know she even lived around here. She was wearing a plain brown dress that almost had a religious look about it. The sort of thing a trendy nun would wear, the sort who does work in the community, visiting prisons, that kind of thing.

If she kept coming, there would be no avoiding a meeting. I think she was contemplating turning round and walking away in the opposite direction, but she knew that that would be even more embarrassing than carrying on. And so, after a second, she carried on, and we approached each other. She was looking down at her shoes. They were as uncool as mine, but in a more plodding, old-fashioned way. If you hit a six-year-old child with one of my shoes (the standard measure for shoe clunkiness), you could probably make it cry, but it would be hard to do any real damage. If you hit the same child with one of Amanda's, you would probably break its skull, and most likely death would ensue. En-shoe. Ha!

That stinks.

And at the last second she looked up. We were a metre apart. She had make-up covering her birth mark.

'Hello,' she said, and it looked like it might have been hard work.

It took me a few seconds to think of a clever response, but when it came it was a classic.

'Hello.'

She was blushing. I was blushing. It was a blush-a-thon, a blush-off, hardcore blush-on-blush action. So, we had something in common. But I couldn't leave things at just hello and blush.

'Do you live around here? I haven't seen you before. Here, I mean. I've seen you at school. You're called Amanda, aren't you?'

That all came out a bit too quickly, say eighty-five miles an hour in a thirty-mile-an-hour zone. But she smiled, and both of our blushes began to fade.

'Yes. I mean no. My name is Amanda, but I don't really live here.' Her voice was very quiet, but precise. 'I was just going past on the bus and . . . I thought I'd get off. Don't know why.'

Did she mean that because she'd spotted me from the bus, and got off just to meet me? But then she'd seemed surprised to see me, surprised and dismayed. Sometimes the more you think about people the stranger they become. Sooner or later you always hit a layer of mystery.

'I know you're called Hector Brunty. And I know that you're kind . . . that you did a kind thing, once.' And then, after a moment, she added, 'You look different,' and the blush came back. 'Your hair. I like it.' And she looked down at her clunky shoes again.

'Thanks. Um, yours is nice too.'

I can't listen to this. Look, Heck, we've got to ditch this girl. Look at her! She's a—

I shut him out.

Amanda gave a little laugh and pushed back some strands that had fallen in front of her face.

There was another silence, and if you think this sounds like there were too many silences and that this must have been terrible, then you think wrong, because it wasn't. It was so pent up with things, *feelings*, I suppose you'd have to call them, that this silence, this space, was about the most exciting thing in the world.

'What were you doing here?' she asked.

'I don't live far away. And I came with Stan – you know Stan, little guy, my best friend – to have a look at—' The great big willy. Don't say that, don't even *think* of saying that. 'Er, just to hang out.'

'Where are you off to now?'

'Nowhere. Nowhere special, I mean. Want to come?'

Amanda smiled and nodded, but didn't say anything. And then we set off across the field away from the path and the beck. The ground was uneven with little mounds and troughs and soggy places that were almost like quicksand, and Amanda's foot went down into one of the troughs, and I put my hand out to steady her and our fingers touched, and then we were holding hands and her hand in mine felt like the greatest thing that there could be, and thank God Henry T. had crept off somewhere, because I didn't want him around to see this, didn't want to listen to his comments.

And then it was my turn to have my foot sink down into something, and Amanda smiled at me as if I'd done it to make her feel less clumsy, but something went crunch and for a second I thought I'd broken my ankle, except it didn't hurt very much, or at all, really, so we both crouched down to have a look at what had crunched.

My foot had gone through the turf overhanging a cavity in the soil. I pulled it out of the hole, and moved the grass aside so we could see.

Something white. Pottery, I thought. No, bones. White bones. Broken white bones.

For another horrific moment I thought that my first instinct was correct and my leg was smashed to bits, but of course my leg was right there, still perfectly fine.

'What is it?' asked Amanda, with a little shudder of horror. She pressed herself into me, as if I might be the one to save her from bones.

'I think it's an animal.'

A bracelet of bright hair about the bone.

So Henry was still there, watching. Don't know what he meant, though. There was no hair left on these cold bones.

I found a stick and had a bit of a poke around. The bones were pure white and as dry as chalk. Old bones. Ribs. Legs. Small bones. Amanda was close beside me, her strawberry hair touching my face. Her lips had parted, and she was breathing through her mouth. I moved some more grass with the stick and kicked aside the heavy soil and found the creature's head.

It was a dog, some kind of little dog.

Webster was much possessed by death, and saw the skull beneath the skin.

Lipless, it grinned at me, and that should have been

creepy, but it was really just kind of sad, as if the little dog was trying to be friendly, even in its death and decay, waiting, as the years passed, to wag its tail, fetch a stick. To play dead.

And then I saw something that really *was* creepy, and Amanda saw it too, because she gasped and pulled away from my side, and put her hands to her face. It was an arrow. A short arrow, the kind they use in crossbows. Thick and heavy, with a steel point. A bolt, that was the word, and it was in the neck of the little dog. Someone must have shot the poor creature and left it here to die. I stood up, but I couldn't escape from the bones and the grin and crossbow bolt and I had to fight the urge to sob, but then Amanda took my hand and pulled me away.

The wound's invisible that love's keen arrows make.

Shut up, please.

As you like it.

'It's really raining quite hard now,' said Amanda, and we ran to the bus shelter, still holding hands, and we sat on the seats, which were specially designed to stop you getting comfortable in case you felt like moving in. And there we chatted for a while, with the rain drumming its fingers impatiently on the asbestos roof, and we talked about the bones of the dog and the arrow in its throat and it brought us together in the way that a shared experience of something fatal can, and I nearly told her about my head stuff, but I didn't, because I thought it was too early to lay that kind of heavy shit on someone.

And there was something else I didn't tell her about.

I didn't tell her about my hot date with Uma Upshaw, and you can probably guess why that was.

'Do you want to go somewhere else?' I asked after about an hour. I knew it was about an hour because I looked on my watch, but if you'd asked me to guess I would have said about ten minutes.

'I should get home, really. My mum and dad will wonder what's happened to me.'

Three buses had already gone past, slowing as the drivers saw us waiting, then accelerating away with a belch of black diesel smoke when we didn't move.

'What are they like?'

Amanda rolled her eyes.

'A pain. They both work at the university. So we haven't got a telly.'

'That's terrible. Even we have a telly, you know, just a basic one. What do you do instead?'

'We read, mostly. Sometimes my parents read plays out loud and I have to join in.'

'Man, that's awful.'

'Not so bad, really.'

'You probably play chess and bridge as well. Or sing madrigals together.'

She laughed: 'We're not that weird.'

So she said, but I still guessed there was a madrigal or two in her past.

'Do you have any brothers or sisters?'

She shook her head. 'My mum had a difficult time with me, so they decided not to have any more. What about you?'

'Nah, just me and Mum. I haven't got a dad. Not one here, I mean. Everyone's got a dad somewhere.'

Amanda didn't ask anything else about my family, but I think we both came away with the idea that we were equally strange, in that respect.

Another bus trundled by. There were too many buses today.

'I'll get the next one.'

While we were waiting I asked her what she was doing tomorrow.

'Nothing.'

'Do you want to meet up again? Just, you know, hang out for a bit.'

'Yes, I'd like that.'

'Shall we meet here?'

She nodded again. 'What time?'

'Whenever you like.'

Please say never.

'Three o'clock. My parents like us to have lunch together.'

In the ten minutes until the next bus came, we talked about music. (She liked classical, but also some olden-days stuff like The Beatles, and she said the greatest albums were, in order, *Pet Sounds* by the Beach Boys, *Revolver* by The Beatles and *Forever Changes* by Love. I wasn't sure if the last one was real, or some kind of code. I said that I liked The Libertines and Franz Ferdinand but, to be honest, I was winging it, and I was relieved when the bus came and saved me from having to do any explaining.) When the doors sighed open, Amanda put one foot on the step-thingy, and then turned and gave me a kiss. Not the sort of deep tonsil-tickler I'd had from Uma Upshaw, but infinitely more wonderful.

CHAPTER 35
THE DARK KNIGHT RETURNS

I opened the door and knew straight away that things weren't right. It was the laughter.

Clytemnestra.

I'd forgotten about her.

I went into the living room and there she was, lying on the sofa wearing some sort of flowing black membranous garment attached at both her wrists and her ankles. She looked like a crashed pterodactyl. Mum was in the good chair and there was a bottle of wine open between them and the spent husk of a second lying next to it. As soon as Clytemnestra saw me she flapped and writhed and finally managed to stand up.

I was transfixed by her hands, which were brown and wrinkly, but tipped by lethal red talons. Her hair was dyed Goth black, and there was a ring of black something around her eyes.

'Hector, Hector,' she said in a moaning, sighing way, like a dead thing, coming towards me with her wings outstretched, her talons twitching. 'Come embrace me, my poor, good, beautiful boy.'

Every instinct told me to run, to hide.

'Hi,' I said. 'Hello, Mum.'

The second bit was over Clytemnestra's shoulder as she hugged me. I expected at any moment to feel her talons sink in to extract my life force.

'Your mother and I have been having a long talk.' Clytemnestra now had me firmly gripped at arm's length. She was looking deep into my eyes, like a hypnotist. I felt myself growing weaker by the second. Soon I'd be a zombie, willing to fulfil her every wish. I had to fight loose, had to escape. 'And now so are we.'

It was useless. Resistance was futile. The end was near.

'I've made some soup,' said Mum. 'Moroccan bean.'

The next hour was pretty grim. Clytemnestra asked me all sorts of questions about how I was and how I felt and all that kind of stuff, never letting her eyes drift from my face for even a second. After the questions (my answers: 'I'm all right', 'I feel OK', 'No, not sad at all, really, can't complain, you know how it is', obviously weren't the ones she wanted, but I wasn't going to go sharing my feelings with any old vampire), came a load of talk about how hard it had been on Christabel, and how we must all stick together. Mum and she carried on drinking the wine, and I had some soup, which wasn't bad, actually, in a Moroccan beany kind of way, and, let me tell you now, there are worse ways than that when it comes to my mum's cooking, and, for that matter, beans in general.

It was only later that I realized why, in fact, it wasn't bad.

Finally I managed to escape up to my room. This was no

time for the enlightened, progressive world of *The Watchmen*, or even the aestheticized utopianism of the Justice League. No, this situation needed the near-fascist vigilante. It had to be *The Dark Knight Returns*. Batman has been in retirement for ten years. A gang called the Mutants has taken over Gotham City. The police are corrupt, the streets are meaner than a polecat with a toothache, and the old, familiar villains are more psychotic than ever. So out comes the cape. But Batman is out not just to right wrongs: he's here to reassert his dominance, to show the world that he is still a player. It's brutal stuff, especially when Batman takes on the leader of the Mutants, and his job isn't so much to defeat, as to humiliate him. It ends with a death, a funeral, a heartbeat.

Once I'd got that out of my system, I started to think about Amanda. And about Uma.

Beauty and the Beast. And we all know who the beast is.

She isn't a beast.

No, not a beast. I'll tell you what she is. You've just been reading about them. She's a mutant.

'SHUT UP!' I'd been trying to internalize all my conversations with Henry since the moment of humiliation with Uma, but now my anger took over.

I can't, I won't shut up. This is too important. She's a freak. We can't have her. We must try again with Uma. She's the one.

'She isn't the one.'

I give up.

'Good.'

Your funeral.

'I know it is.'

Silence.

Sorry, I didn't mean . . . it came out wrong.

'And you seem to forget about the fact that *my* funeral means *your* funeral as well. Unless you know something I don't, and you're planning to beam out or some such shit, you know, just before we crash. I can see it now. The shuttle's heading into a black hole, or maybe a star about to go supernova, and we see the sweat on the pilot's forehead, and someone screams "Pull her up, Jack", because, well, the hero's always called Jack, unless it's a made-up science-fiction kind of name like Svoron 17, and then we cut back to an outside shot of the shuttle, now just a black spot against the orange of the star, and next there's a massive explosion, or maybe it's just a little blip against the background, because sometimes that can look pretty cool in a bleak, how-small-a-thing-is-man way, and we think he's a goner, and you get some reaction shots of the team back on the mothership, and one of them's probably Jack's girlfriend, who's half Mulvanian, and they have four breasts, but as she only half-Mulvanian, she has three, but anyway then when they're all despairing (the crew, not the breasts, because not even Mulvanians have sentient breasts, for those you have to go to the warrior maidens of Kroyttzer VII), they pick up the *bleep bleep bleep* of the distress signal, and it's all OK because he got out in the escape pod at the last second.'

Finished?

'Yeah, sorry, got a bit carried away there.'

No, I won't be beaming out, and I haven't forgotten that our time is limited. It's why I keep trying to get you to find someone suitable to continue the line.

'Well maybe I have.'

She doesn't count.

'She counts. And I've told you I don't care about the line. And while we're on the subject of continuing the fucking line, you do realize, don't you, that you're not the only one trying to kill me? That psycho Tierney's probably going to thwang me with a crossbow on Monday. Through the throat, like that dog.'

I did a quick mime of someone getting it in the neck, adding a pretty good squelching thud sound effect

No, he isn't.

'Really?' Dripping scepticism.

Really. We're going to take that mother down.

That made me laugh.

'How, exactly? He may be a runt, but he's a better fighter than me. And that's before we even get to his gang. What am I going to do, knock him out with quadratic equations?'

I've got a plan.

'A plan? What plan?'

Look, you think I've just been sitting back here with my feet up? I've been working on this. I've been playing through some old tapes back here, and it turns out, if I am correct, and, let's face it, I am, that Tierney has a weakness, an Achilles heel.

And then Henry Tumour told me his plan, and I almost forgave him for being a bastard about Amanda and, almost, for being the brain tumour that was killing me.

And it was then that I thought again about the bean soup. It wasn't bad, because it didn't taste of anything. Anything at all. Or smell of anything. And then I remembered one of the things it had said on a brain-cancer website I'd looked at with Stanislaw. It was under a heading: SYMPTOMS. It said: 'You can lose your sense of taste and smell.'

CHAPTER 36
SOME PROFOUND REFLECTIONS ON LOVE AND DESIRE

My mum and Clytemnestra went out that night. Hideous though the pterodactyl was, I had to admit that she was good for Mum. I hadn't seen her looking as cheerful and normal since . . . well, *ever*. It must have been hard for her to pack in the Valium, and there was no one around here who she could lean on. Maybe at another time I might have been able to help, but I had my own troubles. And I'm only a kid. Clyte was a link to her past, a link to a time when things were better, before things had gone pear-shaped. Sometimes that can be a bummer, you know, when you're confronted with what a mess you've made of things, and your true crapness shines through. But other times it can be a beacon, showing you that things don't have to be the way they are. Sometimes the light behind us illuminates the way ahead.

Thanks for that, Socrates.

So I spent the evening reading and thinking and talking to Henry. His plan was a dandy, and we ran through it a couple of times, more just to enjoy it than anything else, because it wasn't even that difficult, you know; we weren't talking *Mission Impossible* here.

But even after he'd gone over the plan and we'd discussed it, and I'd added a couple of elaborations, and we'd laughed about it, Henry couldn't help but stray back to the old subject even though, this time, he tried to come across as all sweet reasonableness.

But, Heck, my friend, he said, his voice as fluffy as a dandelion clock, *why that Amanda girl? I just don't get it.*

'Why?'

Yes, actually, why? It wasn't really such a stupid question. From the first time I'd noticed her, standing alone, looking lost and helpless, but also somehow not needing or wanting help, I'd felt strange inside. It wasn't something as simple as just fancying her, because at first glance she was quite hard to fancy, with that birthmark and her shapeless, flapping clothes. And it couldn't have been her personality because, as far as I was concerned, she didn't have one back then. I didn't know her. She was just a space. Was it that I thought she was like me? Lost and helpless, like me? A freak, like me? That sounded plausible. Birds of a feather gather no moss and all that. But I didn't quite get the psychology, and if you want to trade clichés, then don't opposites attract?

I wish I could say it was because I saw her inner beauty, was drawn to her goodness or purity, and that the outside of people didn't matter to me. But it did. It does. Matter, I mean. The outside.

I think it must have been that her face, her eyes, her hair, her skin, were so beautiful (and I don't mean pretty, because she wasn't pretty) that it overcame the horror of the port-wine birthmark. Birthmarks, disfigurement, they've always been associated with evil, been seen to be symbolic of something foul and misshapen within. But if the multitude had been able to ignore that one blemish, been able to close their minds to the clamorous bullshit, then they too would have loved her. Yeah. The people who only saw the birthmark weren't being superficial *enough*.

Could that be it? Was it my lack of depth that made me love Amanda Something?

Thinking about feelings never gets you very far. Thought isn't the right tool for the job. Like hammering in a nail with a screwdriver.

'Because . . .' Well, I thought about running through the love stuff with Henry, but I was tired, and I didn't feel up to it. '. . . because she's stacked.'

Stacked? You're kidding me? How did I miss that?

I'm telling you, body of an angel. A bad one.

Bad, huh? Bad angel. Well . . .

And then he sort of chuntered and mumbled to himself until I went to sleep.

CHAPTER 37
A SECOND JOURNEY TO THE UNDERWORLD, THIS TIME WITH PERSEPHONE, RATHER THAN APHRODITE

I was at the bus shelter at two o'clock, an hour before we'd arranged to meet. I was wearing my new clothes again, which I hadn't been the day before. I wasn't early because I was nervous. I didn't feel nervous, or at least no more than was enough to give me that pleasant tingly feeling. There was a rightness about it all, a *fitting-togetherness* that made the kind of shattering, nerve-jangling tension of my Uma date simply unnecessary.

I was early to escape the Pterodactyl.

Really?

No, that's just a lie. I was early because I wanted to be in the place where we had spent that perfect hour yesterday, the place where I was going to meet her again today. The bus shelter had become for me a sacred shrine, a place of pilgrimage. There ought to be some kind of sign. Yeah, a plaque:

HERE SAT

HECTOR BRUNTY

AND

AMANDA SOMETHING

ON 12 APRIL

AND NOTHING WAS EVER THE SAME AGAIN

AFTERWARDS

You are so losing it, man.

Hey, it's long gone.

The time moved slowly and exquisitely, like a jewelled python. Each second she wasn't there hurt, and yet it was filled with expectation, and hope and joy. It was like the opposite of waiting for the dentist. And each bus that came was the bus that might bring Amanda Something to me, and I felt an affection for them that was out of all proportion to the sort of feelings you really ought to be having for buses.

You said it.

And it wasn't even raining.

Because it was Sunday there weren't many buses, only two in the hour, but then, at five past, there came the good bus, the true bus, the beautiful bus that was carrying Amanda Something to me.

The door opened, and there she was. She was wearing a pretty dress that didn't suit her, and her hair was pinned up, and she had make-up covering her birthmark and, all in all, she looked much worse than usual, but that made me love her more, and I'd say the increase was between twelve and fourteen per cent, and don't go asking me to work it out to

233

six decimal places, because love isn't about mathematical precision.

I put my hand out and she took it as she stepped down from the bus, and it felt like something from the days of lords and ladies, and I was handing her down from her carriage or her palfrey, whatever that is or was.

A little horse.

The moment was ruined, but only a bit, by a large lady who squeezed past us onto the bus, tutting like a Geiger counter.

'I thought you wouldn't be here,' Amanda Something said.

'I didn't have anything else on. And, you know, Sunday telly . . .' Despite the fact I said it with a smile and was looking into her eyes, which were a kind of greeny colour, like pond scum but beautiful, I saw that part of her believed that a person would only ever want to see her if there was nothing else to do and nothing on the telly, and even then they probably wouldn't really want to see her, but might out of duty or because they felt that they should as a good deed. And I tried to answer her by blasting her with a high-intensity beam, a bit like a supervillain's Doomsday device, except in place of death it dealt love. But she didn't seem to feel it, on account either of her having some kind of protective armour plating – love kevlar, say – or me not really being able to beam out anything except wind after one of Mum's bean extravaganzas. I wanted to be able to say something reassuring, something that expressed what I was feeling, but I just didn't have the words, and there was no way I was going to ask Henry to help out on this one.

'You look . . . pretty,' I said, and her hand went up to her birthmark in that unconscious way you always draw attention to things you want to hide. 'I like your dress.'

'Thanks. I . . . I made it.'

'Wow!'

Oh, Christ, why did I have to say 'Wow!'? Why couldn't I have said something cool, or maybe just raised one eyebrow, and smiled seductively? And then, maybe because it sounded a bit like 'wow', and was therefore in my head, I said, 'Why?' which was probably worse than 'wow'.

'My parents don't give me money for clothes.'

'Who needs clothes?' I said, not at all meaning, 'Who needs clothes, when we are young and can take them all off and romp around COMPLETELY NAKED before thrashing ourselves into a frenzy of frantic, exhausting, extravagant, flamboyant, gaudy, baroque, eye-boggling, COPULATION?'

Steady on.

But I think that's what she thought I meant, because she gave a modest little smile accompanied by one of her modest little blushes.

OK, get back on track.

'Do you want to go and see a film?'

'Yes,' she said unsurely, 'that would be nice.'

Mmm. Obviously she didn't want to go and see a film.

'Or we could go to the new Starbucks up in town. Nice muffins.'

Damn! I'd forgotten that 'muffins' entirely contains the word 'muff'.

She smiled encouragingly.

No, Starbucks clearly held no appeal. Or the muff.

It all felt a bit groundhog day, you know, reliving the Uma experience. And what was it Marx said about history repeating itself, the first time as tragedy, the second time as farce? But I'd already got the farce out of the way, so that left tragedy. Or more farce. Or something else. But probably tragedy. Which is why the next thing I thought of was my weeping willow.

'I know a nice place where we could go.'

Amanda's eyes suggested that she liked this vague new idea much more than the old specific ones.

We weren't coming from the same direction this time, so at least I didn't have to retrace my steps, or go back into the Spleen and Marrow. But soon we were on the same narrow lane leading up to the wrought-iron arch that led into the churchyard.

'We're going to church?'

'No, no. Not at all. In the graveyard. There's a place.'

'But why?'

'I like it. It's a secret. Nobody knows about it. Just you and me.'

And every other girl you've ever snogged.

It was the afternoon, so there wasn't a service on, which would have spoiled things. We stopped in front of some of the older, prettier graves. There were stone angels for the children. Mary Pullinger, d. 2 Nov. 1902, aged 11. John Bunyan. d. 23 Feb. 1899, aged 2 years. We held hands in front of the sad monuments. Deeper into the churchyard we came to older graves, which must have belonged to an earlier church. Most were unreadable, the letters smoothed against the stone, or buried under moss and lichen. But some were still legible. We read the dates: 1769, 1804, 1799, 1777.

'All these people,' said Amanda dreamily. 'All of them gone for ever. No one left who remembers them. No one left who'd remember even their grandchildren.'

She traced a name with her finger, brushing away the dust and grit from the carved grooves.

'But we're here. We're alive.'

For now, I didn't add.

And then I took her to the willow bower, and we sat beneath the branches on the dry ground together, and I didn't even have to try to block out the images of Uma.

'This is beautiful,' she said. 'I love the way the world is still there, but blurry. As if the whole world is a rockpool, and we're here looking down at it.'

Ergh. You two deserve each other. She'll be telling you next that the stars are God's daisy chains.

Even though the ground was dry I took off my jacket and spread it out. I was close to her now and I could feel the heat from her skin. I put my arm round her, and she was looking up into my eyes, all trusting, hoping, fearing. And the make-up on her birthmark had begun to flake, and I put my lips to it, and I felt her pull away, but I wouldn't let her.

And we spoke, our foreheads touching. She told me how lonely she had been, told me how she had once been happy, and how she had changed when she was six and another girl at her school said to her that she looked horrible, like a monster, and before that she hadn't even thought about her birthmark, but after that she thought about nothing else. She said that in a year she would have laser treatment to make it fade, and that she had been told that it would be virtually invisible, one day. I almost said that she shouldn't change herself, but how could I say that to someone who had lived her life, put up with everything she'd had to deal with?

'I don't care about it,' I whispered in her ear. 'I think you're beautiful, and I don't care about it.'

The skin of the birthmark wasn't like the rest of her skin. Its texture was a little rougher and it felt warmer to my lips.

And then I looked at her eyes again, and they had become liquid, and I kissed the tears as they spilled, and drank the salt tears, mixed with the make-up from her face. And then I wiped away the tears and the make-up with my sleeve, and I felt through her hair to the nape of her neck, and I pulled her closer to me and we kissed, and after we'd kissed I told her that I could stop time and she, wonderingly, asked me how, and I said watch, and as we lay together, face to face, I stilled the spinning world and stopped time, and there were only the two of us together.

And that's all I can tell you, because the rest is private.

Don't worry, you haven't missed much.

CHAPTER 38
ABBA ABBA

I opened the kitchen door, not knowing what to expect. I'd heard the distressing tones of 'Dancing Queen' as I came down the road, but it wasn't until I reached our house that I realized that here was the epicentre. It was enough to bring me down to earth, which was probably a good thing as I was as high as a weather balloon, and we're not talking solvent abuse here, but, well, you know.

The kitchen was clear. I moved cautiously towards the door to the living room, my presence covered by the racket. I opened it.

The sight before me was truly shocking.

The bottles of wine, the gatefold sleeve of Abba's *Arrival* by the side of our ancient music centre. Mum and Clytemnestra were in the middle of the room. They had hairbrushes in their hands. Hairbrushes they were using not for their noble, God-given purpose of making your hair look less stupid but as dummy microphones. They (Mum and Clyte, not the microphones) were wearing some ancient nightdresses of my mum's: long floaty nylon items that hadn't been worn in decades. They were dancing and miming, throwing the kind of shapes you see on re-runs of olden-days *Top of the Pops*.

Yes, they *were* Agnetha and Frida.

Frida, I mean Clytemnestra, was the first to spot me. You'd expect embarrassment, a hurried hiding of micro-phones, the covering up of pink nylon nighties with cushions or rugs.

Instead: 'Hey, Heck, come join us. You can be Benny. Or Björn. Doesn't really matter.'

Benny or Björn? The original rock and the hard place.

I don't know if it was because I was still on cloud nine after my afternoon with Amanda, or if it was some special power that Clytemnestra had but, and God forgive me for it, I joined them, playing air keyboards (which made me Benny, I think) to not only 'Dancing Queen', but also, and yes, you are right to quake in your boots as I call the roster of shame, 'Knowing Me, Knowing You', 'Money, Money, Money' and 'Fernando', not to mention the long-forgotten album tracks in between.

By the end, I'll admit that I was laughing with them. This may have been helped by the fact that Clyte poured me a glass of red wine, which I drank with one hand whilst continuing the air-piano with the other. When it was over we all flopped down on the sofa.

'You seem in a very nice mood,' said Mum when she'd got her breath back. 'What you been up to?'

'Just hanging out. The usual.'

She looked at me as if she knew that something more than that had been going on. It was amazing how she'd changed. In the old days, meaning just a week ago, she wouldn't have noticed if I'd been abducted by aliens and given the full anal-probe treatment and came back twenty years later but not a day older with the anal probe still sticking out of me.

Then Clytemnestra said, 'You two settle down for your talk and I'll go and make supper. Something special today.' And then she swept out into the kitchen.

'Talk?' I said, when the door was safely closed.

Mum was suddenly very serious, after the silliness of the Abba concert. I hadn't sat together with her like this on the settee for a long time. Years, maybe. When I was a little boy, seven or eight, say, she sometimes used to let me stay up late with her to watch a film or a documentary about animals. But that was a long time ago.

'Abba,' she said. 'It means "father" in Aramaic. Did you know that?'

I did know it, or at least I'd heard it before, and it was lodged back there, somewhere behind Henry Tumour. *Abba abba sabba labectori*. Something like that. I've only heard it spoken. *Father forgive them, they know not what they do*. Jesus on the cross.

So, that was what this was about.

'It's Clyte that convinced me. Convinced me that I have to tell you. About your . . . father.'

I sat back against the settee. My ears had gone a bit funny. Sort of echoey. And I was cold. I've already said that it was a bit of a non-issue in our house. Well, a big issue, really, but not one that we could talk about, beyond the, you know, Great Spirit Who Is Father to Us All, sort of line.

I gulped to try to get my ears working properly. I wanted

to encourage her, but I didn't want to seem too eager. I'm not trying to come across all saintly here, but I knew that, despite being a bit of a spacer, and not really quite all there, head-wise, Mum had worked hard for me, given me everything she could. And I didn't want her to think that all the time I was wishing it wasn't just her around, but some guy as well. The complete stranger known as my dad. Especially not now she was a bit more back on the rails, or at least nearer the rails, like when you have a road that runs next to the track and you can race the trains.

Calm down, Hector. Even I know this is important. We're about to find out who our father is. Or was. The man who started the line we're trying to carry on.

Mum took some deep breaths. Her fingertips were touching her lips, like a child praying.

'I told you about the Valium, how it happened. It wasn't just because of world peace. The camp, we were all women. And it was wonderful, all sisters together. But sometimes, you know, it would get a bit, samey.'

She gave me a little smile, a nice smile, where her mouth went slightly down rather than up, and I saw her as a teenager, or maybe she was twenty, at the peace camp.

'So some of us would go to the pub in the village. Or the next village along. And that's where I met him.'

In a village pub. So, my father was a local yokel, a country bumpkin, a turnip head, his face red from being out all day in the sun driving his tractor.

Nah. No way. We're not sheep-shagger stock. We're city slickers, sophisticates, cosmopolitans. Anyone can tell that.

Hey, I could live with that. But why couldn't Mum?

'He wasn't from the village. He . . . worked at the base.'

The base.

He worked at the base.

'How do you mean, like a gardener or something?'

Mum looked confused for a moment.

'No, he was a pilot.'

Jesus. He flew the damn things. Nuclear bombers. Jesus.

'But how could you?' I said.

I didn't want to sound disapproving. I wasn't disapproving. I was too stunned to feel anything really, and the words just came out as a way of filling up space. Still, it was all a bit like Luke finding out that Darth Vader was his dad, although that was always on the cards, especially when you learn that Vader is Dutch for dad (thanks for that one, Gonad).

'I mean,' I continued, still in a fog, 'everything you were there for . . . the camp . . . the women. I don't understand.'

Mum took some more deep breaths, getting up the nerve to go on.

'When I first saw him, sitting there in the pub, I knew there was something special about him. He was so . . . young, and he had such kind, smiling eyes. Some of the locals were in, and they were giving us a hard time. I've told you before how they hated us, really hated us. The local squirearchy, the councillors, the fox-hunting types. They were worse than the Americans. They wouldn't serve us that night at the bar. We couldn't even get to the bar, in fact. The local men would form a kind of barrier with their backs, and move whenever we tried to get round or through them. It was nasty. It was me and Clyte and another girl, I can't even remember her name now, but I think she was from Wolverhampton. And then *he* came over and bought our drinks. And it was such a shock that we accepted. He wasn't in uniform, but you knew he was American before he spoke. There were three of them as well. All clean-cut and handsome, but he was the only one who looked ... nice as well as handsome. So I began teasing him, and he wasn't like the others. They were so earnest, tried to tell us that what we were doing was irresponsible, that they were protecting freedom. But he ... he laughed, and made fun back, but there was no hate in him. He was from Iowa, and he just loved life. And he was so handsome. I already said that. Sometimes I look at you, Heck, and I can see him ... Anyway, he said he would be in the pub again the next week, and he was. I came without the girls. And he was alone. And after that I began to see him whenever I could. He didn't have long to go. I mean, before he left the United States Air Force. We didn't make any promises to each other, but we both knew.

'None of the women knew what was going on. Except for Clyte, and even she didn't know everything. And then one evening he came to see me at the camp. In my tent. It was silly. We shouldn't have. But it was ... exciting. He tried to sneak away afterwards, but someone saw him. There was an argument. Men weren't allowed. They thought he was there to cause trouble. They were near the road. He was in the middle of a group. A car was coming. A four-wheel-drive thing. A Range Rover, I think. The driver was a woman from the council, one of the ones who hated us for being unfeminine. She'd done this before.

Driving past us too quickly, too close, her horn blaring, laughing, trying to make us jump out of the way. We were used to her. But he didn't know about that, and he was talking to the women and they were shouting at him, calling him a fascist, and when the Range Rover came, all the women knew to move out of the way. It was raining, I remember. He was wet. He was enjoying the argument, I think, enjoying being the reasonable one. He hadn't even been to college. He was going to go after he left the air force. And all the women moved out of the way and the Range Rover hit him. The woman, the woman who was driving, Olga something she was called, said she didn't feel it, and she drove on, but there was a dent in the side of the car, and those cars don't dent easily. Built like tanks. Not that she was ever charged with anything. She said it was our fault. And the women just stood there, looking at him.

I didn't understand what had happened for a moment. And then I realized it was all wrong, the way they were standing, and I ran to him, and he was on the floor. His legs were all bent, and at first I thought it was just a broken leg, something like that. I knelt beside him and held him, and I thought he was going to open his beautiful blue eyes. His face was fine – nothing, not a mark, except for the mud – but then I felt the blood on my legs, seeping in, and the back of his head wasn't really there any more. Just a pulp, like rice pudding. And I knew that he was dead.'

My mother's face was cold and still and blank.

'What was his name?'

'His name? His name was Hector.'

And that was too much for me. I folded up into my

mother, and she wrapped herself around me, and that's how we stayed.

In the middle of the night I woke up and remembered about my mule. We might not have had a computer but I had earned my spurs, all right, on Gonad's Playstation. You need a mule in Dungeon Siege to carry your inventory. That's weapons, armour, health vials and magic spells. Without the mule, you can't carry as much stuff. But the mule can be a bit of a pain. He follows along behind, and can be a liability in a fight. I was deep in a warren of caves and caverns and passages. There were Krug waiting in ambush round every corner. Krug, and worse than Krug. I had picked up a pretty competent team of warriors. I had a sexy archer girl called Ulura, and a big ox-like character called Tog, plus a dwarf and, naturally, an elf. I wanted to explore an area with the team and then come back for the mule. But I lost my way in the caverns and accidentally went up a level. I couldn't find a way back. I could go on, but not back. I was in the light, but my mule was lost to me. The worst thing was that I could change screens and see my mule waiting patiently in that dark place, laden with my stores. It would wander backwards and forwards, never losing faith, never giving up hope that I would return for it.

I lay for a long time with the night breathing about me. I revisited those caverns alone, without Ulura or Tog or the others, and I searched for my mule. I was sure that I could find him again, lead him into the light. There had to be a key or a switch or a lever. But I couldn't find it. And I felt Henry big and heavy in my head.

When I woke up in the morning, I was lying on the floor in a pool of my own vomit.

Beats the hell out of lying in a pool of someone else's.

Another seizure.

I cleaned up the mess, showered, and put on my school clothes.

CHAPTER 39
MIXED FEELINGS

Mixed.

Definitely mixed.

My feelings about going to school that day.

As well as the usual bad things about Mondays (the arse-kicking, the nipple-squeezing, the triple maths in room G2 where the windows didn't open and your brains boiled like offal in a pan, just the very fact of being at school and a full week of it ahead of you), I now had a whole new thing to dread: the public enjoyment of my sexual humiliation, not to mention the general appreciation of the fact that I was now known to be the kind of person who

    TALKS

        TO

           HIS

              BRAIN

                TUMOUR.

And maybe worst of all, the whole betrayal of Smurf thing, which combined so many bad things: me *feeling* like a shit, me actually *being* a shit, and then me being *treated* like a shit by the few friends I had. Of course, all that was assuming that Uma would blab and, well, who could blame her if she did? I mean, you'd need to be pretty special, in the keeping-of-secrets line, not to spread a story as juicy as that. And it wasn't as if she owed me anything. I, or rather Henry, had felt her up, and then felt her down again. After she had said to stop. Not good. Not good at all.

How was I to know? Someone told me Earth girls are easy.

Welcome back. Where've you been hiding?

Nowhere special. Just keeping my own counsel for a while. And don't forget, we need to stop off for our munitions.

I haven't forgotten.

The good bit of the mixed feeling (the diamond in the ash? the walnut in the whip? the carrot in the sick?) had everything to do with Amanda, and I kept switching to her channel whenever the other material was getting me down.

The trouble was that the two things couldn't be kept separate. Nice Amanda thoughts were contaminated by bad Uma thoughts, because when the Uma bomb exploded, shrapnel was going to land everywhere.

Despite having to stop off on the way, I got in early. The ginormous willy still hadn't been cleaned off, a fact which I found comforting, even if it was fading, sinking slowly back into the wall. It had become a kind of totem for me, and as long as those elegant lines were there, however faintly, hope remained.

Because it was early there were no monstrous sentinels on the gate, and the only person I knew in the playground was Flaherty, who came scampering up.

'Hey, Mr Lover-Man. Saw you, saw you.'

My heart sank.

'Saw me where?'

'In the street.'

'Big deal.'

'Not alone.'

'Some of us have got mates.'

'Not a boy friend.'

He'd seen me with . . . which one? Uma or Amanda? God, but it was hard being a stud. (I'm being ironic.)

'Did you then?'

'Did I what?'

'Did you snog her?'

'Snog who?'

'Fanny Eldritch.'

Mrs Eldritch was a tiny ancient sewing teacher, called 'Fanny' because it was widely accepted that she didn't have one. (Flaherty was being sarcastic, which is much less cool than being ironic.)

'I can honestly say that I've never snogged Fanny Eldritch. Have you?'

'Yeah. She tastes of dog meat. She must eat it, and it gets stuck in her dentures. So you did then?'

'You've lost me, Flaherty. I wish I could do the same for you. Please go away.'

'Hey, Gonad, Hector Brunty snogged Uma Upshaw. Probably had her too, dirty monkey.'

Well at least that answered the 'who' question. For now.

I turned round. Gonad had just arrived, his bag over his shoulder, his small ears all a-flicker. His mouth fell open at the news.

'Snogged . . . I thought you were sick?'

Big groan. From me. There was no way I was going to be able to control this.

'Look, it's a long story. Nothing happened. I just went down to get some chips, and she was there, working, and she had to go out, and we were walking in the same direction and . . .'

It wasn't sounding convincing, even to me.

'I saw them, I saw them,' said Flaherty, doing one of his stupid little jigs. 'They weren't just walking in the same direction. They were on a love cruise. Heading for the cemetery. And we all know what happens there.'

'The grave's a fine and fateful place,
But none I think do there embrace.'

'You what?' said Gonad, looking puzzled. Flaherty had stopped his jigging as well. I must have spoken the words. Bloody Henry T.

'Love poetry, that's what that was,' said Flaherty, the irritating little shit. 'He's got it bad if it's come to love poetry. He'll be gazing at flowers and sighing next. *Aaahh*, nature.'

'I'm off to registration,' I said, stumped for anything better. 'I've got to give in my sick note for last week.'

Flaherty followed me in his flitting, scampering, dancing, mosquito way, and Gonad trudged along as well, looking vaguely annoyed. Snogging girls like Uma Upshaw wasn't playing by the rules. It was cheating. It was unnatural.

It was entirely without historical precedent.

Shouty Mrs Conlon, who used to be nice Miss Walsh, decided to mix and match by becoming nice Mrs Conlon, for the morning at least. She asked if I was OK and how I felt, and that sort of thing, and she asked if Mr Mordred had really slipped and fallen arse first into the pool of puke (she used different words), and you could see her trying not to laugh when I told her that he had, and the kids who were there all laughed because nothing was stopping them, certainly not nice Mrs Conlon.

But that was about as good as it got that day.

CHAPTER 40
SHE WHO GATHERS
ALL THINGS MORTAL

I made it through the morning lessons. There was little alternative. Unless I stopped time again. But I felt that my time-stopping powers were weak today. I *did* entertain a fantasy about a sniper on one of the local tower blocks. He was, obviously, going for a headshot, but he failed to account for the curvature of the Earth, the slight breeze, and the gravitational effect of the moon and so the bullet only grazed my ear. But it was enough for another glamorous hospital run, plus an interview on Sky.

And after that I became the prime minister's special adviser on teenage assassination attempts.

Oh, and a recording deal with EMI.

It was a fantasy, remember. Be grateful I left it there.

Morning break. Recently whittled down from twenty to fifteen minutes for the purposes of advancing the three great causes of numeracy and literacy. Not very popular, in general, but joy to we nerds as it meant five fewer minutes of intimidation and battery.

Up until break it had been nose-to-the-grindstone (assassination fantasies excepted), and there hadn't been a chance to talk. Smurf was acting normal, his usual half-smile and slightly dazed expression fully in place as his bendy body swayed gently in the breeze. So he obviously hadn't heard. That was something. As soon as we were outside I took my chance and got hold of him and dragged him to the tuck-shop queue.

It was hard to get out the things I had to say, and I had to blink and swallow and wiggle my ears a bit before I got going.

ME: There's something I have to tell you, about thingy. Ummm, Uma.

HENRY: *Never apologize, never explain.*

SMURF: You didn't tell anyone, did you?

ME: No, but I . . . But it's just that . . .

SMURF: Because I feel a bit of an idiot.

HENRY: *That's because you are an idiot.*

ME: No it's me that's an idiot . . . What? Why? No, look, I've got to tell you. I went to see her.

Smurf: You didn't say something to her, did you? Jesus, Heck, I wish you . . .

ME: No, I didn't tell her about you. It wasn't supposed to . . .

SMURF: Because I was wrong.

ME: Wrong? What do you mean? Wrong about what?

SMURF: About fancying Uma Upshaw.

ME: How can you be wrong about fancying someone? Either you do or you don't.

SMURF: There's no logic to it, Heck. I did, for a while, and then I sort of didn't.

ME:	You mean you just went off her?
HENRY:	*Heartless bastard.*
ME:	Heartless bast— I mean, that's a bit, er, fickle.
SMURF:	Well, it's more that I sort of fancy somebody else now. You know, instead. Hey, don't look at me like that. It's something that happens. It doesn't make me a monster of depravity. And stop laughing.
ME:	Sorry, I can't help it. And I know you're not a monster of depravity. I'm just relieved is all.
SMURF:	Relieved, why?
ME:	Well, just relieved. And who is it, anyway?
SMURF:	You swear you won't tell?
ME:	For Christ's sake, Smurf . . . Have I ever let you down?
SMURF:	Well, er, OK. It's Stella Mulrooney.
ME:	Stella! But she's almost as bad as Uma.

Stella was, in fact, one of Uma's gang. She was long and lithe and ruthless on the netball court.

By then we were at the front of the queue, and the prefect in charge – a heavy-set boy called Vass who'd once famously put a whole Melton Mowbray pork pie in his mouth – was looking at me impatiently. I'd planned to buy Smurf a packet of crisps and also maybe a Snickers or a Twix to pay him back for snogging the love of his life, but now that seemed a bit excessive, so I just got him a KitKat, and he was still thanking me for this inexplicable act of generosity when the others all came round.

Stan, of course, already knew. About Uma, that is. So

now, carefully watching Smurf the whole time, I filled in the others.

It was tough getting the tone right. I had to convey the greatness of it, snogging the most famously glamorous girl in the year, etc., etc., but without bragging, and without rubbing Smurf's nose in it. So I capped it off with an account of the final catastrophe, dwelling on my incompetence and embarrassment. This also had the advantage of being true, and it's always nice finding yourself on the high ground, truth-wise.

Smurf, generous-spirited waif that he was, looked genuinely delighted with the business. He seemed incapable of holding a grudge.

Or he holds his grudges close, until the time of execution.

'Put it there,' he said, holding out his lank, long-fingered hand, and we shook. 'It's like you're doing it for all of us.'

I tried to detect a tone of melancholy or resentment in this. It was hard to tell.

'We didn't *do* it,' I said modestly, and truthfully.

'Yeah, well, but, as far as I can see, kissing counts as *it*, sort of.'

'No way,' I replied, 'kissing isn't *it*. It is *it*. But, listen, there's . . . something else.' I turned to Stan. 'After you left on Saturday, I—'

'I think you ought to . . .' said Gonad, doing a turn-round sign with his finger. I felt a physical jolt, as though someone had exploded a tiny bomb in my lower intestine.

Uma or Amanda?

I turned.

Uma.

And friends.

The Fierce Ones.

Pitiless girls.

Including Stella Mulrooney.

They even looked vaguely hawk-like, with their sharp faces and swept-back hair. Hawk-like, but not hawk-like like Hawkgirl was hawk-like. She was hawk-like in a much nicer way, which didn't stop her from kicking alien butt big style when that was necessary. Maybe it's the wings. It's hard not to love things with wings. Unless the wings are leathery, in which case the opposite is true.

She, I mean Uma, looked magnificent – her head held high, her black hair heavy as a sea lion coiled around her shoulders, her long skirt billowing behind her.

I thought about Tierney and the wallop she'd given him. I wasn't going to duck, wasn't going to cringe, wasn't going to beg for mercy. I was going to take it, and hope I didn't cry like a dying swan when the slap hit me.

Pale beyond porch and portal,
Framed in white light she stands,
She who gathers all things mortal
In cold immortal hands.

What? Had I said it? No, my friends weren't staring at me.

                                        Other women cloy
The appetites they feed, but she makes hungry
Where most she satisfies.

'Yum yum.'

'What d'yer say, Heck?' asked Stan, but he was as

engrossed as the rest of us in Uma's stately progress, and when I replied, 'I said I'm hungry, yum yum,' he just nodded.

Uma finally stopped about two metres away. That was a good sign. Too far away for a punch. Unless she wanted a run at it. Or maybe she was going to throw something at me. A tomahawk or one of those cool ninja death-star things.

Yet again I found myself at the centre of a circle of attention. All these years of no one knowing who the hell I was, and now suddenly I was always the one in the middle of stuff happening. Why couldn't stuff happen to someone else for a change?

But one good thing: Amanda wasn't there.

'I'm sorry you're sick.'

'What?'

'I said I'm sorry you're sick. My mum talked to your mum. She said you were really sick. I'm sorry. That's it, really. See you.'

Boy, she fights dirty.

And with that she turned round and walked away again. I felt sort of relieved and crushed at the same time. The watching faces dissolved back into the air, and it was just the four of us again. Or five, including Henry.

Some seconds of silence passed, as each of us absorbed what was relevant in the exchange. Smurf focused vaguely on the retreating rump of Stella.

'OK,' said Gonad eventually, 'just what *is* up with you? The fainting and spewing. And nice one, by the way, for spewing on Mordred. Cos I didn't say, before.'

I looked down, and then up at them.

'I honestly don't know what's wrong with me. I've been having these headaches, and sometimes I feel a bit faint, and then I spew. Not just on Mordred, unless he's around. I've been to the doctor and the specialist, and I had some tests last week when I was off. They'll tell me today or tomorrow if there's anything in there.'

'In there?' Smurf looked anguished, almost on the edge of tears. He knew what I meant. Stan was quiet. But then Stan was always quiet.

'It might be a brain tumour. But they hack them out no bother these days. Piece of piss.'

I couldn't resist it: dramatize it, and show how I could laugh in the face of death. What a hero.

'And it might be why I've been acting a bit weird. So, sorry if I have been.'

'S'all right,' they said, in unison.

STAN:	What about Tierney?
GONAD:	Oh yeah, he's going to kill you.
ME:	I don't think he is.
SMURF:	Are you going to tell the teachers?
ME:	Nah. Got something else in mind.
HENRY:	*That's right, you take all the credit.*
ME:	I intend to.
STAN:	Intend to what?
ME:	What? Oh, ah, sort him out.
GONAD:	You've got a plan?
ME:	Oh yes.
ALL:	Tell us!

ME: No. It'll probably never come off.

STAN: You're not going to fight him, are you?

ME: He doesn't frighten me, not any more.

GONAD: Anyway, it's time he was taught a lesson. You saw how Heck dealt with that mutant what's-'is-name last week. Heck's going to kick ass.

STAN: It isn't right, Heck. You know it isn't. You can't deal with violence by using violence. You just keep the cycle going.

ME: He started it, Stan. He's a bully.

STAN: But if you beat him, it means that you are.

ME: How do you make that out?

STAN: A bully is someone who picks on the weak.

ME: Yeah?

STAN: If you beat Tierney in a fight, it means he must be weaker than you. It means you'll have picked on someone weaker. QED.

GONAD: WHAT? You are a crazy man. That means you'd never stand up to anyone. QED my arse.

SMURF: I sort of agree with Stan. Maybe not in the logic, but in the meaning behind it. Fighting isn't the way. Especially if you've got a brain tumour.

ME: I'm not going to fight him.

GONAD: Aw!

STAN: I'm glad.

But Stan didn't look convinced, and he was right not to be. I had in mind something much worse than fighting Tierney. I was just waiting for the right time.

And then old Mrs Trimble rang her handbell (*unclean, unclean*), and it was time to go in, and still there was no Amanda.

CHAPTER 41
AT LOVERS'
PERJURIES, THEY SAY,
JOVE LAUGHS

After break nothing much happened. Corridors, class-rooms, shuffling bodies, a yellow stink in the toilets. Until I was sitting in the physics lab, and it was hot. Equations, calculations, vectors. The numbers that map the universe. And if numbers can tell us everything there is to know about stars and atoms, about nebulae and quarks, why should they be silent about the other things that matter, our emotions, our dreams? Surely there was an equation some-where that would give me the answer to the question of love.

No, not singular. Multiple. The questions of love.

Who?

Where?

Why?

When will it start?

When will it stop?

And there, looking out of the window over the damp coarse grass of the gypsy field where we had found bleached bones of the dog, where I had touched the hard metal at the tip of the bolt, and then touched her fingers, I thought I had that equation within my grasp, and I reached for it, and the numbers and symbols danced translucent around my fingers, and I could feel them, slippery, jellied, but I could not hold them.

Hang up philosophy! Unless philosophy can make a Juliet.

Hey, Henry.

Hey, Heck.

Feeling a bit not-so-good again. Any chance of you easing up back there? Pull in one of your – what did you call them? – tendrils.

    I

          need

    more

           time.

Time. Shall we stop it? I think not. You know that only lived time is precious.

There are so many things. To do.

The time of life is short; to spend that shortness basely were too long.

Base? Isn't it you who wants me to . . . ? Is it just me or has the world gone funny? You have stopped time again, haven't you, without asking me?

And the kids in the class, and Mr Harker teaching, were not moving, and there was no noise – not the droning of the teacher or the whisperings and murmurings of the class, or the sounds of chairs scraping or the buzzing of the dying fluorescent light.

OK, not good.

Panic in his voice.

Heck, wake up.

He's gone too far. He knows he's gone too far.

I'll sleep. You wake.

And then I came back into myself and the noise of the classroom returned. I'd been in some kind of a trance. There was drool on my chin. Nobody had noticed. At least I hadn't pissed my pants. Or fallen off my stool into a foaming fit on the floor.

'With us again, Brunty? Try to stay awake.'

'Sir.'

Amanda. I'd begun to wonder if Amanda had decided not to come into school today. The horror of seeing me. The shame. Something like that.

I went out for lunch with the gang to our usual niche, but I wasn't hungry. Which, it turned out, was a shame.

GONAD: Look at that! Heck's got some food. I mean, food you could eat.

SMURF: Looks like a real sandwich with, let's have a look, yes, cheese and pickle.

GONAD: It'll be chopped pork next, and other similar delights.

SMURF: And, look, a Wagon Wheel. Awesome. And a packet of crisps. Whale and bacon – my favourite!

GONAD: The nation's favourite.

Well, the unexpectedly edible lunch should have been a

pleasant surprise, but as I said I wasn't hungry, plus it added to the general doom and gloom. If Mum (aided, no doubt, by Clytemnestra) had thought things were so bad that I needed a real lunch rather than horseshit fritters, then, well then things were really bad.

The playground began to fill up as the school-lunchers filtered in. Stan said to me, 'Did you hear about Flaherty?'

'That he's a stupid wanker?'

Gonad and Smurf laughed.

'No, that his dad's been put away.'

And I half laughed, and then stopped.

'That's bad luck.'

'He's in trouble,' said Gonad. 'The only reason he hasn't had a serious kicking is that everyone's afraid of his dad. If it is his dad.'

'Yeah,' we all said. Flaherty used to annoy us, but he was a major goad to the hard bastards and they hated him.

'He can take care of himself,' I said, but without much conviction.

I handed out my food, and when everything was gone except the crumbs brushed off for the sparrows, we got up to find somewhere else to slouch. It was then that I saw her, and the gloom of the day lifted and I instantly felt sixty-seven per cent happier. (I rounded up, of course, from sixty-six point six recurring.)

And then my focus widened and I took in the scene around her. There were other girls – the hawk-like hand-maidens of Uma. For a moment I thought that the scene was a happy one, that the girls were enjoying some joke together. And for a while that might have been how it was.

The fierce girls were smiling, and Amanda was smiling back uncertainly.

But no.

It was changing.

They were laughing. Amanda was looking around. She saw me. The uncertain smile returned and she began to walk towards me.

Walk away.

No!

There's nothing in this for you. Look around. People are watching again.

I don't care.

You should.

Amanda was searching my face as she came, trying to find an answering smile there. But I was busy with Henry, trying to shut him up, trying to make him go away.

He wouldn't go away.

Foul.

No.

Misshapen.

No.

Poxed.

No.

And Amanda was here now, talking to me, but I couldn't hear.

She is as ugly as a warthog's scrotum. She is diseased.

'Shut up!'

She is a MUTANT.

'Fuck off. Fuck off. Fuck off.'

She is pollution, contagion, death for us.

266

'Shut up and fuck off!' I was screaming. I knew I was screaming.

Look at her. She's—

Finally, despairingly, I cried out, 'Go away and leave me alone, please.'

And the girls who had been laughing stopped laughing, and I don't know if what remained in their eyes was satiation or disgust, and the crowd of people around Amanda – around me – parted and she ran through, covering her face with her hands and, as in a kind of echo, as a replay, I heard what she had been saying.

'Tell me it isn't true, tell me you didn't see her, tell me you didn't go there with her, tell me you didn't take her to the place where we were together, tell me you didn't.'

And what she had heard in return, as she stood imploring and desperate before the crowd of tormentors, was: 'shut up', 'fuck off', 'go away' and 'leave me alone, please'. And, for all I knew, 'pollution', 'contagion', 'diseased' and 'mutant'.

And I looked at the faces in the crowd, and I could not see my friends, but I did see Tierney and his followers, and he was grinning like a skull, and they were nodding and their eyes met mine, and they knew me.

Tierney, Johnson, Murdo, No-Name, Brunty.

The new gang.

CHAPTER 42
THINGS CAN ONLY GET BETTER

The horror of it. And I was rescued by, of all people, Mordred. Of course, I didn't know he was coming to rescue me to begin with – I just saw him scampering on his little feet towards me across the playground.

'Brunty . . . ah, er, Hector. Your mother has telephoned' – his voice here broke and quavered a bit, strongly suggesting he was shit-scared of Mum – 'and, er, she would like you to go, as it were, home.'

'Now, sir?'

'Yes, now. Of course, now. Straight away. Immediately. In a word, now.'

Mordred left, his hand making meaningless gesticulations, as if he were mentally rehearsing a speech to a Nazi rally.

'I'll come with you if you like.'

Stan was there again.

'It's OK, Stan. I'm good. I'm good.'

'It'll get me out of RE. Father McGuire's coming in, and you know the smell of whiskey makes me feel sick.'

Father McGuire was one of the two priests serving the parish and the school. McGuire was ancient and scrofulous, and he didn't like the kids at all. He regaled us with what would happen to us in Hell, which involved a lot of burning, and a grab-bag of inconveniences ranging from impalement (bad) to being forced to read the works of J. K. Rowling over and over again for all eternity (v. bad). McGuire obviously looked back fondly on the good old days when he could strap boys for failing to look suitably religious, but now he had to make do with coming up close and shouting into your face with his brown teeth all over you and the spray flying out and with it a sulphurous stench, and most of us thought that the strap would have been better.

The other priest was Father Conway, who liked to be called Jim, which may well have been his name. He was young and nice and never shouted at us or threatened us with Hell if we 'interfered with ourselves' (a favourite topic of Fr. McGuire). Because he was nice, he was generally thought to be gay, although I never heard a report of any actual interference or even inappropriate ogling. His RE classes took the form of meditations on some moral problem, such as why it might be nice to be nice to each other, and how it was not nice not being nice to each other, and he rarely mentioned God at all except in a very back-groundy kind of way, along with the suggestion that he might well be nice.

But McGuire was a good enough reason to get out of school. So we went and got our school bags and coats and set off back to my house.

'OK,' said Stan, 'what the hell was that all about?'

'That?'

'That girl, the one who came over. I don't know her name. It didn't seem too good, what happened.'

More explanations. I told Stan about meeting Amanda after we'd parted company on Saturday, and I said that I really liked her.

'So why were you so nasty to her? In front of everyone?'

I knew, I knew. My heart ached for her, ached for what I'd done.

Yet each man kills the thing he loves.

I pointed to my head: 'This makes me do stupid stuff. I'm not in control any more.'

'Do you want me to carry your bag?'

'I'm not a crip, you know.'

'Yeah, sorry.'

'Anyway, you'll stink it all up,' I said, and I shoved him and he shoved me back, and we laughed until we reached my house.

'Do you want to come in?'

'Nah, I'll just . . . Oh, hello, Mrs Brunty.'

'Hello, Stan.'

She must have been watching from the window. Her face was rigid. Stan wandered away, either back to school or off into town.

We went inside. Clyte was there, looking serious. There was no hugging or emoting, which was a relief.

'Doctor Jones called,' said Mum when I'd thrown my bag in the corner and taken off my coat. 'Not his secretary, but himself, which was good of him, because he must be a busy man.'

Twittering.

270

'What did he say?'

I knew it wasn't good. If it was good they'd already have told me. Hey, they'd be wearing party hats and doing the Highland fling.

Pause. Pain.

'They found something on the scan.'

'I knew they would.'

'They want you to go into the hospital on Thursday.'

'For more tests?'

Hopeful. Not really hopeful.

'No . . . yes, well, they . . . Oh, come here, Heck. I wasn't going to do this. I was going to be strong. But I'm not. I'm not. I'm not strong.'

And then she was hugging me, and kissing the top of my head. And I had to comfort her and say 'there, there' and that sort of thing, and finally she was able to carry on.

'They want you to go in on Thursday, and then they're going to operate on Friday. Doctor Jones said it was urgent . . . that they had to take out what they could.'

'What they could?'

'No . . . all of it. They'll take out all of it. He said it would all be fine, he said they would get all of it. All of it, he said.'

The heartless swine.

'They're good now,' said Clytemnestra. 'They zapped my breast. Not a trace.'

'Of what, your breast?'

'No, my— Oh, you're joking. That's good. That's very good.'

'I'm not frightened, Mum,' I said.

Well I am. It's fine for you to be all blasé about this. You're not the one that's going to be sliced.

'Well I am, actually, when you think about it.'

'Think about what, Heck?'

'Nothing, Mum.'

I took the rest of the day off school, and lay on the bed trying hard to think about nothing at all, because none of the things I might be able to think about were good things, and most of them entirely fitted the description of fucking terrible.

CHAPTER 43
VERY ROMEO AND JULIET

The next day I had a choice: go to school and take whatever punishment awaited me there from Amanda or Uma or Tierney or fate. Or stay at home and look at Mum trying to keep herself together, with nothing to take my mind off Henry T. and the other shitty things in my life except for *Celebrity Antique Challenge* (or was it *Challenge an Antique Celebrity?*) and the other crap on daytime telly. Caught between the poo and some soft stuff.

Despite Mum's protests and Clytemnestra's claims that we could have a fun day together, I opted for the poo. I mean, school. I was going to explain everything to Amanda. She would understand. Who wouldn't? I had a brain tumour. They were about to crack open my skull like a walnut and spoon out bits of my brain. *Of course* I was acting strangely.

I decided to try to enjoy my last couple of days, so I kicked a stone to school. I didn't care if it wasn't cool.

Hey, Heck.

Hello, Henry. I mean, goodbye, Henry. You've done enough damage for one lifetime, haven't you?

Don't be like that. I'm here to make it up. I've been thinking. I was wrong about Amanda. I'm big enough to admit that now. If that's the best you can do, then we'll have to live with it.

Will we?

Will we what?

Live?

No morbidity, not today. Let's have some fun.

I don't see how. Tierney still wants to kill me, even if you don't. And I can't even imagine how to make it up to Amanda. She's probably taken an overdose herself.

Very Romeo and Juliet.

Yeah, I've seen the movie.

You're forgetting my plan.

Yeah, well, I was thinking about that. I know Tierney's a dog but, well, isn't what we planned a bit ... serious? And you heard what Stan said about bullies. If I beat him, then I am one, because he must have been weaker. QED, he said.

Tricks with words. Fighting evil never makes you a bully.

Well, I don't really care. It all seems a bit ... unimportant now. Compared to the other stuff. Amanda. You. What they're planning to do to me in hospital.

Us.

Eh?

Do to us.

Then I realized I'd forgotten about my stone and it was nowhere to be seen. But I was at school anyway. On the way in to the gates I got jostled a bit by the bruisers there. And when I looked back I saw why.

The huge knob was gone.

A fresh layer of grey paint covered it up like a pair of giant underpants. So they hadn't just let it fade away, dwindling to a shadow and then a memory. No, they had to kick a knob when it was down. I felt as though I'd lost a friend.

And then I found a few more. Stan, Gonad and Smurf were all there, and I slotted into the group. There was none of the usual piss-taking and messing about, but nor was there any obvious sympathy. They'd probably worked it all out in advance.

'Didn't think you'd come in today,' said Stan.

'Couldn't stay away. You know, double chemistry, head kicked in at break, what's not to like?' And although I piled on the sarcasm, I wasn't joking about the double chemistry.

But for once I wasn't really in the mood for Mendeleyev and his marvellous invention. I was desperate for break, so I could go and find Amanda and try to explain things. And then I saw that the rain had started, drops as big as crab apples hitting the windows, and then hail, and then a steady, drenching shower, and I knew that we'd be confined to our form rooms.

I was on my way down there when I suddenly found that I wasn't on my way down there. I was going in the other direction altogether. I was heading for the language rooms, and I knew which one.

If we're going to do this, we're going to do it right.

Whatever you say.

Amanda's form teacher was the dreaded Mrs Allworthy, recently promoted to head of French. Her base of operations was the language lab, a sad and desolate place, and not just because Allworthy was such a callous bitch. Half of the space was taken up with the soundproofed audio booths where kids were supposed to be able to Listen-and-Speak, using what was probably cutting-edge technology in 1972. They hadn't been used in living memory, or at least not for the teaching of languages. Now they were isolation cells where Allworthy sent the kids she didn't like to look at. The booths were made of nice crumbly asbestos, and some of the school drongos were convinced that if you ground it up and snorted it you could get reasonably high before you perished from asbestosis.

I pushed open the door without knocking. Mrs Allworthy had her back to the class, with her feet up on the windowsill. She was smoking a thin cigar and had on a set of earphones. She had once been, it was said, an attractive woman. Now her short sleeves showed off her bingo wings (or nan flaps, if you prefer), and her eyes were lined with resignation and contempt. She didn't know I had come in. Or didn't care. The class all stared at me. Fights were frozen mid-punch. Pencils poised mid-stab. Even by the standards of The Body, this was a rough class.

I looked around. There were many faces, glittering like the facets of a diamond, and I couldn't take them in. I couldn't see Amanda. But I did see a couple of the members of Tierney's gang, and one of them was Murdo.

Don't give up. We have waded so far in blood, it's as well to go on as back.

Blood?

Figure of speech.

276

I strode through the desks to the booths at the back. There were four rows of them. I found her in the third row, in the far corner. First I saw the back of her head with its strawberry-blonde hair, and then the side of her face, the left side, the side without the birthmark. She was biting her bottom lip and looking down at an exercise book, her whole being absorbed in what she was doing. It was only when I was almost upon her that she saw me, or felt me, and she turned towards me, startled, and she began to rise, but I came down to her, and knelt by her and took her face in my hands and kissed her and whispered into her ear that I was sorry, so sorry, so sorry, and I felt her tears flow over my hands.

'It's OK,' she whispered in my ear. 'Stan told me. Stan told me you were sick.'

And then I heard the loud jeering. I stood up and turned round. Murdo was there, and the rest of the class was behind him, clustered into the narrow spaces between the lines of language booths. Hard faces, both boys and girls. Some showing spite, some disgust, some still neutral.

Murdo was trying to get the class on his side, trying to get them to join him in ridiculing us. Ridiculing, and then worse. A year before it would have been easy. A year ago most of the kids didn't have girlfriends or boyfriends, or even particularly want them. Sex was funny or filthy or shameful. It was something other people did. Now, although there was still a residue of that, it was normal, or at least within reach. But still, Murdo wanted blood.

'Givin' her one, eh? At it like fucking polecats. Go on, shag her, shag her. No one else will, ugly slag.'

Murdo was big. And he was hard, and his fists looked like huge iron gauntlets at the end of his long arms. I decided then that I was going to try to land one punch before he got me. One punch would be worth it. My muscles were tensed, ready to spring.

In close. Make him flail.

Yes, get in close, one punch. Didn't care after that. He could do what he wanted.

And then a sharp face appeared over the top of one of the booths. It was Flaherty. Just what I didn't need – I mean, he was hardly going to add to the dignity of the proceedings. I imagined he was going to make some mad chattering commentary on what was happening, taking the piss out of everyone there, including me.

I was wrong.

He was carrying a waste-paper bin and, with as much force as he could muster, he slammed it upside down over Murdo's head.

'Stop looking, you dirty pervert,' he said in his sing-song way. And then he jumped down next to Murdo and started whacking the bin with the wooden edge of a board duster.

It was funny. It was very funny. The class joined in pushing and belting Murdo, and he was bellowing inside the bin, lashing out blindly with his fists.

I took Amanda's hand and pulled her towards the back of the classroom where there was a second door, and soon we were out and running along the deserted corridor, suddenly free and full of joy. Down the stairs, two flights, and then we were outside into the rain, and still running.

'Where are we going?' Amanda shouted, smiling, rain drenching her face and hair.

'Nowhere,' I said, and we stopped in the middle of the playground with puddles all around us, and I didn't know what to do next. But Amanda did. It was her turn to kiss me, and I felt the presence of a thousand pale faces clamped to the windows and I didn't care.

CHAPTER 44
THE DUEL

From the playground we went to the new Starbucks that used to be a picture-framers, and she had a cappuccino and I had a latte, which was nice but not very butch and I tried not to think about how upset Mum would be about me throwing my weight behind globalization and the terrible effect it was probably going to have on the rainforest and the ozone and peasant farmers in the High Andes.

Amanda wanted to know everything, and I told her everything. Told her about my dad, about my head, about the voices I sometimes heard, about how I had a good chance of pulling through. She didn't say much back. She didn't have to.

I thought about taking the whole day off, spending it with Amanda, hanging out, talking, dreaming, but then decided against it. I wanted to see my friends again, wanted another afternoon of classrooms and corridors. Because soon they'd be gone.

'You can come and have your lunch with us,' I said.

From everything she'd said, it was pretty clear that Amanda had no real friends in the school. Except me. I was her friend. And that made me feel proud.

Amanda smiled shyly. 'The others wouldn't like it.'

'They'll love you. Just don't talk about girl stuff, OK?'

It was a joke, because Amanda never talked about girl stuff – you know, dresses, hair, the stuff you put in hair, that kind of thing. She talked about music and books. She'd fit right in. Might even be a civilizing influence. Maybe Gonad would cut down on his moose-like belching, and Smurf might get some odour-eaters for his trainers, because boy his feet stank, and that was all wrong for a poetry-loving type like him.

So we got back in time for lunch, or a bit late actually, because the playground was already half full. And things weren't normal. There was a cluster over against the fence on the beck side of the school. A strange noise was coming from them – a low grunting, sound.

Heck?

Yeah?

Ready to rumble?

I don't know.

I told Amanda to wait. There was a feeling of horror, of blood in the air, and I didn't want it splashing on her. I glanced back as I walked towards the group. Amanda looked thin and young and frail against the background of concrete and glass. She was biting her bottom lip. She waved, and I smiled.

The noise grew as I approached. An ugly noise. The noise of a blood rite or ritual. The sounds of people working at pain, and the sounds of others egging them on.

A circle had formed. That usually meant a fight. I wasn't alone in approaching. This sort of thing always attracted a crowd. For the past week I had usually been in the middle of it. Now all I could see was a wall of purple blazers.

Then I saw Stan and Smurf and Gonad, looking on helplessly. I was relieved that at least none of my friends were in there, getting tortured.

'What is it?' I asked.

'It's Flaherty,' said Smurf.

Flaherty. I'd almost forgotten his antics this morning. Binning Murdo. And he had no protection. And they hated him.

I pushed through the wall. Elbows jabbed at me, big boys pushed back. But I was through.

It wasn't a pretty sight. Murdo and No-Name had hold of Flaherty, forcing him down onto his knees. Murdo had a fistful of hair and No-Name was squeezing his cheeks, trying to open his mouth. Sean Johnson was hovering around as well, looking gormless, needing someone to tell him what to do. Flaherty's nose was bleeding and his face was red and blotched from hard slaps and sloppy punches. But that was nothing compared to what was about to happen.

Tierney had a stick. A thin branch torn off one of the willow trees by the beck. At the end of the stick was a used condom, impaled on the splintered wood.

'Open his fucking mouth,' snarled Tierney, and his eyes were burning.

No-Name squeezed harder and Flaherty's lips began to part. He didn't make a sound. Nothing. He might be about to have a stinking used condom shoved in his face, but he wasn't going to whimper.

Maybe Tierney was never really going to make Flaherty eat condom. Maybe it was just part of the humiliation. I wasn't going to take the chance.

'Stop it.'

Tierney spun round, still holding the stick like an obscene spear. When he saw it was me his face showed a second of uncertainty before it hardened.

'Oh yes, this is good. Come to help your bum chum?'

Sniggers from the crowd. Guffaw from Murdo. Out of the corner of my eye I saw Stan help Flaherty up. Nobody else was paying him any attention now. Things had moved on.

'You're the one going at him with a condom. Bit of wishful thinking?'

There was another quieter snigger at that. This crowd could go either way. Tierney responded by jabbing the johnny-stick at me – nothing like smearing someone with used-johnny juice to set the multitude against them. I managed to sidestep the thrust and grabbed the stick halfway along its length. I wrenched it from Tierney's grip and then threw it, javelin style, over the fence and into the beck, where it drifted downstream with the lazy current. HMS *Condom*'s maiden voyage.

'I said I was going to kill you, and now I am,' said Tierney. And his hand moved, and I saw that he was carrying a knife, long-bladed and thin.

Knife. Bad. Time to run?

'You really are chicken shit, aren't you, Tierney?' I said, ignoring Henry.

Whether or not Tierney was chicken shit, *I* was certainly

afraid. I so didn't want Tierney to stick his knife into me. I didn't want to feel the blade slide through my skin, glance off bone, find my liver or my lung or my heart. Stabbing is not a good way to go. But I was angry, and I had my plan, and my mind was clear.

Henry had given me this clarity. His words, partly. But more his presence. The presence of the thing that really would kill me. The other times that he had helped me in situations like this, he'd sort of taken over, shoved me out of the way. But now we were together, and our thoughts and actions were one.

'It's you what's afraid. Shitting your pants, are you? Don't worry, might only give you a little nick, something to remember me by.'

'You're a coward, Tierney. And I can prove it.'

And then I took out *my* weapon, and it wasn't a knife or a gun, or a rocket-launcher, or a cunning blowpipe with curare-tipped darts.

It was a packet of Revels.

Six different flavours: toffee, coffee, orange, coconut, honeycomb, each wrapped in a chocolate coating, and sold in a neat little pack for thirty-eight pence.

Six. I said six, and yet I named only five. And the sixth is the one that counts.

The Peanut.

You might think you could spot the peanut, easily telling it from the others by its irregular ovoidal properties, but you just might make a mistake and, as I'd learned, that was a mistake you really didn't want to make if peanuts were your nemesis, your Kryptonite.

'What's that?'

Tierney was looking at the Revels dangling from my hand. Knife against packet of sweets. Could have been funny. *Was* funny.

But both of these could kill.

'I think you know. Want one?'

'What's he on about, Chris?' said Murdo. 'What's he got them for? Have 'im.'

'Don't fucking like 'em.'

Tierney's voice had now lost its sly, wheedling tone. It had been a gamble, but I was right.

A-hem?

OK, *Henry* was right.

Yes, it was Henry that spotted that Tierney never thieved anything with nuts in it.

Obvious, really.

To a genius.

'This scares you, doesn't it?' I said, waving the packet in front of him. I could sense the interest of the crowd. Some of them were getting it, understanding the line of attack. I made it clear for even the real thickos. 'Fancy shitting bricks over a peanut . . .'

'It's you what's afraid of nuts. We all saw you spaz-out when you ate one of them before. Fucking foaming and twitching. You're the poof here, you're the freak, the one with the allergies.' Tierney was blustering now.

'Come on, then,' I said, 'let's share.'

I opened the packet, praying my hands wouldn't betray my nervousness. The rustle and tear was loud against the silence.

'One for you, one for me.'

Here it was.

Everyone knew that I was allergic to nuts, just like Tierney said. But he'd hidden his allergy, thinking it was something to be ashamed of. If he backed out then his sham was exposed and he'd be condemned on his own terms as a gay freak.

But if that didn't happen, then it was going to be a duel.

Revels Russian roulette.

And that would show who the coward was.

The trouble was that Tierney still had the knife and as a defence against a knife a chocolate-coated peanut is, all things considered, inadequate.

The balance of power was, however, about to change.

A kid burst through the circle. He was from the year above. Conor O'Neil. Everyone knew him. He'd had an embarrassing encounter with an ice-cream van last year and since then he'd turned into a weirdo. I mean, the kind of weirdo who sees stuff that isn't there, not just a social misfit. He talked to himself. And his hair was really, really bad. But the weirdness made him a bit scary, and none of the thugs bothered him. Gonad said it was like the Sioux and other warlike tribes, who always respected loonies.

Anyway, O'Neil just came up and took the knife out of Tierney's hand, the way you'd take something sharp away from a toddler so they didn't hurt themselves. It was like Tierney was in some kind of trance – he didn't resist at all. Everyone stared at O'Neil. O'Neil stared at the knife. I thought he might throw it over the fence the way I had with the johnny-stick, consigning it to the depths, and maybe a hand would come up and catch it like *Excalibur*. But instead he put it in his pocket and wandered off without saying a word to anyone.

So that just left the Revels.

'One for me, one for you,' I repeated.

'What if you cheat? You've got the bag, it's not fair.'

That was funny – hearing Tierney use the words of the underdog, of the oppressed.

I looked around, focused on Tierney's crew. Murdo, No-Name, Johnson. Murdo hated me. No-Name was unpredictable.

'Come here, Sean,' I said to the hulking Johnson.

He did as he was told.

'You hold them. Take one out at a time. Give the first one to me, then the next to Tierney. Then carry on. Until one of us says stop. You cool with that, Tierney?'

What could he say? It was a fair test of courage.

Or a stupid, irresponsible, dangerous prank.

But there was no way he could back out. His gang was all in favour.

'Go on, Chris.'

'Show him.'

'Make him choke.'

'Me first, then Sean,' I said to Johnson. He emptied the first Revel into my hand, making sure with his grimy fingers that only one emerged.

Without looking I put it straight in my mouth. The crowd gave a little gasp.

I bit.

I chewed.

I smiled.

'Orange cream. A touch sickly sweet for my taste, but not bad. Your turn.'

Tierney was close enough for me to see the sweat glistening on his upper lip. Johnson shook the packet up, and held it out. Tierney's hand went to meet it. A chocolate was deposited. Tierney scrutinized it carefully. I could see the strain in his face. He suddenly threw it into his mouth. I thought he was going to spit it out or puke. Then his face lit up.

'Coffee. I knew it.'

His mob gave a little cheer. Emphasis on the little. I wasn't the only one who had noticed his alarm.

Johnson wriggled another free. Without hesitation I put it in my mouth.

'Toffee. Better watch out for my fillings.'

All eyes swung again to Tierney. He was faster this time, a touch feverish, his hand shaking.

'Malteser,' he said.

He'd been chewing gingerly, trying to keep everything at the front of his mouth, so some of the crumbs sprayed out as he spoke.

Again Johnson served me. Now my heart was pounding and my mouth was dry. The previous Revels had formed a hot sticky coating and I didn't have enough spit to wash it away.

'What do you know – another Malteser! Well, Chris,' I said, with mock sympathy, 'five down, and no nuts. Could be this one. You never know your luck.'

Johnson was wearing his idiot grin. He freed another Revel. Tierney could barely stand to look at it. He fumbled the sweet and it fell to the wet earth. Johnson picked it up for him.

I looked around at the crowd. Smurf and Gonad were there. And Stan. He was smiling, which seemed a bit odd, what with the life-and-death struggle being played out before him. There was no sign of Flaherty. But I couldn't think about him. I had to concentrate.

'Go on, Chris, what you waiting for?'

'He's bottled it,' said someone, didn't catch who.

'I haven't. Give it here.'

And it was in.

No!

It was out again.

Tierney had tried to chew, but couldn't. He'd spat the Revel back into his hand. His eyes were watering and thick brown drool was hanging from his mouth. The crowd emitted a sort of snorting jeer. It wasn't a good performance.

'It's not a nut. It's a raisin. I don't like raisins.' He sounded pathetic. 'Look, I'm eating it.'

He lapped up the raisin-and-chocolate sludge from his palm.

'That's not right,' said someone at the back. 'He thought it was a nut one and he spat it, and then when he knew it wasn't he ate it. That's cheating.'

'I can live with it,' I said. 'Johnson – another.'

I was in a frenzy now. I was on a roll. It wouldn't be a nut, and even if it was, it wouldn't hurt me. Nothing could hurt me. I was immortal.

Well, I was dying of cancer.

Tierney had been looking at me, his face full of hope that I would get a nut: that I would be the one choking; that it would be my throat that would begin to itch; that my trachea would be the one to bubble and flame, closing itself off, leaving the tiniest space for air to squeeze through; that it would be my whole body that would begin to close down, going into anaphylactic shock. Well, it wasn't, not this time.

I spoke without a flourish, my face a mask.

'Orange.'

The bones in Tierney's face collapsed inwards. He fell to his knees.

'Here, your go.'

Johnson now sounded gruff. He was annoyed, embarrassed by his chief. The gang was losing face. Hell, its face was well and truly gone. Tierney had to pull it back. Johnson shoved the packet at Tierney. Tierney didn't speak, didn't do anything. And then we heard the noise – a thin, keening, close-mouthed wail.

'Take it! Don't be so shit soft.'

'Mmmmmmmmmmmmnnnnnnnnnnnghhhhh,' went Tierney, whimpering, crying. It was a desolate sound, like the cry of a marsh bird.

'Have it,' said Johnson, screaming now, and when Tierney still refused, he crammed the packet into his face, and pushed him back onto the ground. Some of the crowd came over. Someone spat at Tierney. Murdo. Someone kicked him. No-Name.

It was over. It was all over. And now my friends were

around me, and I felt a soft pressure on my hand, and it was Amanda.

'That was the best thing I think I've ever seen,' said Gonad. 'It was like something out of a film. It was like *The Seven Samurai* crossed with *Charlie and the Chocolate Factory*.'

And Stan said quietly in my ear, in a tone that made it uncertain if it was a question or a statement: 'You knew, didn't you?'

'Knew?'

'About the change?'

Sage Heraclitus
Trying to spite us
Said all is in motion
Like a river or ocean.

'Don't know what change you mean.'

'To the Revels.'

Stan was smiling, but watching me closely.

'They changed them?'

'Got rid of the nuts. Replaced them with raisins. There was no danger. To either of you, I mean.'

'I haven't the faintest idea what you're talking about, Stan,' I said, meeting his smile with a broader one of my own.

I looked around for Flaherty. I saw him alone on a bench.

'Gonad, Smurf, this is Amanda. Amanda, be gentle with them. You already know Stan.'

Smurf blushed, Gonad stammered, Stan smiled.

'I'm going to have a chat with Flaherty. You lot go ahead

and warm up the concrete for me. It's the least you can do, what with me being at death's door and all.'

I walked over and sat down beside Flaherty, leaving the others to overcome their embarrassment. His face was completely blank. Only his sniffing gave anything away.

'They won't bother you again,' I said, trying not to sound too heroic.

Nothing from Flaherty.

'And thanks, by the way, for this morning. At break. That thing with the bin. God, that was funny. I wish I could have seen his face. But there was a bin on it.'

A half-smile, perhaps.

'Did they touch you with it?' I meant the johnny.

'Nah.'

'Could have been worse then.'

'Yeah.'

'We're off to eat our sarnies now. Wanna come over? Do me a favour, though. Don't do your thing with Amanda. She's a bit shy.'

And Flaherty stood up with me and we went to our usual place, and Amanda was there, and Flaherty, after a quiet beginning, did his thing, but Amanda seemed not to mind.

CHAPTER 45
THE END OF DAYS

I was shivering. I'd been hoping it might be the same technician as before, the one I called Barry Cunliffe. But it wasn't him. It was someone else. She wasn't wearing a badge, so I had no idea what she was called and for some reason that made me sad and depressed and lonely. I tried to believe that it might have been her lab coat the other Barry was wearing, and that she was a female Barry, which was short for Barryella, or, um, Barryeeeeesha. But then why wasn't she wearing the badge now? Perhaps the other Barry was out robbing a bank and was trying to throw suspicion on to the real Barry so that she would be arrested and he'd get her job, which was one notch further up the nerd pole. Plus he'd have the money from the robbery, say £25,000, which could buy you an awful lot of circuit boards or postage stamps or whatever it was that Barry (the fake Barry) collected.

Then I thought I'd better stop thinking about the Barrys and for the rest of the scan I relived the day before, which was, officially, the Best Day of My Life.

I didn't want to go to school, because I'd gone out on a high with my triumph over the Forces of Evil. I mean, how was I supposed to follow that up? In a graphic novel, such a triumph would be followed shortly by a reversal. I'd either be taken over by an alien superbeing using, say, mind-control or just old-fashioned blackmail (they'd probably kidnap Amanda for that purpose), and they'd use me to destroy the Earth, or my arch-enemy and nemesis would find a way to rob me of my special powers and crush me underfoot like a worm. Of course, I'd eventually overcome all that but, frankly, there wasn't time for it now.

So, early on Wednesday morning, Amanda and I got on the first bus heading out of town. Technically, she was bunking off, but who was going to stand up in court and deny her compassionate leave in these circumstances? The plan was to get off as soon as it looked nice outside in a grass-and-trees kind of way.

I had some sandwiches in my rucksack, and Amanda had brought an angel cake she'd baked herself, wrapped up in tin foil. I asked her why she'd baked an angel cake as opposed to any other of the world's cakes (for a full list see www.cakesoftheworld.com), and she said that it was because it came first in the book as it began with an A. I thanked my lucky stars that no one had thought of inventing a cake with an Aardvark-flavoured topping.

We sat quietly upstairs, watching the red-brick estates give way to posher houses, which thinned until there were flat fields and out-of-town hypermarkets, and then the road became winding and the land swelled and breathed until it felt like a good time to get off. We were on the outskirts of a village, but we turned our backs on it and walked down the road until we found a green sign that said PUBLIC FOOTPATH pointing along the edge of a field that was growing nothing but brown earth. The sky was solid grey, but something about the complete uniform drabness of it suggested that it would not rain, and that was all we asked.

And talking of asking, I'd begged Henry to let us have this day together, alone. He grumbled a bit, said that he'd get bored back there, that he was entitled to a bit of fun on what just might be his last couple of days. He promised to behave himself, said that he'd learned his lesson, and that he was going to be accentuating the positive from now on. But I was adamant, and in the end he said he had to stay in and wash his hair and, anyway, the countryside was boring and so was I.

We walked until the field of earth became one of knee-high wheat, green and young, and we looked at each other (that's me and Amanda, not me and the wheat), but it wasn't quite right because the ground beneath the wheat was rough and furrowed. And then we came to a little wood about the size of a football pitch, and the path forked and one part went through the wood, and we followed it, and on the far side there was a field of soft grass and the field rose to meet the sky and the wood was at our backs, so it felt like a world that we had all to ourselves.

And then we'd walk down to the orchard,
Through brambles and weeds to the grass
And ever so perfectly tortured
The days and the lifetimes would pass.

Henry!

Sorry, sorry, I'm just going.

And we ate the cake first, which turned to perfumed air on my tongue, and then we laughed at the tofu sandwiches, which were actually quite nice. And after that I put my head on Amanda's lap and she stroked my hair, and we pretended that the sun was beating down, and whenever I said something funny or clever she bent and kissed my mouth, and I was reliving her kisses when the voice of Barryella came though on the intercom and told me that we were through, and that I'd done very well for staying so still for so long.

I was in a special neurological ward, so most of the other beds were surrounded by monitors going beep and trolleys with wires, which was all pretty interesting. I guessed I'd be plugged in too, after my operation. None of the other patients were much in the mood for chatting, on account of the whole massive brain injury thing that most of them had going on.

That evening everyone came: Smurf, Gonad, Stan, Amanda, Mum, Clyte. Even Sister Winifred rolled in from her usual ward to say hello and wish me luck. Smurf presented me with one of those huge embarrassing cards from school, signed by lots of people I didn't know. Everyone was cracking jokes, and even Henry got in on the act. And then the time for visitors ended and my friends left, and then Clyte, and then Amanda, and last of all Mum.

I felt Henry heavier than ever in my head.

Hey, Henry, you need to lose a couple of pounds.

Well, kid, you could do with putting a few on.

Let's rest now.

Yes, I'm tired.

Goodnight, Henry. I love you.

The words came out of nowhere.
My father.
I'd been thinking about my father.
Young and handsome in his uniform. And dead.
I love you too.

CHAPTER 46
THIS MORTAL COIL

They were coming to get me. Monsters. The faces of pigs. Forked tails. Teeth, curving like scimitars. I was running through the corridors, but my pyjamas were tangling me and my feet couldn't grip on the polished floors. And finally there was no more corridor and I turned to face the monsters. They were in the shadows now, coming slowly, and their eyes glowed red, and they were going to tear me apart, they were going to put their snouts into my flesh. But that would only be the beginning, because they were going to take me away to a place where I would be theirs for ever and the terror and the pain would never end. And I looked beyond them, because it should have been now that they came to help – the Justice League. Hawkgirl should have been there to spread her wings over me; The Flash should have been a blur of pure energy; Superman, my rock; Batman glowering, clever, indomitable.

But they were not there, and I was alone.

Heck, Heck. It's me. Wake up. They don't exist, they're not here.

The voice came through into the dream, and to begin with it seemed that the monsters spoke with the voice of Henry Tumour, and then I was awake in the grey hospital dawn and an old man was coughing somewhere, and there were curtains around a bed across from me, and voices murmured their concern and the patient gave a groan as though they had performed some act of terrible sacrilege upon his body.

Henry, I'm scared.

Me too.

Do you know anything about . . . about what comes after?

After the operation?

After everything. After life.

Don't think like that.

How else can I think? Tell me, what is next?

How could I know?

I thought you knew everything.

I'm sorry, Heck, I don't know that. But I'm afraid of the dark. Philosophers have said that we should not fear death, because it is not a state. It is an absence, a nothing. But that's exactly what I'm afraid of. I don't want to be a nothing. I want to be with you.

When you speak like that . . . tell me, is it me speaking? Are we truly the same?

I don't know. I don't know. I don't feel well. The drugs they gave you. They make me feel bad. I cannot feel my hands.

I'm sorry. It'll be all right. It'll be fine. We'll be OK.

And I think I fell asleep again. Winifred woke me, and explained that I couldn't have any breakfast because of the operation, and all the old men of the ward knew that today was my day. An hour before my time a Chinese lady doctor gave me an injection in the arse, and after that I felt myself float slowly above the bed, and although the fear and the sadness were still in me, their grip was weak and I felt detached from them, as though they were something I was trying to remember.

And I drifted not only above the bed, but in other dimensions. I was back in the playground near my house. I was on the swings – the baby sort with a bar. Someone was pushing me. Too high. I strained to see who it was. I couldn't see. But I knew it was him, my dad. And then I was in the field with Amanda, my head in her lap, looking up into the pearl-grey sky, and she was speaking into my ear, telling me the secret thing. And then I felt a pressure on my hand and I opened my eyes to see Sister Winifred.

'It's time for you, my love.'

Not yet, please not yet. Only a little longer.

'Yes, my love, you have to go. The man is come for you.'

Don't let him take me.

But the man was here. The porter.

Let it not be the porter, the porter is drunk, the porter is death. Lechery, sir, it provokes, and unprovokes; It provokes the desire, but it takes away the performance.

It's OK, Henry, we're nearly there.

The old men frailly waved their liver-spotted hands, and the nurses gathered to wish me luck. Tiny ones from the Philippines, big ones from Jamaica and the Ivory Coast. They'd come so far for me. And then it was a lift with the drunken porter and then a new part of the hospital, a part I'd never been to. And then the operating theatre, and if I'd had my wits about me I'd have checked out the stuff they had in there, the gear and the gadgets. I saw that I was wearing a green gown but I couldn't remember when I'd put it on. The same Chinese lady doctor was there again, but now with a plastic bag on her head and a white mask across her face. Anaesthetist, yes, that's what she was. Other doctors were there, the ones who would do the cutting. Grave, grey men. The lady doctor was talking to me, but it was hard to hear her over Henry. He was whimpering, jabbering, making no sense, and I wished that I could comfort him.

I looked down and saw that there was a thing in the back of my hand. A tube thing with a valve.

'Can you count for me, backwards from a hundred?'

Maths.

Good at maths.

I could tell her all the prime numbers, walk with them into infinity. She put a syringe into the tube in my hand. This was how they did it.

'One hundred.'

The room was darker. And in the shadows I saw shapes.

'Ninety-nine.'

Not the pig men. The shapes of my friends. And then larger shapes, sleek with power. And I knew that at last they'd come to help me: the Justice League.

'Ninety-eight.'

I saw The Flash, glimmering like starlight.

'Ninety-seven.'

I saw Hawkgirl, saw the spread of her velvet-soft wings. Saw more figures arriving – superheroes I didn't even recognize, from every corner of the known galaxies and beyond, all coming to help me . . .

'Ninety-six.'

And that was my last number, and the darkness drew down like a blind and all I could hear was Henry. Green fields, green fields. He babbled of green fields.

And it was then that the thought came to me that life is the process by which you discover all the things you can't do. And at the end you finally discover the last thing you can't do: live for ever.

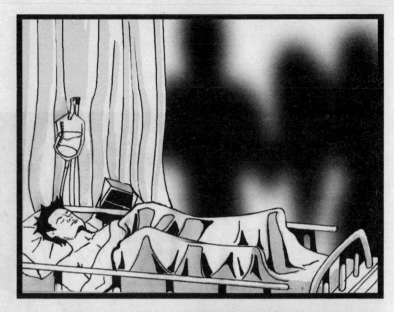

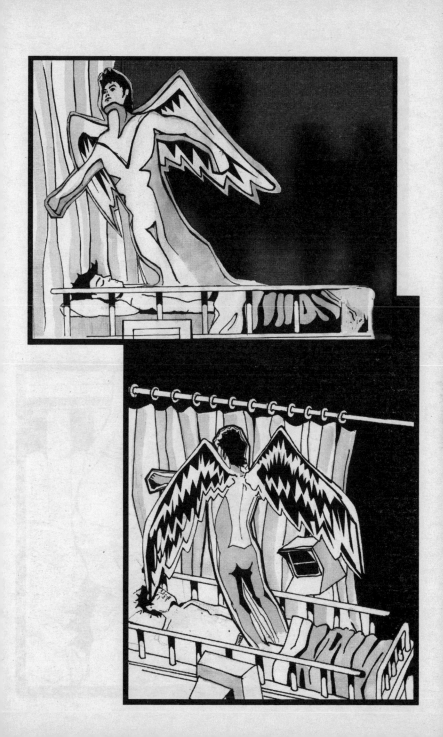

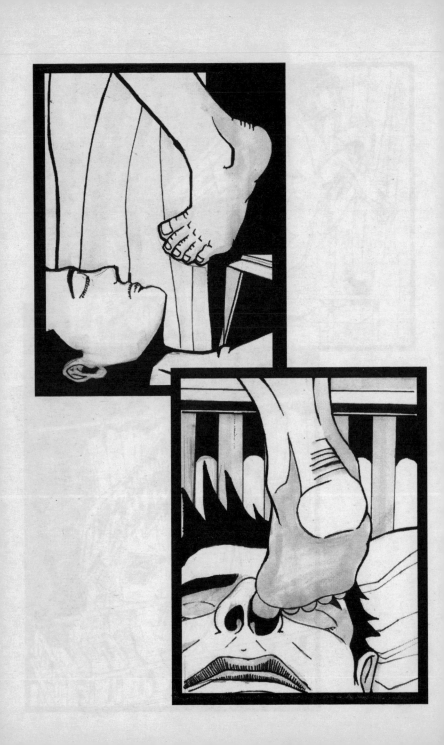

ACKNOWLEDGEMENTS

I would like to acknowledge the inspiration provided by two outstanding works of reference: Iona and Peter Opie's *The Lore and Language of Schoolchildren*, and *The Law of the Playground* by Jonathan Blyth.

Thanks also to Shannon Park for her editorial élan, to Stephanie Cabot for her support and to Rebecca Campbell for everything else.

ABOUT THE AUTHOR

Anthony McGowan was born in Manchester, brought up in Leeds and lives in London.

Author photo copyright © Jerry Bauer

Henry Tumour is his second novel for teenagers.

Also available now in Definitions paperback:

ANTHONY McGOWAN

Hellbent

The shame, the horror, the ignominy . . . I'm about to be
run down by an ice-cream van.

After the embarrassing circumstances of his untimely
teenage death, Conor is sent to Hell when it turns out
he's three lies over the limit for good behaviour. His
custom-made torture is to spend eternity in a bleak cave
filled with dusty philosophy books and classical music.

But what if Conor's version of Hell is someone else's
idea of Heaven, and vice versa? Could he escape his
torment by swapping places? With his hideous pet dog,
Scrote, at his side, Conor sets out on a mission with his
personal devil and enforcer of evil, Clarence, and a
melancholy Viking called Olaf. Together they embark
on a revolting, repulsive and riotous search for
Conor's match made in Hell . . .

'A wisecracking helterskelter' OBSERVER

978 0 099 48213 0
DEFINITIONS

THE BLACK TATTOO

SAM ENTHOVEN

Esme's hard brown hands lifted fractionally from her sides. Her amber eyes glittered as she faced her enemy.

'No tricks,' said Esme. 'No more lies. You and me are going to fight this out to the finish. Right now.'

Jack doesn't know what he's got himself into. One minute he and his best friend, Charlie, were in Chinatown having crispy duck with Charlie's dad, then suddenly they were in a mysterious room above a theatre, with some of the strangest characters they'd ever encountered. And they were about to take The Test . . .

The Test transformed Charlie – leaving him with the distinctive markings of the Black Tattoo. The boys' meeting with Esme – a young girl with the most impressive martial arts skills this side of Bruce Lee – her huge and hairy father, Raymond, and the mysterious Nick, seemed to have swept Charlie and Jack into a world they had no idea existed. And it was only going to get weirder . . .

978 0 385 60965 4
DOUBLEDAY

CLASH
OF THE
SKY GALLEONS

PAUL STEWART & CHRIS RIDDELL

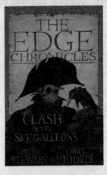

'Not even here in this place of ghosts and demons and half-formed things,' bellowed the wild-eyed sky pirate captain, '... will you be safe from my vengeance!'

After many years, Turbot Smeal, treacherous quartermaster, arsonist and destroyer of the Western Quays, is back. The taverns, league palaces and boom docks are awash with rumours. Quint Verginix, knight academic, is called away from his studies in the great floating city. Together with his best friend, Maris, he finds himself caught up in his father, Wind Jackal's, obsessive quest for vengeance against his former quartermaster.

From the sky-ship yards of Undertown to the deserted quarries of the Edge cliff, from blood-drenched bloodoak glades to the horrors of an abandoned sky-wreck, Quint, Maris and the crew of the *Galerider* are drawn into an increasingly deadly pursuit – a pursuit that will ultimately lead to the clash of the sky galleons.

THE EDGE CHRONICLES – Over 1 MILLION COPIES sold!

'Stunningly original' *Guardian*

978 0 385 60721 6
DOUBLEDAY

The **BARTIMAEUS** trilogy

JONATHAN STROUD

A roller-coaster ride of magic, adventure and political
skulduggery, set in a London where spells and demons
are part of everyday life. Young magician Nathaniel, fast
rising through the government ranks, must summon up
the troublesome, enigmatic and quick-witted djinni,
Bartimaeus, if he is to hang on to his job. Or his life . . .

'A hilarious read with a stroppy young wizard
whose demon, Bartimaeus, is funny, cynical and
totally out for himself' *OBSERVER*

Book I: the Amulet of Samarkand
978 0 552 55029 1

Book II: The Golem's Eye
978 0 552 55027 7

Book III: Ptolemy's Gate
978 0 552 55028 4